PHILIDA

André Brink is the author of several novels in English, including *A Dry White Season*, *Imaginings of Sand*, *The Rights of Desire* and *The Other Side of Silence*. He has won South Africa's most important literary prize, the CNA Award, three times and has twice been shortlisted for the Booker Prize.

ALSO BY ANDRÉ BRINK

The Ambassador
Looking on Darkness
An Instant in the Wind
Rumours of Rain
A Dry White Season
A Chain of Voices
The Wall of the Plague
States of Emergency
An Act of Terror
The First Life of Adamastor
On the Contrary
Imaginings of Sand
Devil's Valley
The Rights of Desire
The Other Side of Silence
Before I Forget
Praying Mantis
The Blue Door

Mapmakers (essays)

A Land Apart (A South African Reader,
with J.M. Coetzee)
Reinventing a Continent (essays)
A Fork in the Road (memoir)

ANDRÉ BRINK

Philida

A Novel

VINTAGE BOOKS
London

Published by Vintage 2013

2 4 6 8 10 9 7 5 3 1

Copyright © André Brink 2012

André Brink has asserted his right under the Copyright, Designs
and Patents Act 1988 to be identified as the author of this work

First published in Great Britain in 2012 by
Harvill Secker

Vintage
Random House, 20 Vauxhall Bridge Road,
London SW1V 2SA

www.vintage-books.co.uk

Addresses for companies within The Random House Group Limited
can be found at: www.randomhouse.co.uk/offices.htm

The Random House Group Limited Reg. No. 954009

A CIP catalogue record for this book
is available from the British Library

ISBN 9780099578758

The Random House Group Limited supports The Forest
Stewardship Council (FSC®), the leading international forest
certification organisation. Our books carrying the FSC label are
printed on FSC® certified paper. FSC is the only forest certification
scheme endorsed by the leading environmental organisations,
including Greenpeace. Our paper procurement policy can
be found at: www.randomhouse.co.uk/environment

MIX
Paper from
responsible sources
FSC® C016897

Printed and bound by CPI Group (UK) Ltd, Croydon, CR0 4YY

This book
is for my wife
KARINA,
with love and gratitude,
for more than I can ever say

I am indebted to the University of
the Western Cape for awarding me the Jan Rabie/
Marjorie Wallace Bursary in 2010 for the research
and writing of the novel.

I am
God knows
A free fucking woman

Antjie Krog

PART ONE
~
COMPLAINT

I

On Saturday 17 November 1832, after following the
Elephant Trail that runs between the Village of Franschhoek,
past the Farm Zandvliet to the small Town of Stellenbosch
near Cape Town, the young Slave Woman Philida arrives at
the Drostdy with its tall white Pillars, where she is directed
to the Office of the Slave Protector, Mijnheer Lindenberg, to
lodge a Complaint against her Owner Cornelis Brink and
his Son Francois Gerhard Jacob Brink

Here come shit. Just one look, and I can see it coming. Here I walk all this way and God know that is bad enough, what with the child in the *abbadoek* on my back, and now there's no turning back, it's just straight on to hell and gone. This is the man I got to talk to if I want to lay a charge, they tell me, this Grootbaas who is so tall and white and thin and bony, with deep furrows in his forehead, like a badly ploughed wheat field, and a nose like a sweet potato that has grown past itself.

It's a long story. First he want to find out everything about me, and it's one question after another. Who am I? Where do I come from? What is the name of my Baas? What is the name of the farm? For how long I been working there? Did I get a pass for coming here? When did I leave and how long did I walk? Where did I sleep last night? What do I think is going to happen to me when I get home again? And every time I say something, he first write it down in his big book with those knobbly hands and his long white fingers. These people got a thing about writing everything down. Just look at the back pages of the black Bible that belong to Oubaas Cornelis Brink, that's Francois Gerhard Jacob's father.

While the Grootbaas is writing I keep watching him closely. There's something second-hand about the man, like a piece of knitting gone wrong that had to be done over, but badly, not very smoothly. I can say that because I know about knitting. On his nose sit a pair of thick glasses like a bat with open wings, but he look at me over them, not through them. His long hands keep busy all the time. Writing, and dipping the long feather in the ink, and sprinkling fine sand on the thick paper, and shifting his papers this way and that on top of the table that is really too low for him because he is so tall. He is sitting, I keep standing, that is how it's got to be.

In the beginning I feel scared, my throat is tight. But after the second or third question I start feeling better. All I can think of is: If it was me that was knitting you, you'd look a bit better, but now whoever it was that knitted you, did not cast you off right. Still, I don't say anything. In this place it's only him and me and I don't want to get on his wrong side. I got to tell him everything, and that is exactly what I mean to do today, without keeping anything back.

He ask me: When did Francois Brink first . . . I mean, when was it that the two of you began to . . . you know what I'm talking about?

Eight years ago.

You sure about that? How can you be so sure?

Ja, it is eight years, I tell you, my Grootbaas. I remember it very clearly because that was the winter when Oubaas Cornelis take the lot of us in to the Caab to see the man they hanged, that slave Abraham, on the Castle gallows. And it was after we come home from there, to the farm Zandvliet, that it begin between Frans and me.

How did it begin? What happened?

It was a bad day for me, Grootbaas. Everything that happen in the Caab, in front of the Castle. The man they hang. Two times, because the first time the rope break, and I remember how the man keep dancing at the end of the rope round his neck, and how his thing get all big and stiff and start to spit.

What do you mean, his thing?

His man-thing, Grootbaas, what else? I hear the people talking about how it sometimes happen when a man is hanged, but it is the first time I see it for myself, and I never want to see it again.

And you said that when you came back on the farm . . .?

Yes, that was when. We first come past the old sow in the sty, the old fat-arse pig they call Hamboud. The Oubaas say many times before that he want to slaughter her because she is so blarry useless, but the Ounooi keep on saying she must stay here so her big arse can grow even bigger and fatter. And afterwards, when we get home, we come past the four horses in the stable, and the two good-for-nothing donkeys, and then the stupid *trassie* hen that Ounooi Janna call Zelda after her aunt that *skinder* so much, the hen that don't know if she is a cock or a hen and that can never manage to lay an egg herself but always go cackling like a mad thing whenever some other hen on the farm lay one. And then in the late afternoon when we are all back on the farm where we belong I first go to Ouma Nella, her full name is Petronella, but to me she is always just Ouma Nella.

And what happened then? ask the tall bony man, beginning to sound impatient.

So I tell him: Then Frans take me with him, away from the longhouse, through the vineyard where the old cemetery is. Down to where the bamboo copse make its deep, dark shade in the elbow of the river, that's the Dwars River that run across the farm, and there I begin to cry for the first time and that is when Frans —

You mean *Baas* Frans, the tall bony man remind me.

Yes, Baas Frans he take me to where the bamboo copse close up all around you, and when he see me crying, he get so hot that his thing also jump up, just like the dead man on the gallows, and that is when he get onto me to ride me.

Behind the dusty thick glasses the man's deep eyes seem to be looking right into me as he ask: Yes, and what did he do then?

I can feel myself going blunt inside, but I know I can't stop now, so I bite on my teeth and tell him: He do what a man do with a woman.

And what would that be?

I'm sure the Grootbaas will know about that.

He say: I want to know exactly what he did.

He take me.

How did he take you? I have to know all the particulars. The law demands that I must find out everything that happened. So that it can all be written down very precisely in this book.

I tell him: He *naai* me.

The tall thin man with the bald head give a cough, as if his spit is now dried up. After a while he ask: Did you resist?

Grootbaas, in the beginning I try to, but that is when Frans begin to talk to me very nicely and tell me I mustn't be scared, he won't hurt me, he just want to make me happy. If I will let him push into me, then he will make sure to buy

· 6 ·

me my freedom when the time is right, that is what he promise me before the LordGod of the Bible, he say he himself will buy freedom for me. But I remember thinking, how can it be that a thing like freedom can hurt one so bad? Because it was my first time and he didn't act very gentle with me, he was too hasty, I think it was his first time too.

And then what happened?

When he finish, he get up again and tie the *riem* of his breeches.

It is just as well the man don't give me much time to think, because the questions start coming again and they getting more and more difficult.

Philida, I want to know what happened *afterwards*? ask the man with the ploughed field on his forehead. Did you . . . I mean, were there any consequences to the intercourse you had in the bamboo copse?

I don't know about that intercourse thing and the consequences, Grootbaas.

This thing you did in the bamboo place. Did it *lead* to anything? He getting very red in the face. What you did together in that bamboo place . . .? Did anything happen inside you – to your body?

Not right away, Grootbaas. Only after he lie with me a few times, I start to swell.

How many times?

Many times, Grootbaas.

Two times? Three times? Ten? Twenty?

I fold my hands around my shoulders. And once again I say: Many times, Grootbaas.

Unexpectedly he ask: Was he the first man that was with you?

I just shake my head because I don't feel like answering. I already told him *mos* it was my first time.

He change the question a little bit: Have you had a lot of men?

I tell him, It's only Baas Frans I come to complain about.

Look, if you have a complaint, you've got to tell us everything now. Otherwise you're wasting our time.

Once again I say: It's just about Baas Frans that I am here.

Did he hurt you?

No, Grootbaas. It was a bit difficult but I can't say it hurt me too bad. I had badder things happen to me.

Then what are you complaining about?

Because he take me and he promise me things and now he is going away from me.

What did he promise you?

He say he will give me my freedom.

What did he mean when he said he would give you your freedom?

He say he will buy me freedom from the Landdrost. From the Govment. But now instead of buying my freedom he want going away from me.

How is he going away from you?

They say he want to marry a white woman. Not a slave or a Khoe but one of his own kind. So now he want to sell me upcountry.

How do you know that?

I hear him talking to the Ounooi about it. They want to put me up on auction.

Why would they want to do that?

Because they want to take my children away from the farm before the white woman come to live here.

What can you tell me about your children?

That's *mos* why I am here, Grootbaas.

How many children do you have?

There is two left, but there was four altogether.

What happened to the other two?

I think by myself: Now it is coming. But after a while I just say: They die when they are small. The first one didn't have a name yet and the second one was Mamie, but she only lived three months, then she also went.

Who is their father?

Frans and I made them.

Baas Frans?

Baas Frans.

He keep on asking: And the two who are still alive? Where are they?

One is at Zandvliet where we made them. She's Lena. My Ouma Nella look after her. The last one is this one I bring on my back with me.

For some time he say nothing more. Then he get in a hurry and he ask: When did the other two die?

I don't look at him. All I can say is: When they was small. One was only three months old.

And the other one?

I have nothing to say about the first one.

Why not?

He die too soon.

He look hard at me, then he sigh. All right, he say. What can you tell me about this one you brought with you?

I don't say anything. I just turn sideways so that he can see the child in the doek on my back.

I tell the man: He is my youngest. He was born only three months ago. His name is Willempie.

And you say it is your Baas Francois's child?

Yes, that is the truth, before the LordGod.

Can you prove it?

I ask him: How can I prove a thing like that?

If you cannot prove it I cannot write it in my book.

The Grootbaas must believe me.

To believe something, he says, does not make it true.

Grootbaas, I say, there are things about you that I also cannot see, but I believe they are there and that make them true.

He laugh and I can hear it is not a good laugh. He ask: What you talking about?

It is getting more difficult to breathe, but I know I have no choice and so I ask: Will the Grootbaas give me permission to say it?

He say: Look, we're getting nowhere like this. So all right then, I give you permission.

I nod and look straight at him and I say: Thank you, my Grootbaas. Then I shall take that permission and say to the Grootbaas that I am speaking of the thing on which the Grootbaas is sitting.

Are you talking about my chair?

I am talking about the Grootbaas's *poephol*. That is, his arsehole.

I see him turning red first and then a deep, almost black purple. He pant like a man that climb up a steep hill.

Bladdy meid! he say. Are you looking for trouble?

I am not looking for trouble, Grootbaas, and I hope I won't find any.

For God's sake, then say it and have done with it.

Then I shall say it with the permission the Grootbaas give me.

Well, what is it?

I just want to say, that thing the Grootbaas is sitting on: I never seen it and with the help of the LordGod I hope I never will. But I know it is there and I believe it, and so it is true. And it is the same with my children. I know Frans made them.

Very slowly he get up from his big, beautiful chair with the armrests that I can see is carved very carefully by hand. Now he is trembling. And he say: Meid, your cheek will land you in more trouble than you have ever been in.

My Ouma Nella always tell me that will happen to me one day. But I only say this to the Grootbaas because you ask me and you give me permission.

What the hell do you expect of me now? he shout.

I can only ask the Grootbaas to do the right thing that Frans promise me.

Baas Frans.

Baas Frans.

The trembling man move his books and papers aside, put his long feather pen on top and get up.

Willempie start wailing and I smother him with my breast.

Is that all now? I ask.

What makes you think it's all? ask Grootbaas Lindenberg. We haven't even started. All you have done is to lay your complaint. We still have to investigate. Now we must wait for your Baas to come and make his reply.

I feel my chest go all tight. So what do I do now? I ask.

We will let your Baas Frans know. You can wait here in the jail behind the Drostdy until he comes.

My whole body feel numb, but I can see there is no way out.

He call one of his helpers, the ones they call the Kaffers, who do all the dirty work here around the Drostdy, to take me to the jail at the back.

Once again I ask him: What do I do now?

You don't do anything. You just wait until your Baas comes. The Protector will send a messenger to your farm.

When we go out on the back stoep I ask the man who

is come to fetch me: What do I do about food? That can take a long time.

They will look after you here in the cells, say the Kaffer. He look like a Khoe man and his face is wrinkled like a sour plum.

Thank the LordGod, I am now taken to a cell with five or six other women. They act friendly to me and make room for me and give me some of their food. From that first day the women share with me all of the little bit they got. There's dried fruit and aniseed bread and sometimes a few fresh apricots or early peaches or a dried fish. In the beginning I feel scared, because I got no idea of what is going on and what can happen to my child. But I soon find out that they look after me well in that place. Once a day the Khoe man with a face like a sour plum come to take me round the big white building to the backyard to stretch my legs. It is a long wait and I soon get tired of having nothing to do except to think, but it give me good time to make sure what I want to say if the day come.

What keep on going round and round in my head is everything that happen to bring me here where I am now. Was it really worth all the trouble? Because it wasn't just the long walk, and not knowing, and feeling scared, and wondering about what is going to happen. It was the being here.

Because it's not just deciding to come and complain, and then to walk to this place and get it done and go back home. I know only too well what it take and that's a lot. Everything that ever happen to me is here in my two hands, and for all I know it's for nothing. It's not much of a life I had at Zandvliet, with the beatings and the knitting and the working day and night and always doing what other people tell you to do and everything else. But it's all I got, it's all I am and all I can ever be. It's my whole blarry life. Because after this, coming to Stellenbosch to complain, it may be over for me. If this do not work out it's to hell and gone for me. But there is nothing else I can do.

What have I got at Zandvliet? You can't really call it a life. It's not clear like day or night, or like sun and moon, it's somewhere in between. If I can be sure of Frans, that can make things different, but I'm not. Today, there's nothing sure about anything for me. But this little chance I got to use, otherwise it may be gone for ever. I mean, you can say the law give me the right to come and complain. But if you ask me, it's not the law that speak the last word in this land. It's everything that happen behind the law, and around the law. That is what matter for the big men of the Caab. Ouma Nella already told me about slaves that went to complain with the whole law in their hands, and then afterwards, when they get back to their Baas, they get beaten to death or they get hanged upside down or they get starved to death, and there's no cock that crow about it, no dog that dare to bark. There's many ways to kill a cock or a dog or a slave. Even Ouma Nella tell me to stay out of it, but for once I do not listen. Because no one can tell me to let go, not even she. For once I cannot listen to her or to anybody. Now it's heaven or hell for me. To hell I refuse to go. And to the kind of heaven I got to know at Zandvliet, their kind of heaven, I swear to God, I will not go either. Not now. All I got is to sit here in the cell and wait, with the baby on my lap.

II

*Philida's Thoughts wander back to the Secret that
did not drown and the Promises left unfulfilled*

At Zandvliet it all begin. Almost as far back as I can remember,
it always been the farm, nothing but the farm. I remember
an earlier time when we were still living at the Caab. But
mostly I think about the farm and its people, its early people
and later people, all the way from the beginning to today.

I remember my Ouma who always been there. And everybody that come afterwards. All of this Ouma Nella tell me.
She got stories for everything, and many of them come from
a long way back. Because Ouma Nella keep her ears open
for everything that sound like a story. And she talk to everybody. I often hear her talking even to God. Most people,
the Oubaas and them, go down on their knees when they
want to talk to him. But Ouma Nella can speak any time
she want to. She speak to God the way others speak to a
man you know well and don't quite trust, because she keep
saying he's a bit of a cheat and he'll tell a lie if it suit him.

My head remember this and that and lots of other stuff
as well, but the thing that really remember is my body.
Everything leave its mark there. Some you can see, others
you can't, but they all there. Burns and cuts and bruises.
The scrape marks on my knees and my elbows and my
heels, all kinds of marks. The beatings and the falls, the icy
water of early winter mornings, mud on my feet, chickenshit
or rotten figs between my toes, I remember Frans's hands

on my body, on my shoulders and my back and my buttocks, my feet in his hands, I remember him hard and swollen between my legs, and I can hear him talking softly in my ear: Come and lie with me, Philida. My body will make yours happy. It will be good for you, you'll see. I shall buy you free, I shall go to Stellenbosch and speak to the Landdrost, I shall walk all the way to the Caab if I have to, and pay whatever they ask so you can be free, then you can walk everywhere you want to. With shoes on your feet.

That I remember specially well. The shoes on my feet. What he say about the shoes he promised me from the very first day. Because he knew, as I knew, as the whole world know: the man or the woman with shoes on their feet, they cannot be slaves, they are free, shoes mean that they are not chickens or donkeys or pigs or dogs, they are *people*.

I remember walking, with my two narrow feet, walking and walking and walking for days on end. Along the old Elephant Trail that go back to the time before time, when they say big herds of elephants used to trek past this place, first from deep inland and over the mountains where the village of Franschhoek is nowadays, and then past Zandvliet to Stellenbosch, and from there across the Flats to the Caab, all those years since that time before time, when there was no people yet, just the track that seem to move along on its own below my feet, farther than far. It's a road that come from the beginning of the world and don't ever really end. Yet at the same time you may say that it's a road that start this morning before sunrise, from the sands of Zandvliet in the grey dust. That is the farm, it's Zandvliet. That's the place they bring me to when I was nine years old, they tell me. I was the knitting girl, with fingers as thin as twigs, but as clever as hell. And I had no choice, otherwise Nooi Janna would have stripped the skin off my arse; Oubaas Cornelis taught her everything about flogging. With a thong, a shoe, a *kierie*, a switch or a sjambok, if you wouldn't listen, and Nooi Janna never had a soft touch. Not in the Caab where the Oubaas had the wine shop and the big cellar, nor among the mountains at Zandvliet when they came to live here.

Zandvliet, in the shadow of the mountains that blue off in all directions – to the clouds and the cliffs of Great Drakenstein, or the heights and caves of Simonsberg opposite. Mountains on both sides, further and further away, blue and pale blue and paler blue, like old bruises getting fainter on your body. Mountains that echo with cries and calls, of the bateleur eagle and the brown bustard, the thin shrilling of the lark like a twine of cotton among the others, a shy tacking stitch. The noisy screams of the hadeda, like messy red and purple and green stitches on a new cloth, the crows like dark patches in the bright sun, black threads in a field of white or blue, or a peacock yelling like a thing that know all about death, but so beautiful with its bright feathers when it open up like the rising sun, growing as stiff as Frans's thing when the lust grow in him, always the birds, or the bats at dusk, the owls at night tearing your innards out in shreds with their hoots and hoos. All of them calling out Zandvliet, Zandvliet, deep into the secret places of your body until you learn at last to know where you come from. Because their sound is like thin twine or yarn through your head and your stomach and your ribs, reminding you that this is where you belong, this is Zandvliet. Zandvliet is sand, it is stone, it is deep earth covered with white grass and green grass and grey grass and longing and anger and happiness and vines and wheat and rye and oats and misery and joy and weeds and once again vines.

Zandvliet go back very far, and Ouma Nella love telling the stories of the place, for days on end, and especially nights. Often she go back to the woman called Fransina, who lived

here long before Oubaas Cornelis bought this farm, before
we came here from the Caab, the white people on their
wagons, along the road from Klapmuts, past Simondium and
Stellenbosch, and the rest of us on foot, we the slaves, barefoot
across the Flats and along the valley and over the mountain,
following the Elephant Trail, three days' walking, four days,
and the little ones – I was nine, remember – sobbing snot and
tears because our feet are bleeding and the Oubaas refuse to
stop or rest except for a few hours' sleeping at night, he is
always right there beside you or behind you on the big black
stallion, the riding crop in his hand to spur you on whenever
he think you are malingering, bleeding welts on your back
and your dusty bare buttocks, nine years old, and at that time
there's some even younger children walking too, all the way.

Even before that time, long before Fransina is working
here on the farm, as the story go, she must have been about
the same age I am now, and then she run away, she and the
slave Klaas run off together, the name of the Baas on the
farm in those days is Marais, and they run away because
Fransina cannot take it any more, all those beatings from the
Ounooi, who beat her every day. With anything she can lay
her hands on, *rieme* or knotted *entjies* or quince switches or
even a piece of firewood. Every single day she got beaten,
at sunset to punish her for what she done wrong during the
day, at sunrise for what she will do wrong in the day ahead.
And yet she meekly take whatever came her way, she was a
slave after all, what happen to her is the will of the Lord. All
she care about is her children, her two girls, Philippina and
Emma, they are all she got, those two daughters she got from
her previous Baas, Dominee Schutte. He make her lie down
for him and break into her night after night, and that is how
Philippina happen, and later Emma, two pretty girls. What
make her lie down for him, is that the dominee promise with

his big white hand on the open Bible, promise her before the God of Abraham, Isaac and Jacob, that he will free the children she give him from between her legs, so that is how she give him Philippina and Emma. The same way that Frans later promise me also that he will free our children, he promise it before God, even though he didn't have his hand on the Bible. But when the time come the dominee forget all about his promise and he sell Fransina and both her daughters to Baas Izak Marais. And after all the trouble Fransina had with her Nooi, and all the beatings, there was an auction in Stellenbosch one day and the Nooi sell the two girls to a farmer from deep in the inland, somewhere in the Sneeuberge, and no one even know for sure where that was.

Fransina will never see her children again. So that is why she run away with Klaas, after another bad beating in the farmyard, first by the Nooi and afterwards by Baas Izak too, with a piece of wood and a *riem* and a *kierie* over her head and neck and shoulders, wherever he can reach; those people was just as bad as Oubaas Cornelis who come later.

So Klaas and Fransina run away, outlawed and banished as the Landdrost say, they want to go to the Sneeuberge where the two girls was taken after the auction, but they got no idea at all of where that place is. They only get as far as the Steenbrazens River, where they got to live on fish. First there on the Steenbrazens River and afterwards at Saldanha Bay, where they sometimes find vegetables in somebody's garden. After a while there come another runaway, Afrika of the Caab, and he take them to two other slaves, Philander and Fleur, that was living near Stellenbosch for some months, stealing and breaking into houses and so on. For a while it was all right, but then they steal two sheep and they got caught by a commando just as Afrika was skinning one of the sheep. All of them off to the court.

Klaas was tied to a pole behind the Drostdy and there his back was beaten to shreds with canes and then he was sent to Robben Island to do hard labour for ten years. Afrika, Philander and Fleur was burnt with irons and their legs was put in chains. But there was one good thing: when the Landdrost hear about Fransina's children he only send her to the jail for six months. Afterwards she don't have to go back to the De Villierses, but I don't know what happen to her after that. Anyway, that is how I got here. Because when I hear that Frans Brink is going to sell me in the interior, and my children too, little Lena who is only two, and the baby here at my breast, Willempie, I decide no, they not going to do that. Because where is Fransina's Philippina and Emma today?

So for me Zandvliet is the place where Fransina and them once lived. But Zandvliet is more than Fransina. It is also the birds and the little bushbuck and the trails of snakes and the tracks of meerkats, it's porcupine and aardvark, it's the jackals in the night, it's the sun shining through the ears of a hare, it's the dry cough of a leopard on cushion feet.

But what to me is most special about Zandvliet is Kleinkat. How it start is when Langkat get six kittens and the Ounooi say they must all be killed, we already got too many of them on the farm. Not in eight weeks' time as it usually happen, not tomorrow or the day after, but right now, today. And it is Frans who must put them in a bushel basket to drown them in the Dwars River just down from the longhouse. I tell him he cannot do it, not to Langkat's babies, because Langkat is my cat, the Ounooi say so herself the day I knitted her the red-and-blue cardigan, the pretty one with the double moss-stitching, so she say I can keep Langkat for myself, and so the kittens is also mine. But then Frans say she told him to drown the litter in the Dwars River and all he can do is follow orders. I go and stand before him and ask him if he always do what his ma say. He just pull a face and say, What else? I ask him again must he always do what his ma tell him, can't he just say no? Frans say, She is my ma. I tell him those kittens also want to live, don't they? He ask me, How can I say No to her? If I don't listen to her she will tell my pa.

I ask him: Are you a slave then who must do everything she say?

Her word is her word, he say and he pick up the basket. I can hear the little sounds they making inside and I grab the basket too.

He say: Give me the basket, and he try to pull it from my hands.

I grab it back and we pull it this way and that way. The basket fall. Inside, the kittens are screaming and mewing in thin little voices like needles in our ears, and the lid begin to slip off. Frans dive closer to grab the basket and push back the little ones, but one of them, the smallest one, the little grey-striped one, she jump out. I pick her up and put her in the pocket of my apron and hold her tight.

Philida! he say, and his voice sound like crying. Give it back! I'm going to get into bad trouble.

Then it's *your* problem, I say. I'm keeping this one. I'll make sure the Ounooi won't get her.

Philida, you a shit. Give it back!

You a shit too!

I'm going to tell my ma!

This time I say: Let me be, dammit! And I promise him: Look, I won't tell anybody. Nobody will ever find out.

When Frans see he won't catch me, he stop.

You promise before the LordGod you won't tell anybody?

I promise before the LordGod.

Then it's all right, he say, you can have the little one.

Before he can change his mind, I run off and rush to Ouma Nella's room where I cannot hear the other kittens outside mewing and crying for help when he drown them.

For a whole day I stay just there looking after the striped kitten and Ouma Nella give it some milk to suck from her finger and then all is peace on earth again, as the Ounooi always say.

It's only four or five days after that, as I sit outside our room with the little one on my lap, that Frans come back to me. He is standing out of the way.

You still angry with me? he ask.

It's not you I'm angry with, I tell him. It's the big people. Thank you for helping me to keep the kitten.

He say: You better make sure nobody ever find out about her.

From that day Kleinkat is our secret. And oftentimes Frans come to play with us if I don't have knitting to do or if I can slip away when we sure that Ounooi Janna won't see us. And from playing with the kitten he and I also start playing together. Like we played when he was very small and I look after him and change his nappies and get him to be quiet, the way Ouma Nella showed me. Those games go on until Frans is no longer a baby. And it's always the two of us together, with Kleinkat, but often without Kleinkat too, in the deep shade of the bamboo copse.

It's only after the day they hang the skinny man in the Caab that I know everything is now different, and for ever. Because from that day, whenever Frans come to sit with me and we go off on our own, behind the longhouse, or to the deep well in the backyard, or of course to the bamboo copse, it happen over and over that, when I think of that day, I *sommer* begin to cry. I was never a cry-baby-tit, not even when the Ounooi took the strap to me, over my dress or on my legs or on my bare bum; I clench my teeth and swear to the LordGod I won't cry, I won't cry, even if they beat me dead. But those days I find that the tears come by themselves, just like that. Every time I see that thin man hanging by his neck, the crying start all over again. And the pee also, down my knees, no matter how hard I try to keep it in. That is when Frans put his arms around me and start to rub my back, my back and my arms, and at first I try to stop him, but soon I no longer try, and I can feel his arms moving all over my body, first my back and my arms, then down across my stomach and between my legs and between my buttocks, everywhere, while I just cry and cry, and his hands keep moving. And after some time I no longer cry, and I just let him do whatever he want, now I can feel him pushing into me, into the deepest deepness of myself, and then he begin to shake like a sheep that got its throat cut, and then I know that this is it, he is *naaiing* me, and I cannot and will not stop him any more, I just go on crying in his ears, no, no, no, crying no, no, yes, yes, yes, and then I no longer know or care what is happening. That is how it happen every time from that day on. If I start crying he will push himself into me, until I no longer care any which way, I just do whatever you wish, you are the Baas, just push into me, I no longer want or wish anything, just stay inside me, just keep on, don't stop.

And from this beginning what happen for us is not just the thing in the bamboo copse, but everything we do, everything we say, everything we think about. It is the thing, Ouma Nella tell us, that we call love. And not just because it make his thing stand up and push into me, but because we want to be together, he and I, and because he care for me and I for him, and because the world can only happen for us because we are together.

And I think that is why, when we are together and he

move into me, that he keep saying, Philida, I shall care for you, I promise you, I shall make it worth your while, I shall make sure that you're made free, I'll talk to Pa, and to the Landdrost, and to everybody in the whole wide world, from Zandvliet all the way to the Caab, I promise and I promise and I promise, from now on you are mine, for ever, for us there will never be a slave and a baas any more, just you and me, I promise and promise and promise, from now on we shall both wear shoes, for ever and ever, amen.

And every time Frans start telling me these things, I have questions that must be answered: How can such a thing ever happen? All these things you promise me, how can they come true? You are white, I'm a slave and a *meid*.

That is when he start explaining, over and over, how those Englishmen that are baas in the Caab, they may be bad, but they are not just bad. Remember, they brought their law with them, he tell me over and over, and what that law say is what must happen, not just in the Caab but in Stellenbosch and Paarl and Worcester and everywhere in this land and even over the sea. And what that law say is that this thing about baas and slave is wrong and it must stop, and soon there will be a day when everything will be different.

And will we all wear shoes then? I ask him.

Then Frans say, Yes, that is how it will be. Shoes on our feet so that we can go where we please, we can walk all the way to England if we wish. I shall go and talk to the Landdrost in Stellenbosch, he say, and to the Council of Justice and to the Govment. The world will be a very different place from today, you'll see, we must just be patient and bide our time, you and I and everybody.

And Kleinkat too?

Yes, Kleinkat too, he say.

III

Francois remembers his Childhood with
Philida and the Stories about the early Days of Zandvliet
before MaJanna married into the Brink Family

Yes. To Philida I would promise anything, ever since we were children. She was the first person I really wanted to be with. By the time I was about eight, so she must have been eleven or thereabouts, I already had the habit of filling a wooden barrel in the kitchen with hot water from the hearth so that she could take a bath while I kept watch at the outside door, because I didn't want anybody to see her without clothes. As if that could make much difference! Her poor little dresses were just rags and tatters. Philida with the cut and bruised feet, barely a toe or nail unscathed, covered in dust and dirt and chickenshit and cowshit, but I still remember how carefully I used to hold them in my hands and rub lard on them and how much she liked it. Such small, thin feet, but she could run like a steenbokkie if she wanted to. What I wished above all else, and what I kept promising her for years and years, was to give her a pair of shoes. I'd have loved to make her a pair with my own hands, it's a skill Pa taught me, one of the few things I can really do properly. I'm not big and strong like some of my brothers – KleinCornelis or Lodewyk, who are like tree trunks in the dusty yard. I myself always prefer to be indoors rather than out, and from the time I was only a couple of hands tall Philida taught me to crochet and make quilts. But then Pa decided that was too girlish and it was time to move outside. I learned to manage the fields and the orchards and especially the vineyards with their hermitage and hanepoot and steen grapes and muscadel and a bit of shy cabernet. I have to attend to all of this while my pious brother Johannes Jacobus spends his Friday evenings at an address on the Kreupelsteeg in Amsterdam where he habitually drains a *borrel* before spending a sedate hour with a plump prostitute whom he casually mentions in private letters to me, not sparing me any details, such as his insistence on wearing his bladdy home-made socks knitted by Philida to ward off the cold. To our parents he presumably pretends to be gathering information which may be of use in future sermons to his congregation once he is back home.

In those early days, before I was forced to work outdoors, I saw Philida the most, because she was the knitting girl. But we never got as far as shoes. For she was a slave child and slaves and shoes had nothing to do with one another. That was why I kept on promising to buy her freedom one day, so she could get those shoes she wanted so badly. I'm sure she never cared as much for freedom as for shoes. And I swear – I really swear – that was what I wanted for her. How could I know that PaCornelis would once again put his foot down? He set Petronella free so many years ago already, the old woman in whose room Philida still sleeps. So why couldn't he do the same for Philida?

Or perhaps I should have known it all along, he's my father after all. Still, I never thought that he'd find it so bloody difficult to agree to buy the freedom of a slave girl. She was always so small, with those narrow little feet, what difference could that really make to Pa, one skinny girl less on the farm, there have always been such a lot of them around, always under one's feet.

But the real problem wasn't the shoes or the work. The problem was MaJanna. When she met Pa, she was the widow of Oom Wouter de Vos, who was an important man at the Caab, and MaJanna always reckoned that Pa could never stand in the shoes of such a man. He was a Brink and everybody knew, she said, that the Brinks were rather ordinary people. All we have is money. Not class. Which is why MaJanna decided right from the beginning that her children should marry well one day. If MaJanna hadn't been in such haste to get her children's future settled, I might still have stood a chance of putting in a word for Philida. But then she set her sights on a white girl for me and all I could do was to say Yes and Amen to everything. And now Philida is stuck with Lena and Willempie, our children, my slave children, apart from the two who died early, little Mamie and the one she does not want to talk about, the baby, my four children and hers, so what can I do now?

It will bring shame on the family, and MaJanna would like for our farm to be counted among the best in the Drakenstein. Look at how it began. Conceived and born in sin, to say it outright. For in about 1690, when the farm was first handed out by the Governor, there were stories doing the rounds. It had been given to two young men, a Hans Silberbach and a Callas Louw. Silberbach had fourteen cattle and more than two hundred sheep and a blunderbuss, and Louw had no more than a blunderbuss to his name. Both had to make their way through the world weighed down by shadows. Silberbach got married to a freed slave woman, Ansela, who'd been deported from Java after murdering her white lover. On the neighbouring farm someone called Arij Lekkerwijn moved in with a young Frenchwoman, Marie de Lanoy. But somehow things between the neighbours turned sour and for some dark reason Silberbach bashed in Lekkerwijn's skull with a piece of firewood and he was forced to run off into the deep interior with a price on his head. A stain of blood on the farm, right from the start. Which is why I said it was conceived and born in sin. And it may be that this event kept hanging over Zandvliet like a black cloud. But in all that darkness Kleinkat was here like a small ray of sunlight.

IV

*In this Chapter Philida's Thoughts continue to
dwell on Zandvliet and the House of Ghosts and Cats in
which she lives with her Ouma Petronella*

It is because Kleinkat is with us that I know something is still
good on the farm. Whether I'm alone in the longhouse or with
Ouma Nella in her room, or when Frans is with me, I know
that there's always something special, something different about
her. Sometimes I think she must be one of the greyfeet that go
about in the dark, for often when I hold her in my arms, I can
see her lifting her little head to stare over my shoulder, and then
I know she can see things that no one else can see. Or while
she's lying quietly on the bed, half asleep, she would suddenly
sit up and start playing. Not the way other cats play, jumping
and charging and grabbing at things, but as if she's really playing
with another cat, like one of the little ones Frans was supposed
to drown. I tell you, she can play like that for hours on end,
with something that isn't there, that little striped thing. She will
wriggle herself into my arms until she fall asleep. Otherwise
she'll suddenly run away, her back straight, her tail all stiff and
stretched out, walking about in circles on long, straight legs as
if she don't recognise anybody and don't belong here, and her
eyes – that start off a deep blue, then turn yellow, then green,
then greener, then grass-green – they look as if they come from
somewhere else, somewhere very far from here, further than all
the farms of Drakenstein, on the far side of the world itself, the
other side of England, the other side of the whole world.

Sometimes when I'm working, knitting or something, she go outside, and when she come back I can smell the garden on her. She smell of green grass, and of the sun, she smell of birds and their feathers, and of the young wind, her little feet smell of buchu. Then she come to lie against me, or she get hold of a piece of knitting and unravel it, and many times it lead to a quarrel with the Ounooi, a bloody awful quarrel that leave me with my tail on fire and make me feel I can murder the cat, but the moment I pick her up and I see her staring right into me with those grass-green eyes and I smell her little buchu feet, I forget all about the trouble; as long as Kleinkat is here with me the world is the best of all places to be in. One day, I know I'll no longer be here, I'll be far away in a place of my own, a place like Zandvliet but different, with Frans and Kleinkat, and our children, just us, free for always and always, and with shoes on our feet.

Of course Zandvliet will still belong to Oubaas Cornelis Brink, it's a white man's farm, and we are only the hands that work here, the feet that tread the grapes in the big vat, or churn up dust on the wide yard around the longhouse, we are the backs that bend until they feel like breaking, we are the necks that get throttled, the stomachs that get hollow from hunger, and mine are the hands that keep on knitting and knitting and honest-to-God never stop knitting, and then stop for a moment to unravel a piece that went wrong, or to pick up a fallen stitch, morning and noon and night. Knitting and knitting and knitting, longstitch and plainstitch and purlstich and tacking stitch, and unravelling everything when you drop one or make a mistake with your in-and-over-and-through-and-off, and doing it all once more from the beginning if there is one wrong stitch in it, even if the day burn out into night and your fingers get numb in the dark yellow light of the candle that get smothered in its own wax and your eyes feel as if someone throw a handful of sand into them, and every time, every single bladdy time, it ends with Ounooi Janna's *riem* on your shoulders or your backside, and nothing for supper before you go to bed.

So Zandvliet is where it all begin, and from there you go past Lekkerwijn, and L'Ormarins, past Boschendal, then Rhône and Languedoc and Goede Hoop, and Bethlehem, which must be the Bethlehem of the Bible where the Lord Jesus was born, all the white people's farms, all those strange and pretty names that come from faraway places that no one can ever reach, and open spaces in between, void and something as the Bible say, and up and up along the Helshoogde from where I can look back to see the whole world open up behind me like a piece of knitting that is not yet sewn up, all the colours and colours, with bits and pieces of wool and twine and fringes and trimming and buttonholes and loose flaps, up to the very top, and then slowly down into the valley until I get to Stellenbosch where I am now waiting in the dirty cell for Frans to come.

So many things you pass along the way. Near the end of the first heights, below the blue mountains of Great Drakenstein on the left, there's the fountain that lie waiting for the girls to come and fetch water so they can watch their own faces in the bright deepness. Some of the girls stare so hard that something at the bottom slip loose and begin to stare back at them, and then a Water Woman with very long hair come up to the surface and grab one of them and drag her down and never let her go again. For a little while the water keep bubbling and then it is over. From time to time it spill over the edges and then I can hear dark things moving about on the bottom. But sooner or later it draw back, like a story that get lost along the way, and that you may never find again. And the fountain keep on unmoving above the darkness of its own depths and that will remain a secret forever. And all it can do is to keep reflecting the sky up above, and all the clouds and the stars and the sun and moon. The water from yesterday, the water from all time – water that may never see my face again.

From there I walk on. Always further and further. Until I can no longer move and simply lie down just where I am and fall asleep, a sleep as deep as an old fountain that is dried up and can no longer remember anything. When I wake up again in the early dawn I see something moving far below me, something that may be a man: and if it is a man, it must be someone that learned to live alone with his thoughts, with his will and his wishes, all his desires and his suffering, all the power he got inside him, however little that may be, and his sadness about the world and everything that happen inside it; a man that once upon a time was a baby, like the one in the *abbadoek* on my back, and later become a child, a child that got to learn to live with hunger and thirst for food and water, but also with the thirst and hunger to know and to understand. The thirst and hunger to taste and to see, to know about what is waiting round the next bend in the road or the next peak on the mountain, someone who is no more than a little sliver of skin that remain of everything he once know and understood, loose from everything that bring him to this place and everything he became, just *someone*, a man, And there he's walking now, and here I am walking, where is he going, where am *I* going?

I am used to walking. When we first came from the Caab to Zandvliet, I had to walk beside the wagon all the way, and it was a bladdy long way, until my feet were bleeding. But this time, when I came to Stellenbosch, it was different of course. This time it was my own choice, and I noticed every little thing along the Elephant Trail. Now and then

I can see a springbok or a ribbok or a civet cat in the distance, but I don't care about them, they move away like shadows as I come closer, they're like the ghosts that come and go wherever I move, some of them are there to look after me, others to try and scare me. I sometimes wish one of them would come to help me carry the baby in the *abbadoek*, he may be barely a month old, but he keep drinking all the way. My breasts are full.

Every step take me further away from Zandvliet. It's like a sharp pain in my chest, because I'm moving further and further from everything that was never mine. What else can I do? Where else can I go to? That was why I keep following the Elephant Trail that bring me to this tall Drostdy where I must now keep waiting in this cell.

So far from Zandvliet, from the farm. The house, the longhouse behind the thin row of palm trees. How well I know that place, every furrow and every stone I know, every bit of field and vineyard, the reeds and the bluegums, the deep shade of the bamboo copse, the small whitewashed cemetery between the longhouse and the bamboos, where the dead lie buried. The copse where Frans take me that first time we go there on our own. Before that, it is only fun and games, like when the boys taking us girls with them to the peach orchard. To climb the trees, they say. But it is always the girls who got to climb up first, followed by the boys, so they can stay behind us and below us, then we cannot run away, they stay between us and the ground. And always, from the time we are small, there is Frans right behind me, his head between my feet, his head between my knees. Just for fun. But that day in the bamboo copse it was not for fun, and it was just him and me. And because of that I got to come all the way along the road with its many bends today, further and further away from the farm and the longhouse.

How well I know that house. The long low stoep and the heavy front door made of coffin planks, and the wide passage, always cool in summer when the cicadas are shrilling outside. The small table in the passage, yellowwood and stinkwood, and the mirrors. Mirrors everywhere inside, one can never get away from them. Which is why the ghosts never go away, they come for the mirrors.

Almost every room got its ghost, some rooms got two, some four or five. In the early days I am too scared to sleep in that house, but Ouma Nella soon teach me not to be afraid. They're our people, she told me, the greyfeet, and they're of all kinds. There's the white woman that drown herself in the Dwars River right next to the bamboo copse, in the very early days of the farm, because her husband beat her so badly. And the slave woman who run away just after she arrive on the ship from Boegies. But the Baas of the farm go after her, it was long before Oubaas Cornelis, and he catch her and chop off her feet. She die soon after that. And now she only walk when the moon is full, round and round the farm, but she cannot find the way back to Boegies. There's a slave man too, they say he lay with the white Nooi of the farm when the Baas was gone to the Caab with two vats of wine. When he got caught, the people say, his Baas took him back to the Fiscal and he had to run all the way there behind the horse, and there they made him sit on a long rod stuck up his back-side, nine days before he died, without food or water. Ghosts, ghosts everywhere, there are nights when they're moving and swarming and moaning and screeching so much that nobody can sleep a wink. Worst of all is the dead baby that cry and cry all the time and never stop, no matter how deep you try to hide under the *karosses*, and that one I know very well, he just cry and cry, it's the ghost of my own Little Frans. He's so small and thin, you can look right through him, but he's there.

It's from the cats that I always know when the ghosts are out and about. A cat know all about ghosts, they say. It can see and hear them when they just beginning to stir in the distance, and then it start growling and hissing and puffing up its hair like feathers. Then you *sommer* know there's ghosts about. Go away, I tell them, move off, *voertsek*, but they don't listen. And some of them can get very difficult, you got to keep your eyes wide open.

Each one of those ghosts got its own story to tell and they walk along all the roads and paths and trails of the land. Perhaps my own story will also learn to find its way. In the end it's only the road itself that stay behind and a road don't talk much to anybody. That's why I'm not expecting too much from this road to Stellenbosch. The most I can do is to go as far as I can, writing my own story in the dust with my two feet, word for word. All the way, from the longhouse to here where I am waiting for Frans to turn up.

And when it's finished I'll go back home. Back to our house and to our room. The room where Ouma Nella live, and I with her. It's not an outroom like those of the other slaves, ours is part of the house. If you go through the wide front door into the *voorhuis*, you turn left and then keep on to the end. There you'll find our inside door. We got an outside door too, but that's just for the two of us and people who visit us, nobody else. Not even the Oubaas. Because Ouma Nella was a slave once, but she's a slave no more. She was set free. And only the LordGod and the Oubaas can tell how that happened.

And then at last, one day, the door of the cell is opened and I am called out. And there I find Frans waiting. Hurry up now, they tell me. Your Baas Francois is come to see you, move your backside.

V

In which Ink and Blood are spilled

Now Philida has gone and lodged this complaint against us and everything is a terrible mess, just because there wasn't time enough before she left to arrange and discuss the situation properly. I was shocked when I heard what Pa and MaJanna were planning for me, but I thought they would see reason and talk about it first. Then, before any of us knew what was going on, we heard that she'd gone to Stellenbosch to accuse us. Accuse me. As far as they were concerned, everything was already agreed and done and my whole future was planned without me. It came like a jug of water in the face when the messenger arrived from the Drostdy to demand an answer to the accusations she had brought against us.

At least I needed to get to know this woman they had decided I had to marry, Maria Magdalena Berrangé. All I knew about her was from the day Pa took the whole family in to the Caab, to the Oranje Street where she lives with her family, and now things have to go as they must, there's nothing I can do to stop or help them along any more. I can say that she is a fine young woman, dressed like the top ladies in the Colony, long dresses and shawls, one over the other, giving one no hint of what may be going on underneath. But she showed a glimpse of ankle once and that didn't look bad at all, a bit bony and very white, but enough to make one curious. It's just that she looks rather uppity, her small pointed nose in the air, with a spread of freckles where the sun of the Caab has got to her. As it happens I quite like freckles, although MaJanna can be vicious about them.

If only I could have spoken to Philida about her before she left for Stellenbosch, just so that she could know and I could hear what she thought, but she was gone before I ever knew about it. And then the summons from Mijnheer Lindenberg arrived out of the blue. A bad time for that, it is summer and the fruit are getting ripe, the early apricots, and the plums, and the grapes beginning to cluster, they need attention all the time. But the folk at the Drostdy cannot care less about a farmer's time and seasons. If they say the word one must jump. And talk is not enough either, everything has to be in writing. In English, mind you, even though I know Mijnheer Lindenberg is an Afrikaner just like me. Not English nor Dutch like most of the other officials at the Caab, but born and bred here in the Colony, so he should know better.

When it comes to writing the officials at the Drostdy are the worst, but of course they get all their orders from above, all of it in writing, it's the English government's way of doing things. Even Philida has caught the bug. For weeks and months she went on pestering me to show her the names and things written about my family at the back of Pa's big black State Bible. Not as big as the one Oom Daniel inherited from Oupa Andries, because Pa is only a fifth son in the line, not the eldest. But this Bible is big and heavy enough.

Over and over, whenever we find a moment without anyone else around, Philida gets me to show her the pages at the back of the Bible, where Pa wrote our names in ink. Starting with Andries Brink from Waarden or Woerden, nobody is quite sure about the name of the place, followed by a date, 1739, and all of that I explained to her. Then in a long row all his children with his two wives. Four of them with the first, Sophia Grové, followed by nine more with Alida de Waal. And from his seventh son, a Johannes, there came fifteen children, of whom the fifth was my father Cornelis. And that is how we got here.

Below the name *Cornelis* in the long row Pa wrote in the names of his own children: from Ouboet Johannes Jacobus, who is in Holland now, learning to be a dominee, and then I, Francois Gerhard Jacob, past KleinCornelis and Daantjie and Lood and the few who died when they were small, down to Elisabet and Alida and ending with Woudrien, the twelfth, who also died as a baby. Our whole family, it seems, has got this dying streak.

And that was where Philida became a real pest. She kept on saying she also wanted to get into the Book. The more I told her it was a book for white people only, the more she kept on: It's just a lot of names, Frans, it says nothing about white people and slaves.

Philida, it doesn't work like that, there's nothing you or I can change about it, this is just the way the world is.

Then we got to change the way of the world, Frans, she goes on nagging, otherwise it will always stay the same.

No, I keep telling her, some things just *cannot* be changed from the way the LordGod made them.

Then we got to start with changing the LordGod, she says.

You don't know that man, I warn her. He's a real bastard when it comes to making trouble.

I tell you I want to be in that Book, she goes on.

I'm telling you, Philida, I keep insisting, it can't be done and it won't be done, and that's the way it is.

Then give the pen to me, she says in a temper one morning, when all the house people are busy outside, it is only her and me in the *voorhuis*. If you can't or won't do it,

I'll do it myself. And she grabs the pen out of my hand and the feather at the tip scrapes against the side of the Book, the shiny side, and her arm knocks over the brown ink jar so that the ink Pa had mixed himself from the powder he ordered from Holland, everything just perfect for writing, is overturned and a huge black-blue blot starts to spread right across the page where she has dreamed of her name written next to mine.

Now they're going to kill both of us, I promise her. But Philida only says, even though I can hear her own voice is getting thin and reedy: Nobody will ever know, man. For all they know, it was the LordGod himself that made this mess.

Until today, as far as I know, nobody has seen it yet, because there's been no need for anyone to turn that page. That will only happen, if you ask me, when MaJanna has another child, and I'm sure that won't happen very soon, I don't think it is likely if one looks at her, or if Pa decides to fill in *Maria Magdalena Berrangé* next to my own name. And by that time, if God wills, nobody will ever know or wonder about the matter any more.

That isn't a day I care to think about a lot. The mere idea terrifies me. To think that by that time Maria Magdalena Berrangé may already be at my side. With her fancy thin ankles. And Philida? Nobody will know about her any more. She's the reason why I got that message from the Landdrost in Stellenbosch. And hard on the heels of the messenger it was Pa himself who called me to the *voorhuis* to talk about it. His tanned face looked like a thunderstorm. I had to listen very closely, he said. Because he is a notable man and in our own way I suppose we're a notable family and he doesn't want his name to be dragged through shit just because I'm too hopeless to deny something a damn slave girl did with me.

Easy for Pa to talk, I said. There was a time when you yourself had a lot of good things to say about Philida. At that time everybody could see that Philida had her first child inside her and they knew it came from what she and I had done. It's the sort of thing most of the men at the Caab do, so you can't pretend you don't know.

That was where he started breathing more heavily from being so angry. I've never had anything to do with a slave *meid*, he said.

I was tempted to ask him: And what about the thing everybody keeps talking about? That it was our own grandfather Oupa Johannes who first took Ouma Petronella nine months before you yourself were born, and that that is the reason you later bought her freedom? But I knew that it would be asking for trouble if I dared to talk about it. I myself had heard him say openly that if anybody on this farm, big or small, slave or white man, ever tried to gossip about that, he would be thrown into the shithouse pit to choke in *kak*. Did everybody understand? So I rather said nothing. I didn't want to lead him into temptation.

What I did ask him very cautiously was: But what if the man at the Drostdy starts asking me questions? What do I say then?

Then you just tell him what you saw with your own two eyes, said Pa. About those two slaves of Izak Marais who *naaied* Philida. That's where her last baby came from, not so? And her previous ones too, as far as we know.

How can Pa say a thing like that? I asked him. When was it those boys lay with her? They could not have had anything to do with the baby because it was only a few months before little Willempie was born.

That is in your own hands, said Pa. I don't want to hear anything about it. All I can tell you is that if you want to drag the Brinks' name through the mud you got to take responsibility for it.

I will.

You'll just mess everything up. Like you always do.

I won't, Pa, I told him. It just came to me. A year ago, I would have stopped right there. But not after that day in the backyard. And I saw Pa waver, saw him look up at me, measuring me. Up and down. Then up again.

This is for me to handle the way I see fit, I said.

I shall go with you, said Pa.

This is not your shit, I told him. It is mine. So I'm going to the Protector on my own. You stay right here at home.

I am still your Pa, Francois, he said firmly, but very quietly.

I said nothing. Just kept looking at him.

And after what felt like for ever, he spoke again: When will you be going? he asked without looking at me.

Tomorrow morning, I said.

We didn't talk any more about the summons. But all the way to Stellenbosch on the back of the big black horse I kept remembering what we'd seen that day behind the homestead in our own backyard. Pa'd called everybody on the farm together, the way he used to do when he thought there was something for us to see or to learn. It was like the day he took us all to the Caab to watch the hanging. This time it was to look at Philida and the two young slaves. Though I still keep wishing God would have chosen not to let me be there on the day the two of them were brought on the donkey cart from the farm L'Ormarins. It was Pa's own idea to send the cart, after he'd discussed it with Oom Izak Marais, the Baas on that farm. The two slave boys had no idea of what was coming and they looked as scared as two chickens lost in the veld when they arrived at our place. None of us at Zandvliet had any idea either.

First Pa goes to call Philida, who sits knitting on the back stoep.

He is waiting in the backyard beside the flogging bench that he has ordered the outdoor slaves to drag out for the occasion, with a long sjambok in his hand while we all stand clustered together in a corner, trying to keep out of his reach.

Take off your clothes, Pa tells Philida. And hurry up, I haven't got all day.

Baas? asks Philida.

Take them off, says Pa, flicking the sjambok against the legs of his corduroy breeches. Today we need you *kaalgat*.

But Baas?

Philida, you heard what I said.

Once more she tries to protest, but then the tip of that long sjambok swishes across her thin blue-grey dress: I'm not saying another word, *meid*.

You can't do that, Baas!

Philida, take off that bladdy dress.

That is when I also dare to speak up: But Pa!

You shut up and stay out of this, Francois Gerhard Jacob! He only uses my full name when he is totally furious.

Philida takes her time removing the blue dress, faded from many washes. I don't want to watch, but something in me makes it impossible not to look. I *see* her. In front of all the others I see what has been meant only for me, ever since that first time I filled the wooden pail in the kitchen with hot water for her to bathe in. Her breasts that fitted so tightly into my cupped hands. Her stomach that was mine, with my child moving inside. Her narrow face with the wide cheekbones. Her big pitch-black eyes. I can see the little flicker beside her mouth. I know that flicker.

Pa motions to her to lie down on the flogging bench.

Flat on her back. There is nothing about her I do not know. And that is how he has her tied down.

I can feel my hands clenching into fists. If he dares to hit her with that sjambok I know the LordGod himself won't be able to hold me back. But this time Pa has a very different idea in his head. He motions to the two young slave boys who are still huddling together to one side. They may be as young as two-toothed lambs, but one can immediately see that Pa has had good reason to select these two.

Move your arse! he orders the first one.

Baas?

Get up on her, man!

The youngster clambers on top of her.

Now *naai* her!

Baas?

The first blow slices open his buttocks as if they've been cut with a knife.

Moerskont! Naai her when I say so. That's all you bladdy randy goats are good for!

For a moment the boy holds back, but spurred on by the sjambok he plunges forward and starts bucking furiously. It is over much sooner than I expected and then Pa steps closer to help him down again. From the thick, dark tip of his thing a drool of slime still comes trickling. Philida doesn't move and makes no sound. For me her silence is worse than anything else. Previously, when she landed in trouble, all beatings were administered by MaJanna, and it always happened inside the *langhuis*, wherever the suspected misdemeanour was alleged to have taken place – in the kitchen or in the *dispens*, in the *voorhuis*, in the dining room or out on the stoep. Whether it was MaJanna's decision or his, I don't know, but Pa generally kept out of the way when any of the slave women had to be corrected. That was the word commonly used at Zandvliet.

On that day I found it impossible to watch any longer. Without losing another moment, I made my getaway into the kitchen and from there through the *voorhuis* to Old Petronella's room. She was the only person I could think of who might still put an end to what was happening.

Petronella! I shouted. Petronella, come here this minute! We need you!

Without waiting, I pushed open her inside door. But there was no sign of her. While I was still desperately trying to think of something to do, one of the house slaves, Sara, came in from the *voorhuis* behind me.

What is Baas Frans looking for? she asked.

I must find Old Petronella.

She's not here, everybody is out in the backyard.

Only then did I learn that Old Petronella had been sent out at daybreak to deliver a *karmenaadjie* to Lekkerwijn. It took Sara a while to explain the situation, and even before she could finish I was on my way again, through the kitchen to where the unspeakable was taking place.

But it was already too late. Through the throng in the backyard I could see Pa standing with the long sjambok in his hand. Philida still lay spreadeagled on the bench. Between her parted legs I could see the second of the young stallions from L'Ormarins huddled over her, his arse bucking and bobbing as Pa's sjambok drew stripes of blood from his buttocks. Almost before he'd properly finished Pa was back to shoo him off from the bench.

Pa! I screamed at him. How the bladdy hell dare you? The LordGod himself, I swear, could not have held me back. Then I saw Pa's arm with the long sjambok jerk back and the blow struck me in the face, just missing my eye. The pain was unbearable and I sank to my knees, covering my face with both hands.

Stop it, you little shit! I heard him growl before I was blinded by tears and blood streaming down my cheeks.

Pure rage took over. In one way or another I managed to stagger to my feet. I came up to him and to my amazement I realised something that had never penetrated my consciousness: how very small he was, half a head shorter than I, strutting about the yard like a little bantam cockerel. Until that day I had always thought of him as just my father, the Baas of Zandvliet, whose word was law, a man just below the LordGod himself. When he said something it was like one of the Commandments in Exodus, proclaimed aloud, straight from God on the Mount Sinai, which you had to obey or find yourself struck down into the fire, sand and brimstone of hell. And now, suddenly and shockingly, he had turned into a small and rather ludicrous person, shorter than me. How could I ever have felt scared of him?

Get away from me! he shouted in a falsetto voice. You have no business in this yard. Why don't you go and help your mother with her sewing?

Shut up, Pa! I shouted, astounded by my own voice.

Listen to me, Frans!

I won't ever listen to you again, I told him. What you are doing here today is an abomination in the eyes of the LordGod.

Shut your trap, you little *poephol!*

Who is the *poephol* here? I asked him.

Francois Gerhard Jacob, today I swear I am going to kill you!

Let's see who gets killed, I shouted back, completely beside myself.

That was when he swung up his right hand to strike out again with the long hippopotamus sjambok. But this time I

· 44 ·

was ready for him and I managed to grab the whiplash and jerk it away with such fury that he lost his balance and stumbled forward, landing on all fours next to me.

Francois! he bellowed. *Moerskont!*

And then I heard MaJanna saying: Now that's enough, both of you. And somehow the pandemonium around us subsided and only MaJanna and Pa and I were left behind, everybody else withdrawing to a safe distance. He slowly got back to his feet. I was aware of my hands still clenched into fists. But what had happened, had happened. For months after that I would continue to be haunted by the memory. For months? For the rest of my life. I can still see the small blunt cart rumbling off through the dust towards L'Ormarins. I can still see Philida sitting on the bench in a small tattered bundle, her thin arms clutching her knees, her rough dirty feet drawn in under her. Those thin small feet I used to fondle in my hands.

Come on, Pa snarled at her. There were traces of snot on his moustache. Put on your clothes. And don't you forget what happened here today. That comes from sleeping around. If you don't know yet you will find out soon enough.

At last he turned to face me again, glowering. Then without another word he left the yard followed by MaJanna.

VI

Which is as True as it is False

There's no way any of us can deny it: that day changed the world. Before that day, whatever happened between Philida and me, concerned nobody but the two of us. If anybody else knew about it, that made no difference, it was not their business. To stand there with all the others looking on while those two boys took turns with Philida, the way she lay there exposed like a lamb brought to slaughter, that was unbearable. In the kitchen, when she had her bath in the barrel, or in Ouma Petronella's room, or down in the bamboo copse, she was always mine only. Now we were a spectacle for all their eyes. And then the stories started, Ma and Pa's stories about Maria Magdalena Berrangé, about what was acceptable and what wasn't; it made me sick. There was nothing left that was only ours any more.

And the last straw came the day Philida went off, with the child on her back, to lay her complaint, to make it known to the whole world that I'd promised to set her free. It was like something snatched away from me and dragged through the mud and shit of the pigsty where that old sow wallowed all day. And all the gossip, like that *trassie* of a hen that kept cackling about the eggs laid by other chickens. Now I had to go and explain it so that the man at the Drostdy could write it up in his book for everybody to see. How could they expect that of me?

Nobody here on the farm had the faintest idea that this

was what she was going to do. How could we? Petronella was the only one she'd told about it, because the old woman had to stay behind to look after little Lena, and Petronella of course told MaJanna, long after Philida was safely out of the way, and MaJanna told Pa. He was all for getting on his horse to go and fetch her back, but MaJanna stopped him. Let the bladdy *boermeid* go, she said. And I hope she never sets foot here again.

But Ma – I tried to say.

Don't you come and but Ma me, she snapped. You have nothing to say in this business.

So when the message came I had no chance to protest or to choose or to think about it. When the Drostdy opens its mouth we've got to move our arses. I was still seething when I set out for Stellenbosch.

Arriving at the Drostdy I was ready for a fight. And it didn't make things easier when the tall sweating man in the office above the high stoep made me wait until he'd finished whatever he was doing. But at long last he was ready to see me and he asked a cheeky young clerk to show me in. Philida already stood waiting inside, with the child on her back. I could see his white curls sticking out from the *abba-doek*. Everything was open and exposed before us. It felt like when the slave bell clangs on the farmyard at daybreak every bladdy morning to get us out of bed and start working. That's the way Pa begins his day. The moment the black rooster crows – everything still pitch dark, it feels like midnight on the farm, with only the smallest, dirtiest little smudge of red in the sky – he leans out over the wide windowsill to bellow: Ring that bell so the work can begin. Ring it!

And if the rooster is the smallest bit late, not even a second – God knows how Pa manages to wake up just so he can check on the rooster – he tiptoes outside on the thick soles of his bare feet and I swear to God he pokes the rooster in the arse with the stick he always keeps beside the bed, and the poor thing gets such a fright that he nearly swallows the crow in his throat, and then it's time for the bell, loud enough to wake up the dead on the Day of Judgement. The bell has often made me think that if the LordGod woke up on that morning and came to his window in his nightshirt to set us working, I'd just turn away and tell him to shove his work up his arse. I wouldn't want anything to do with it.

Philida stood looking away from me as I came into the office on the front stoep of the Drostdy. I also turned my head away. But I did hesitate for a moment to tell her in passing: Good day, Philida. Because I could feel my heart going numb inside me. Look how small she had become in the time she was away. How skinny. Her feet so thin. It wasn't the child on her back that made me feel like that. It was she herself, Philida.

The silence sat heavy between us. And when Mijnheer Lindenberg started questioning me, all I could think of saying was: There is nothing I know about this slave woman, Mijnheer. How could I have ever promised to set her free if she would lie with me? She is not my slave. She belongs to my father. It is not for me to say what must happen to her.

I could feel Philida's growing resistance in the room, but there was no turning back now.

The tall man went on and on with his questions. And what about this child? he wanted to know. Are you not the father?

How can I be the father? Mijnheer Lindenberg, I have never had anything to do with her. My mother would never have allowed anything like that to happen in her house.

Then where do those children come from?

I kept staring straight ahead, still avoiding Philida: That I cannot tell you, Mijnheer. All I know is that she lay with two of our neighbour's slaves. I saw it with my own eyes.

I couldn't look the man in the face either, but told him without any hesitation: Philida whored with any man who came along.

Mijnheer Lindenberg kept on: She told me that you promised her from the beginning that if you lay with her and a child was born you would buy her freedom and her child's.

And then I don't know where those strange words came from, but they were all that made sense at the time: What the *meid* is saying is just as true as it is false.

What is that supposed to mean? asked the man from the Drostdy.

It doesn't mean anything, I replied. It's a slave's word, and mine is a white man's word.

I want to know what it means if you say that her complaint is just as true as it is false.

It means exactly what I said, Mijnheer, I persisted. Her word means nothing against mine because I already told you she is a slave and not even mine. She belongs to my father. I have no say over her, my father is the only one who can decide about setting her free or not. So there is no way I could ever have promised her such a thing. There is nothing, good or bad, I can do for her. I have nothing at all, Mijnheer Lindenberg. I'm standing bare-arsed before you. The *meid* has already brought enough shame on me and our family. If I try to do anything more for her, it'll be finished and *klaar* with me. I'm sorry to have to say this, Mijnheer, but you can see for yourself that she can no longer stay in our family after all her cheekiness and lies and the way she behaved to my mother and the rest of us.

The man kept writing in his book for a long time. Afterwards he turned to Philida and asked her: If all this is true, how can you still expect your Baas to set you free? After all the lies you told?

Philida said: I'm not asking to be set free any more, Grootbaas. I been lied to too many times by too many people. All I'm asking you today is not to make them sell me and my children inland. Please, Grootbaas. They're too small and the inland is too far away.

There's nothing I can do about what happens inland, said the tall, bony man. After all the lies you told there's nothing I can do for you anyway.

Then the Grootbaas must *maar* do what he want, I heard her say. She leaned forward and untied the knot of the *abbadoek*. With a deft movement of her body she shifted the child round to her front and opened her arms to make him sit up in her embrace, as the man moved closer to look straight into those two bright blue eyes.

She said, Here is the lie I told, Grootbaas.

Mijnheer Lindenberg remained standing for a long time, peering at her. Then he motioned with his head towards the door.

I pretended not to hear what she said, but I'm sure she knew very well that I was looking. And at that moment I remembered a passage from the Bible that Pa often read. About Peter who looked Our Lord right in the face when he said: I don't know the man. And about the cock that crowed. But this time, today, it was right inside my own flesh and blood that I heard that blasted cock crowing. And it sounded worse than that *trassie* hen in the backyard, that Zelda that cackled about the eggs laid by the other hens.

As I started walking away, there was something still trying to rein me in, to hold me back, in that office where

I knew Philida must still be standing, waiting with the bundle on her back. *Her* bundle. *Mine. Ours.* What I'd done to her I could never wash from me again. I'd lied myself straight into hell. But what would become of me if I were to take back what I said? It wasn't just about me and her and the child. What about Pa? What about MaJanna? What about our whole family, all the way back to Grandpa Andries who came on the ship? What about the Berrangé family I was supposed to marry into? What about every man, woman or child that was white in this godforsaken land? It concerned everybody and everything that had made me who I was.

Outside the Drostdy I mounted my horse and turned back to the old Elephant Trail. I could feel his chest expanding and contracting against my calves, expanding and contracting, I could hear his wheezing, groaning breath coming and going. He was tiring. But I thought: Just let him. Let him collapse right here under me if he wants to. It's Pa's horse. Everything on the farm belongs to him. It's his just deserts if everything that's here begins to fall apart under him.

All the time I could feel Philida seeping back into my mind, but then I urged the horse on. There was no time to think of her now. How she'd have to walk all this way with her small narrow feet to get back to the farm. But I thought: Good. Let her wear herself out and fall down in a small heap. Don't let her ever come back. What made her bring this shame down on me?

The horse was beginning to slow down all by himself, his breath rattling and wheezing in his throat.

Until at last, at long, long last, we reached the aardvark hole where I had to turn off to the farm. I knew this hole. I was still a boy when soon after we came to Zandvliet from the Cape Pa showed me how to spot it: you look until you can make out where the animal positioned itself at the edge of the hole, its large hind pawmarks close together and the trail of its thick tail right between them, and on either side the hollows left by its balls. That was how one knew it was an aardvark, not a porcupine or a springhare.

And right after the hole one turns left to where one can see the white walls of Zandvliet flashing among the many greens of vineyards and fruit trees and shrubs. The thick white walls that have been standing there for generations, more than a hundred years and for all eternity. But the sweat running down my brow and starting to burn in my eyes caused a strange thing to happen. I couldn't see straight any more. As if I was no longer looking *at* things but at what was happening inside my eyes, as if the walls in the distance were becoming transparent, losing their solidness, like when you're whitewashing a wall and adding more and more water to the lime, until everything turns thin and colourless, until nothing is quite the way it was before, and nothing remains. All the greens of the farm – the vineyards and the plum orchards, the peaches, the quinces, the vegetables crouched on the ground – everything begins to run together in a dull smudge, and disappears in front of your eyes, and nothing remains of all that has been sowed and planted here, until it all becomes void and without form as it must have been right in the beginning. As if there has never been any people around, as if everything we have built and made has been in vain, as if it's only the wild world of the LordGod that remains, leaving no trace of people or animals, nothing at all.

VII

So they stand, without another Word, and with only the
Silence brooding between them, like the Shadow of a Giant
huddling there, and Philida feels the Words spoken by the
tall, bony Man growing thick and swollen in her own
Throat, and turning sour like curdled Milk, but there is no
way she can swallow them, and then their Ways part,
Francois to his Horse, Philida preparing to take the long
Road back on Foot, with all the Thoughts gathered inside her

But just as I get ready to leave, the thin man behind me
say, Not so fast, *meid*.

I stop.

The man say: You made your Baas come all this way just
to listen to a heap of lies.

How can it be lies? I ask. Didn't the Grootbaas see the
child for himself?

Shut up, he say. You're a slave and you've done a wicked
thing to tell all those lies. There's only one remedy for the
likes of you.

I keep silent, but I can feel everything settle in my stomach
like a thick lump of porridge.

He come past me to the door and call outside. Four of
his Kaffers appear so quickly that I feel they must have been
waiting right outside.

Here's the *meid*, say the thin man, rubbing his long hands
with the thick knuckles together. She lied to the court. You
know what to do about that.

My voice find it hard to settle in my throat, but all I can say is: Grootbaas, what about my child?

He call one of his helpers: You can give it to this man.

I want to stop him, but I know that this will only make things worse. To make sure that Willempie will not get hurt, I hand him over, but very slowly.

The two men in the doorway get ready to drag me off by the arms.

But just as they start to move, I hear Willempie whimper behind me and that make me stand still, even though I do not know where this come from. I can only hear my own voice as it break from my throat like a bird flying up from a bush.

Let me go! I shout so suddenly that it make them all stop. Don't touch me!

Behind me the tall man speak very quickly. What's going on here? he ask. These men are acting under my orders. They will do what I tell them.

Yes, the Grootbaas will tell them, I say, as if it is somebody else speaking in my voice. It is like a big juicy plum that suddenly appear on a branch in front of me, for me to pluck and stuff into me without thinking. I go on: And once they finish what the Grootbaas order them to do, yes, then we can all take the road to the Caab to find out what the Council of Justice and the Governor got to say about it.

All I really know about that thing they call the Council of Justice is what Frans tell me on that long-ago day when we first talking about the people in the Caab who got all the power. But after that day I forget all about it and it never come back to me again. Only now, from nowhere, it return and all I can do is to pluck it like a smooth, naked fruit and put it in my mouth. I look at the tall man and this time I can hear my own voice speaking very calm and fast as there is no fear left in me. And from the Caab, I say, from the Caab we can walk all the way to that England place where the laws come from. Then we can talk some more. Because I hear the law is now there to protect us slaves.

Where do you get that nonsense from? he ask.

They say the law in the Govment's books and the LordGod stand together, I tell him, but I still got no idea of how it got into my head.

What on earth are you talking about? he ask.

I just talking about all the walking, Grootbaas, I say. I know all about walking. The Elephant Trail and everywhere else where people walk. And I know the Grootbaas won't like to walk in all those places, but we can walk together if we must.

It is quiet for a very long time. I stand waiting for him to tell the men to get on with their job and give the bladdy *meid* what she deserves. But everything stay very quiet. Until I dare to look up to see for myself what is going on. And that is when the tall bony man say very softly through his teeth to his helpers: Just take the *meid* and let her go. Give her and her white child some food for the road and let them get out of my sight, otherwise I won't be responsible for what happens here any more.

It is a long way I got to walk home now, and it feel much longer this time than when I come here. I try to smooth out the wrinkles from the road by making up a story. It's something Ouma Nella tell me that very first time we walk all the way from the Caab to Zandvliet. And every time I have to walk after that I tell myself my stories again, so now I know them by heart. Ouma Nella's story and the ones I keep on making up. The stories everybody at Zandvliet and on the other farms know. About the fountain up in the mountains where the Water Snake with the shiny stone in his forehead live. Or about the girls that play around after dark and then get caught by the Nightwalkers and are changed into Water Women who come out and catch the boys making clay oxen on the banks and drown them in the deep water. These Water Women have scales on their bodies and when they feel like it they can shed their scales and start again, naked and new and smooth.

But not all the stories are about Water Women. There is one about the long-haired girl in the highest fountain, the one they call the Eye, high up along the mountains near the Elephant Trail, the one with the hair green as slime, and if she get mad with you she braid you into the long ropes of slime and drag you down, down to the darkest depths of the earth. There is another, about the Old Hag with the one shiny eye on her big toe. Or about the Mantis that changes itself into an Ostrich and then the Ostrich into a Feather, and then the Feather into an Eland, and so everything change into something else all the time. Or Ouma Nella talk about the wind that keep on telling his own stories from faraway places, the wind that take our footprints with him when we die, so people think we are not dead, because we all stick to our feet.

There is lots of other stories too, stories that hatch in my head while I walk along the road that never end. Nowadays, when I walk from Zandvliet to Stellenbosch, I start telling myself about a girl that get ill, and every step I give bring me closer to death and hell. But on the way back it turn into a story about a girl who come back from death and open her eyes and come to know her world again until she find herself back in her own place, a story that make me feel alive again.

Along the road I name everything I come past, as well as the things that do not have names yet, and in this way I get to know everything, and my own name as well. I begin with: Flatstone – Kneebreak Bend – Dead Tree – New Tree

– Steep Rock – Round Rock. Then there is Ouma's Rock – Old Man's Bend – Frans's Pissing Place – Ounooi Janna's Hole – Dead Gert's Sitting Stone, and so on. I start knitting them together, joining one row to the next, then the panels. And once the jersey is finished the names also come together, until I can tell in advance what is coming next, what will be waiting round the next bend, where I will reach the underarm, everything. Until I know the place as if I made it with my own hands. I can say: I knit my story to the end. Or I can say: I walk all the way to the last stitches of my story. It's all the same.

I can also change the stiches along the way, of course. I can add new stitches, or I can knit the panel a bit wider. I can use cross stitch or I can choose plain or purl. I needn't stick to other people's patterns. And that is how it happen today that when I get to Klaas's Quick Turn up on the hillside beyond Poor Man's Ditch, I decide to turn off to the Dark Blue Mountain that Ouma Nella first showed me and that no one else know about, just the two of us. It's a long way to go, but it help me to stretch the time so that I can reach Zandvliet later than usual, and I'm really in no hurry to get home. It's just walking and walking, downhill at first along the narrow footpath, the Cobra road where Ouma Nella and I once saw the big snake, down to the Thin Trees, and from there up along the opposite slope, the steep rise along White Thorns, across the Long Neck, past God's Stream, and the lovely straight stretch to the Hollow Cliff where the Eye lies staring unblinking at the sky. Because that is where I want to get to.

This is where Ouma Nella first showed me the overhang of red rocks, and if one bends over to peer under it, because it's very low down and you almost got to kneel to see: a long line of little people walking along the solid rock, or standing or jumping, small thin men with bows and arrows and knobbly knees and spiky legs and sticklike pricks. One of the men is thinner and longer than the others, with a big round head that always make Ouma Nella burst out laughing when she look at him and I can see why.

There are three elands too in the row of little men, elands with very big humps and long straight horns, two or three times as big as the little prickmen, and even a few elephants. Those must be some of the elephants that used to cross these mountains in the dawn-days of the world and that was the first storytellers in these parts. If you ask me, they must have been the storytellers that made these mountains happen.

Many of Ouma Nella's stories tell about the little men under the overhang. And when on some afternoons all the slave women from the farms gather at the Dwars River to spread the shining clean washing white and wet over the bushes and low branches and the rocks where they stretch out their legs and tell the stories they brought from all the places they come from, then it's the story of this long thin Prickman Ouma Nella tell most often.

He is the kind of man, she say, the kind of Godman who once threw all the stars up into the sky and who keep all the winds together until the time is right to set them free. And it's he, say Ouma Nella, who bring death into the world. The people tell many different stories about this, but the one I get from Ouma Nella is the one where his father tell Prickman to wait until the LordGod's wife is asleep, and then he must do the thing to her that will make her just as clever as the LordGod himself. So Prickman wait and wait until he see the woman is now fast asleep, so fast that after some time she throw her legs wide open because the sleep is so good, and that is when he softly crawl to her, with that thick round head of his stuck far forward, and he creep between her legs to where it is all dark and moist, and she moan in her sleep and open herself even wider, and Prickman take off the little *kaross* he use to wear around his hips so that he is now all bare-arsed, and he creep right into her, into the darkness and the moistness of her, until only his two thin little legs stick out between her lips down there. And all the birds in the whole wide world come flying closer to see, because that is a sight one do not see every day. But the LordGod, Prickman's father, he warn them all very sternly not to make a sound: not a squeak or a peep, not a chirp or a burp, not a hoot or a toot, and most especially not to laugh or to giggle or to snigger or titter or twirp, otherwise there will be shit in the world. So all the birds of heaven sit quiet as death, watching and watching, while Prickman creep higher and higher into her, until he is as smooth and wet and slithery as a long thin fish and he begin to see a glimmer of light ahead and he know he is now very close to her mouth, all he need is a last little crawl, and a skip, and a push, and then he will be right in. And he wiggle his long thin toes down there between the lips of her entrance to help him along the last stretch.

But just then the bobtail cannot hold it any longer and he give a thin, pinched little laugh, but that is enough. And the wife of the LordGod wake up and she start pinching, all the way from down there to up here, and she pinch and pinch Prickman until he is as long and thin as an intestine and he can't breathe any more, and that is why he still look the way he look, a prick on the face of the rock. His father, the LordGod himself, pull him out from the woman, with a wet, slurping sound as his thick head break free, but that is too late. Prickman is as dead as a stone. Ouma Nella say that is why a man always feel like dying when he get as far as that, and that is how death come into the world. A real pity, say Ouma Nella. But there is a bit of joy in that dying too.

That is the story I remember as I lie on my back and look up at the overhang above me, until Willempie start fidgeting so much that I got to move out and give him my breast. But while he is sucking as greedy as a little pig, staring up at me with his two big blue eyes, all the walkers up there on the rock keep haunting me. All of them, Prickman and the long row of little men and the elands and the elephants. It give me a funny feeling, thinking of how long ago they were living around here, and how those of us who still live here know so little about that long-ago and faraway time. It's the way I feel at Zandvliet when I sometimes lie awake at night and I go outside from Ouma Nella's warm room to the yard, down to the Dwars River, and I lie down in the thick grass of the bank with my arms under my head so that I can look up at the stars spilled up there against the upended bowl of the sky, all the embers dropped by the dark god Gaunab in the dawn time of the world, the way Ouma Nella tell it in some of her other stories, that time he went to steal fire from Heitsi Eibib and had to run like a mad hare to get away before he got caught.

There are many creatures about on the earth and in the sky when on a night like that I lie on my back staring up at the teeming sky, and down here among the black bushes I hear the ghosts rustling as they go about their business, and I get so scared I can pee myself and yet I am not *dead* scared, because if you really think about it you know that they actually belong here, it is more their place than mine, I only been here for a while, but they been already here when the very first people was walking in these mountains. Now they all gone and only their shadows still rustle and fidget in the dry grass; it actually feel good to know you're never quite alone, not really, there's always the ghosts and the stars and the wind around you. And everything that is here come from a time on the other side of time.

I can sprinkle salt to scare off the ghosts. But I usually don't do it. I prefer to be here with the ghosts, otherwise the world feel too empty So here I am with all my ghost friends. My shadow and I. He come with me wherever I go, usually when the sun shine, but even in the moonlight. Always and everywhere. How many times have I tried to run away from him. But he always stay with me. He copy everything I do. Sometimes I laugh at him. But he don't listen. He just go on, day and night. In a way it feel good, because then we are not so alone. But when you think of how far away he come from, it must be from the time of the people-before-people. And darknesses he bring with him, they bring with them a fear that move right up in your legs, right into the inside of your thighs and it paralyse you. There is a darkness inside a shadow like this that I know nothing about, and I don't want to know, a darkness like the one that live inside an old fountain that come from God-knows-where deep inside the earth. How can I get away from him? He won't be chased away like a bad dog. He make sure I know about him the way he know about me. And if I die one day I'm sure he will go into the earth with me.

Perhaps that is what Frans is trying to do with me now, to get me away from Zandvliet. He want to cut me loose from my shadow. But that I shall never allow him to do. That shadow can scare me, or threaten me, or make me blarry mad, but he is still mine. If I go away he will go with me. To heaven or to hell, just too bad. Your shadow, as Ouma Nella will say, is like your story, he go all the way with you, night or day, all the way to the grave.

*   *   *

Deep in me I know that all the stories playing and tumbling inside me tonight are just to help me forget what happen in Stellenbosch, and what we speak there. What Frans say. That thing he say that really make me know for the first time what he is and what I am. I am a slave. He is not. And that's all. Nothing else matter, not ever. A slave. That is not because of the beatings or the work, it is not being hungry or cold when the snow lie white on the earth, or to feel myself dying in the heat of the summer sun when I cannot lie down in the shadow of the Baas's longhouse, it isn't the pain or the tiredness or having to lie down when Frans – *Baas* Frans – want to *naai* me. It isn't any of this that make me a slave. No. Being a slave, like I was today in that white office in the Drostdy, with all the papers and the buzzing flies around me, mean always going back to the place *they* tell me to go back to. Not because I want to be there, but because they tell me to. I am never the one to decide where to go and when to go. It's always *they*, it's always somebody else. Never *I*.

Willempie is finish drinking, but he is still lying with his small face against my breast, swallowing greedily. I am in no hurry to get up. Tonight I *want* to sleep right here on the mountainside, I can move on in the morning. Above me are the stickmen and the elephants and the elands, and Ouma Nella's stories. This place isn't mine, yet I belong here. Here I know: there is a silence of the night and a silence of the day, and they are both mine. I can hear them both when I am here. It is like my shadow and my stories. They stay with me all the way.

Yes, I know this old Elephant Trail. It draw a line between the mountains, with the sky above. The sky that in the daytime is crossed by clouds and birds and at night by moon and stars and the hooting of an owl. I know this way so well, running past Zandvliet to the Franschhoek and then on, to the farm Radyn, people say. And from there across the plains to the far town of Worcester. And on this side of the mountains he follow the line of the cliffs above, cliffs where the LordGod never came past and people only rarely. Where the stars hang so low in the night sky that you can smell them. I know that smell. They smell clean, like new washing, or like soap, like blue soap. And a bit like nutmeg. And like bruised grass. All that is left in me is a kind of dull sadness, like an old wound that is beginning to heal.

It is a strange feeling to be walking here among the high mountains, day or night. It feel all the time that there are live things around you, moving very close to you, but you never quite see them, they always stay just out of reach. It's like tokoloshes keeping out of sight, but never far away, like mountain people, it's like rocks turning into people and stalking you. But they don't really scare you, it is also a good feeling to know they're there, and that they move very quickly from one place to another when you're not looking, like shadows of clouds or the wind. Out of the corner of your eye you can see them running or floating past, but the moment you stop to stare, they suddenly go very still, as if they never ever moved. Perhaps you think it is a man or a woman, then it suddenly become a tuft of grass or an anthill. Or a Mountain Woman change into a stone or a rock, nothing ever just stay the same, they all keep changing their shape and they keep moving like grass or bushes in the wind, even if there is no wind.

Very close to me is the black water of the Eye where that long-haired woman live. Here you dare not stop to drink, or she will come out and drag you into the depths. Because it is a black hole without end, a fountain that bubble up from the deepest depth of the earth. The water is smooth and clean, you can see right through it all the way to the bottom, even if there is no bottom, because down there it keep all the midnight darkness that will always remain a secret. And it is always ready to reflect the heavens, the moon and the stars and the clouds and the sun. The water been there for ever, the water of today and yesterday and many years before, and yet the water will never see my face again. I am there, right inside it, and yet, if I look again, it is as if I never been here. It is as if even now, at this moment, as I sit here on my knees and look at myself down there, even *now* I am not here, as if I never been here at all and never will be here again. Because the water stay still right where it is, pitch black and filled with the lightest light, yet in a strange way it keep moving, as if something keep stirring it, without ever stopping, ever since the first sun looked down into it until the last moon will rise over it and still will not rise.

And I know that everything around me here, the fountain with its black water filled with secrets, and the shadows that stir and come and go when I'm not looking, and the overhang with the little prickmen, and the moon and the stars, and tomorrow's sun and yesterday's wind, and the tokoloshes and the water maidens, everything will go with me from here, all the way to Zandvliet, to look after me.

Back at the farm down there I shall first go to the Dwars River and make a little hollow for Willempie on the bank, and then walk into the cool water to wash the hot day from me. Washing and washing and scrubbing, so that I'll be ready to start again. Taking my time, time to think carefully about everything, about what Grootbaas Lindenberg said, and about Frans, about myself, all of it. I know that if we ever have time to talk about it again, he will talk differently.

I know he will. Because this is our child, that we made with so much love, like Lena who will be waiting for me with Ouma Nella. And like Mamie who would have waited if she was still with us. And of course like KleinFrans who would also have waited, but I do not speak about him.

Then, once I have washed the long walk from me, I shall go to Ouma Nella's room. Past the chicken run where that mad hen keep on cackling all day long without a single egg to show for it, and past the stupid donkeys, past the old black sow. And when I get to Ouma Nella's room, my Kleinkat will come to me as she always come to greet me. Purring around my legs, over and over, then upside down with her small head resting on one of my feet, with her eyes closed, rubbing the back of her head along my toes, to say: See, you are mine and I am yours, now rub my tummy and around my ears. I shall squat down beside her and start caressing her. I shall press my face against her and sniff in the smell of warm grass and buchu on her small feet. Then I will know I am really home. When the day is ready to be cast off like a good piece of knitting and the night cup its hand over the longhouse, I can crawl in under the *bulsak* with Ouma Nella, cuddling up next to her, her body warm as a loaf of bread, I can slide and sink into the deepest of all sleeps. Except that today I know for the first time ever that even this place, where I live, is no longer mine as I always thought. I no longer belong here. I belong nowhere. What happen to me will always be what others want to happen. I am a piece of knitting that is knitted by somebody else.

VIII

On the Altars of Lechery and Power

We have been sitting here since early morning, even though we did not really expect to see her for a while, as we knew only too well how fond she was of dawdling and how much her mind could wander off to whatever attracted her attention from one moment to the next.

Perched on the stoep we sit and wait. I am leaning against the thick, whitewashed side wall on the right. Next to me Janna fills a space into which three other persons of ordinary size could fit quite comfortably. Three years older than me, she was married previously to the wealthy wheat farmer Wouter de Vos, but he couldn't quite live up to her considerable demands. People say that it was not so much her family, or their connections, that accounts for her standing in the community, but the fact that by anybody's standards she was a handsome woman. That was before she had doubled, if not tripled, in size and suitors tended to become more circumspect. Some people ascribed her increased girth to her excessive mourning of the stupendously rich Wouter's death, on the estate near Tulbagh where they had been farming with fruit and a herd of stud cattle, and even a few flocks of merino sheep after Governor Lord Charles Somerset had begun to develop his interest in that direction; others regarded it as an equally excessive celebration of the stingy bastard's demise which left his widow with all his earthly possessions. Whatever it was, after a surprisingly short mourning period, Janna began to expand at an alarming pace, but I succumbed to her charms anyway and started exploring the considerable appeal of her matrimonial bed with regular additions to the family's prosperity – usually one child every ten or twelve months when times were good, or every other year in times of less prosperity. And there were of course also her children with Wouter to take care of.

For one reason or another, several of our own additions lasted for only a few months or a couple of years at most. But between the two of us Janna and I flourished according to the commandment of the Lord to prosper and increase, as a result of which the third generation of Brinks at the southern tip of Africa dutifully began to fulfil the hopes of the Lords Seventeen in Holland, and subsequently of the incipient British Empire.

Next to Janna, the rest of the family are seated on the long front stoep of the farm – all except Johannes Jacobus, born in the Year of Our Lord 1808 at the first light of day on an autumn afternoon in the lengthening shadow of Table Mountain. An aspiring dominee, he sends regular letters home from the top floor of a canal residence in Amsterdam. He reports how assiduously he attends his lectures in theology, and occasionally mentions something about a set routine which once a week, usually on Fridays, takes him to the Oudezijde quarter, but it has never become quite clear what he does there. He assures us, however, that all the experience he is gathering will later benefit the members of his congregation at the distant Caab.

He was followed on New Year's Day in 1810 by Francois Gerhard Jacob, absent today because of his need to pace up and down the farmyard at Zandvliet to come to terms with the shocks of the previous day at the Drostdy of Stellenbosch. A year younger than Frans is KleinCornelis, the apple of my eye, clearly brought up from his early childhood to stir up trouble with his brothers. After KleinCornelis there are a few hiccups in the row on the front stoep, as the child following him unfortunately died young even before he could be christened. The next member of the family, Daniel, born in 1814, so eighteen years old at this time, already has itchy balls, as far as I can tell, but he is fortunately still too scared of me to do anything about it. After him two more places are empty, the first in memory of Pietertjie, dead at age one month; followed by the late Stefaansie, who made it to the age of two years and seven months. After this blank there is at last another child scalding her little behind on the hot stoep, christened Maria Elisabet, fourteen; followed by Lood, a fat slob of twelve, whose upper lip is permanently disfigured by a fat pale worm of snot; and then two more girls at the far end: Fransien, an unexpectedly pretty child of eleven, with grass-green eyes and long rust-red hair; and lastly, after Woudrien, who has also been laid to rest, the *laatlam* Alida, a cheeky little minx of nine, who is always busy somewhere, cutting small rags into shapes or sorting different colours and lengths of wool into boxes where Philida can pick and choose material for her knitting.

Suddenly, thinking of Philida, I am overcome by a sense of utter disenchantment, my eyes resting on the small band around me. My family, my offspring. What do I know about any of them? And then the unsettling thought: There is so little anyone can ever know. And what does one *do* with what one knows? What the hell does one do with what one *doesn't* know? This woman here right beside me, this lump of flesh? Out of nowhere, I find myself pitying her – and, dear God, I don't know *why*. And even worse, there is nothing and nobody to take it out on. I feel like getting up and flogging somebody. Like kicking a dog or slaughtering the massive old sow in her sty or wringing a chicken's neck. I think of taking my gun and shooting whatever gets in the way, or simply firing a shot blindly into the sky. What difference would that make? And to whom?

A wave of unfathomable terror washes over me as I gaze at the people around me, my mind still preoccupied – with what, with whom? With Francois Gerhard Jacob? With the still-missing slave Philida? The turmoil of thoughts keeps on careering inside me.

I even become aware of a most unfamiliar stirring inside my breeches. So unusual, in fact, that it takes me a while to recognise and acknowledge what is going on. I can hear my breath pushing more emphatically through my open mouth. There are dark spots flickering in front of my eyes. For a moment I feel panic-stricken. What if I am going to have a stroke? But the fear lasts only for that first moment. Then a surge of recklessness overrules all other impulses. Some of my predecessors in our line of the family have been known to expire in this way. Who am I to resist? If I die, I think, I die. And hallelujah! Let God's will be done.

I fumble with the gold watch chain tightly wound between my buttons and my stomach, and readjust the loose pair of thin gold-framed spectacles on my nose. A year ago in the vineyard just when the crystal grapes were ripening, they fell off my nose and I accidentally stepped on them. They broke right in the middle and the left lens splintered like the legs of a nervous spider, after which Frans meticulously tried to fit the two pieces together with a length of thin wire. I swear it was the fault of one of the outdoor slaves whose stares unsettled me that day. He was given a hell of a thrashing. It was high time anyway. Janna had been convinced for a long while that the good-for-nothing was asking for it.

I don't take no shit from nobody and even less from a slave. They fornicate and multiply like rats on the farm and yet one cannot get along without them. That is where the trouble starts and from there it just gets worse. In my child- hood it was easier. They knew their place. All the children had their food together on the back stoep. Got their hidings together, came to prayers together after supper. That was before the bloody English came here and thought they could just take over and started making laws for everything under the sun. So many working hours per day, so many stripes if they need punishment, a Slave Protector to complain to, I ask you. As if a farm, particularly a wine farm like Zandvliet, can keep regular hours. It just doesn't work like that. When there's anything to be done, it's got to be done today. And when a Baas says something it must be obeyed. A child or a slave doesn't talk back.

But I know exactly when and how it all changed. We were still living in the Caab at the time, next to my wine shop and the cellar. I had an altercation with the yellow slave from Boegies, his name was Januarie. I still remember very clearly, he was looking for trouble right from the start and one day he got cheeky with my sister Geertrui and I confronted him at the churn in the kitchen. He talked back. Then I slapped him. He came at me with the spade that stood in the corner, and hit me right across the head so that like that youngster Joseph in the Bible I saw sun and moon and stars all at the same time. Lights-out, and my left eyebrow dented and the eye watering all the time. And as I fell he stabbed me with the sharp edge of the spade in the left calf causing me to limp until this day. That was when Pa arrived with a hedgepole to help me. Afterwards they had to drag me to a bedroom and call the medicine woman from the Greenmarket Square to bring me round and clean and bandage the spade wound and tend to the gash in my head.

Pa ordered Januarie to be brought to the post in the backyard, and had him flogged until the next morning, before they dragged him off to the Fiscal who finished the job. That was before the English came to the Cape, in the early days when a farmer was still the Baas on his own farm. Ever since that day I have no respect for a slave. And that is what I meant to show all my slaves on that miserable day when we all went in to the Caab to see Abraham hanged. What had surprised me then was that the slaves didn't seem to be bothered at all. Which goes to prove that they don't have feelings like us. I think I was the only one there to feel upset. Even though I'd seen that a few times before. And when I took a mouthful of wine to settle my stomach, I noticed that no one else's hands were shaking. True as God. At least I could still taste that the wine was good. The real Zandvliet wine. Not the stuff we sell, diluted with water, fortified with sulphur, but the real thing we keep for our own use and for friends or special buyers. And I needed that on the day in the Caab, I can still see the poor bastard, twisting and turning at the end of his thick rope, his feet dancing just above the ground. Abraham who had to be hanged twice, and who had worked for me for so many years. It was really because of him that I'd bought this farm. Because I'd made a good living from exporting my wines to London and Amsterdam from my cellar in the Caab, but I figured out that it could be more profitable to make my own wine. And Abraham knew about making wine, which was why he cost me such a bladdy lot of money, eight hundred and seventy-five rix-dollars, to buy him from the man who was his Baas at the time, the owner of Nederburg. We got along so well. Why the hell did he then have to run away with those other good-for-nothings? And it wasn't just a matter of absconding: he also stole my good elephant gun, and when the soldiers came to arrest him, he actually shot at them.

The way he looked at me from the gallows that day. With those bloodshot eyes which I shall see in front of me for the rest of my life.

On the road back home we never outspanned and only stopped a few times just an hour or so for a short rest; otherwise we drove on, night and day. I *had* to get home. My farm with its white walls surrounded by so many greens of vineyards and orchards, my farm, my hold on this world, my Zandvliet. I had to get back to the animals that knew me as their Baas. And once we had entered through the wide gate in the ring wall, it was as if the LordGod himself was once again folding his arms around me. *He shall cover you with his feathers, and under his wings shalt thou trust: his truth shall be thy shield and buckler.* I don't know what the hell a buckler is, but if it stands in the Bible it must be a good thing, and that was why I so badly wanted to be back on my farm, with my shield and buckler. I felt I could breathe again.

Every evening when we open the Bible and turn to my favourite chapter, that Abraham comes back to me. He had such a way of leaning back against the wall near the front door, closing his eyes to listen more attentively, even though I knew he couldn't understand a bladdy word. The part where the Prophet talks about Aholah and Aholibah and their paramours *whose flesh is as the flesh of asses, and whose issue is like the issue of horses, the Egyptians that bruise thy teats for the paps of thy youth.* It is a passage that comes back to me whenever at random moments on an ordinary day I open the Bible. And no matter what I do, sooner or later Abraham's red eyes return to pester me. All those years of yes Baas, no Baas, and just look at him now. Where did it get him? I really can't understand any of it. I treated him well, didn't I? I looked after him. I was always ready to give the shit an extra *dop* of wine, wasn't I? I knew he was good at his job, pruning in winter, getting rid of everything we didn't want or need, and cleaning neat paths in the vineyard, then watching the new growth appearing in the spring, all the colours of twigs and twirls and everything, from green and yellow to lilac and red and purple, through the time of swelling and growing in summer, trimming the bunches that grow too heavy, scaring off the birds with tins and pots and scarecrows, until it is time to harvest in baskets and bags to carry to the cellar, to the big vats where the treading is done, then waiting for the fermentation in the buzzing barrels, opening the scuppers, there's nothing that makes a farmyard smell of life like new wine and must, with a touch of sourness at the beginning, going on until it's just right, my God, until everything starts again as if it has never happened before. Not a drop to drink in August, because that is when the wine is weeping in the bottle. Soon it is time for tasting, for running it off into the bottles. Step by step, moment by moment. That, you may well say, is my life.

And all that long time Abraham used to stay with me, he was always the one who just knew what to do and how to do it. Until the time comes to transport the huge vats on the wagon, two by two, like elephants going into Noah's ark, the oxen straining in their yokes, dragging the freight along the rough road up the narrow Drakenstein valley to Klapmuts, then to Stellenbosch, and across the Cape Flats to the Caab, four days there and back. And it takes fifty loads to transport everything, you can calculate for yourself what a hole that makes in your time. For all of that I could always count on Abraham to help me. Until he went mad and the gallows took him from me.

All of which just confirms why I have always figured that with a slave or a child nothing works as well as a good thrashing. And I speak from long and bitter experience. In Philida's case the decision was taken very quickly. Frans returned from Stellenbosch in the late afternoon. His horse was exhausted, I thought he was going to collapse. That's the way I know Frans and I'd told him before that if he ever does that again I'll kill him with my own two hands. The little shit mustn't think that because he's twenty-two he is too old for a thrashing. He was also dead tired and just wanted to go to bed to sleep it off, but I fetched him from the room he shares with his brother KleinCornelis and took him to the *voorhuis* so that he could tell us everything that had happened in Stellenbosch. I'm his father, I am the Baas of Zandvliet, I got to know. So that was where I heard the full story about what Philida had said against us. Everything, about how Frans had lain with her since he was only fourteen and she some three years older. And about the children they'd made together. That's Mamie who lived only for a few months before she died. And Lena, who is two. And the little monkey she still has on her breast. Of course I suspected something like that but on this farm it wasn't anything to be talked about openly. Nothing was ever known officially, and that is how the Caab has always worked.

Frans told the Protector, a man called Lindenberg, about the two slave youths that had been with Philida and that, he said, was how the man recorded it. This is all that matters in the end: that it was recorded. One day in the future, when no one of us is still around, that is all the world will know, and all that needs to be known. We came to this land white, and white we shall be on the Day of Judgement, so help me God. If anybody is still in doubt, I always tell them: Just follow the coast up to the Sandveld, then you will see with your own eyes how we whored the whole West Coast white. God put us here with a purpose, and we keep very strictly to his Word. For ever and bloody ever, amen. Do we understand each other?

But from what Frans told me about what had happened in Stellenbosch, one thing was very clear: that this slave girl had become a threat to us. We Brinks are a boat that has always hugged the coast, no matter what storms have come, but Philida has now cut a hole into it and we may sink if we don't watch out. That is something we just cannot allow to happen. It's the whiteness of our boat that proves we are the children of the Lord. We won't have any truck with Satan's offspring. If we sink here, then everything will sink. Then everything will have been in vain. And that I'll damn well not allow. Over my dead body.

This was how I came to my final decision. What used to be a possibility in the past has now been sealed. It won't be enough just to punish Philida. She has to be removed from among us. The easiest, I'm sure, would be an accident on the farm. A dead person won't talk and a dead slave even less. But Philida is a grown woman in her twenties, her name has been written in the government's books, she can't just be here one day and gone the next. Which means she must be sold, as deep into the interior as possible, so no one can pick up a trace of her again. Books are dangerous things and we must take great care to get past them. Do you understand what I'm saying, Frans?

Yes, Pa, I understand. But –

I don't want to listen to your Buts. This farm has no place for Buts.

And that same evening, after we'd had our supper, I

ordered the whole family and the slaves to stay right where they were. The only one, apart from Philida, who was missing was Old Petronella, but I preferred her not to be there. I know how she feels about Philida. So of the house women only Janna was there. Worse than a fly or an earwig, but that is how the Lord ordered it, so I have no choice. The same with the children around the table. And the empty chairs for the ones who died but who are still with us. The others, I must admit, all look a bit home-made, like one of Janna's baked puddings that didn't quite make it, not much to brag about. I ordered them all to stay seated so that I could tell them about Frans's visit to the Slave Protector's office in Stellenbosch. What was said, and what it led to. And on this blessed day, I concluded, my right hand still resting on the Bible, on this blessed day it is our will, in the presence of God and all his angels, that the maidservant that is within our gates, Philida of the Caab, should be cast out from our company, to the everlasting glory of God the Father, Son and Holy Ghost in the highest heaven. Is there anyone here present who wishes to rise up against the will of Our Lord?

That was when Frans said: Pa, but shouldn't we wait until Philida is back to tell us herself what happened?

You were there, Frans, were you not? I told him. You heard everything that was spoken, so we know exactly what happened in that unholy place. Is that so, or isn't it?

Frans remained sitting without moving.

After some time his mother cleared her throat.

Frans, I said to him, do you want me to strip off the bladdy skin of your bladdy arse? What I said: was that true, or wasn't it?

It's like Pa said.

In that case we are united before the Lord. Let us pray.

I prayed for longer than I usually do. The little ones started fidgeting and after the prayer I had to tell Janna to send them to bed without supper and give each of them a proper hiding to make sure they understood the Word of the LordGod and would pay it proper respect in future.

That Word and I have come a long way together, we know each other's boundaries and respect each other's stone walls. I won't ever do anything without first discussing it with the LordGod. His will be done. Whether it is a year of drought or one of unseasonal rain, I will always ask him first if he thinks the time is right for sowing and planting, for digging furrows, or pulling the husks off the fermenting grapes, for shortening hoops or fitting staves. And I follow his instructions to the letter. Which is why I have always prospered in his eyes.

After finishing the prayer, I knew exactly what passage to read, to make sure Frans fully understood why I try to keep to the Scriptures. It was the passage where God calls Abraham to take his son Isaac, who was his only son after he sent Ishmael into the desert with his mother Hagar, up the mountain of Moriah to bring a sacrifice to the Lord. Together with the boy Isaac and two slave boys they take to the road, and on the third day he leaves the boys and the donkey behind and goes on with Isaac. This is what the Book says: *And Abraham took the wood of the burnt offering, and laid it upon Isaac his son; and he took the fire in his hand, and a knife; and they went both of them together. And Isaac spoke unto Abraham his father, and said, My father; and he said, Here I am, my son. And he said, Behold the fire and the wood: but where is the lamb for a burnt offering? And Abraham said, My son, God will provide himself a lamb for a burnt offering: so they went both of them together. And they came to the place where God had told him of; and Abraham built an altar, and laid the wood in order, and bound Isaac his son, and laid him on the altar upon the wood. And Abraham stretched forth his hand, and took the knife to slay his son. And the angel of the Lord called unto Abraham out of heaven, and said, Abraham, Abraham: and he said: Here am I. And he said, Lay not thine hand upon the lad, neither do thou any thing unto him; for now I know that thou fearest God, seeing thou hast not withheld thy son from me.*

The rest we know. When Abraham looked up, he saw a ram caught with its horns in a bush, and sacrificed the animal in the place of his son. By this time the girls at the table were in tears, so that I first had to send their mother to fetch the strap and give them something proper to cry about. Afterwards we all knelt around the table, and the slaves against the wall at the back door, so that I could confer with the LordGod. After all the others had left I went to confront Frans with a straight question: Do you understand now why I obey the Lord? He always sees to it that the right things happen. You see what a God-fearing father Abraham was.

But Frans was obstinate. You know what he asked? He asked, Who would want a father like that?

That was when I told him, That is exactly the kind of father you've got. And if that isn't good enough for you, I'll give you what you bladdy well deserve. After that we all calmed down again.

And so we came to the decision about Philida. That a simple thrashing would not be enough, but that the time had come to do what we had long threatened to do: to take her to auction and sell her into the interior. This was agreed the evening before she came sauntering along the dust road that descends from the mountains of Great Drakenstein and runs past Lekkerwijn. Even before I moved from the edge of the long stoep I pulled the heavy studded belt from my breeches and stood up. Moments earlier, I had seen Janna slide off the edge of the stoep and grab the basket in which she usually collects the eggs from the hens that avoid the regular nests in the farmyard to find more inaccessible spots. I know what pleasure it gives Janna to outsmart those devious chickens and bring home her booty like priceless treasure. But this morning, when she saw me getting up, she quickly changed course and went round the house past the well towards the kitchen door, leaving the rest of the yard to me. That suited me perfectly. I wanted that girl for myself.

Once more I became aware of the stirring inside my breeches. I could feel my breath pushing more strongly through my open mouth. There were dark spots flickering in front of my eyes. For a moment I felt panic-stricken. But this time it lasted only for a moment before a surge of recklessness overruled all other impulses. Who was I to resist?

I saw her on the dusty white path along the vineyards and realised immediately that she was heading towards the river. I knew why. Didn't I know her since she was only a wisp of a girl? How many times over the years have I watched her skipping through the vineyards and orchards on her way to the river like a bright spot of colour among all the greenery? Already feeling my throat constrict in anticipation, tightening my hand around the belt, I went after her. On the grassy bank beside the Dwars River I found her baby lying in a bundle, fast asleep. Philida splashing in the shallow water. Her clothes folded neatly, that's the way she is, always very tidy, fastidious.

On the bank, next to the bundle of clothes, I stopped.

I call: Philida!

She turns round to face me. One might think she would have bent over to cover herself with her arms, but Philida keeps standing up very straight, so I can get a good look.

The swelling of her breasts with the big black nipples, hanging down like heavy bunches of grapes. Her belly wrinkled like an old bag because of the child, yet still something to look at. And without wanting to, I can feel myself growing from desire until the dumb thing is standing like a beacon pole, something that hardly ever happens to me these days.

Why are you so bloody late? I call out. We've been waiting for God knows how long.

She shrugs as if she cannot be bothered. What is it you been waiting for, Ouman? she asks. It is the first time I have heard her say that: no longer a courteous *Oubaas*, but a crude *Ouman*. This is what happens when they lose all respect.

Even as I try to swallow the confusion of thoughts inside me, I take my time to look at Philida, from top to bottom and then halfway back, before I say: It's you I'm waiting for, you *hoer*. Today you're looking for a proper thrashing.

What for? she asks cheekily. I don't need a thrashing from an old man.

You ran away, I say.

I did not, says Philida. I tell Ouma Nella I go to lay a charge in Stellenbosch, and she tell Nooi Janna and then I walk there and now I am back. No one try to stop me.

Who gave you a pass to leave the farm? I ask her. I certainly didn't.

I do not need a pass to complain.

I am the Baas and you know that bladdy well and you need my permission to go to Stellenbosch or anywhere else for that matter.

My business is with Frans, not with the Ouman.

Come out of the river, I tell her.

I do not come out if you want to beat me.

· 80 ·

Meid! I shout at her. You've got to listen to me.

My name is not Meid, Ouman. I am Philida.

Come out, *poesmeid*.

I am nobody's *poesmeid*. I am Philida.

Come here! By this time I can no longer see straight. But something stronger than myself holds me back and I try to say very quietly: Philida, come out of that river.

At this moment I notice again the baby lying in a small bundle wrapped in its blanket on the bank of the river. And immediately I know what to do, because it is the only way I can force Philida to obey me. Although it is not easy, I bend over and pick up the bundle.

You can't do that! Philida shouts behind me.

You just come with me, I tell her over my shoulder. Or else you'll see what's going to happen to this bladdy monkey.

She is screaming behind me, but by now I am striding along with the bundle in my arms. I can hear her wading through the shallow water. I can even hear her gasping for breath. In my arms I clutch the small, hot bundle. Ahead of me I can see the thick, dark green bamboos clustered together around the dark secret in their midst. And inside my breeches I can once again feel that thrilling, tight, almost painful stirring I haven't felt in God knows how many months. This is it, I think, and I call, Come on now, Philida. Just stay with me. Stay with me.

I'm coming, I hear her say.

Come with me, I say again. I can see that she first considers objecting, but when I turn round she is following me, dragging her feet. She won't allow me to get too far away with the baby, that I know.

I walk a little distance along the white dusty footpath and turn off into the bamboo copse.

Where the Ouman going now?

It's not for you to ask, Philida, I snap at her. You just do as I tell you. And I walk on, pushing the first bamboos out of my way. Then I move deeper into the copse. A few steps further I can hear her footsteps stopping behind me.

Damn you, Philida! I shout without looking round.

This place is Frans's place, she says behind me.

What do you know about Frans's place?

I just know.

Today you're coming with *me*.

She follows me slowly and cautiously. I lead the way with stiff legs, following my half-rampant member that tries half-heartedly to point the way. As far as I want to take her.

The stirring in my breeches becomes more urgent. I can feel my grip tightening around the heavy belt I am clutching in my hand under the baby. The breeches have started slipping. I kick them off. In a heap they cluster around my ankles. It is painful to bend over but with a grunt I stoop forward and use my free hand to disentangle myself.

But only a few steps further she says behind me: I won't let the Ouman beat me.

I turn back to her. Now I have to think very clearly. I don't want to have an argument with a bladdy slave here where everybody can observe us. Even here among the dense bamboos, who knows what they can see?

You want your child back? I ask over my shoulder.

You can't do this, Ouman! she says.

Don't be so sure.

The Ouman is not going to beat me today, she says again, but her voice is wavering.

All right then, I try to soothe her. I won't beat you with my belt today. What you need is a snot sjambok. Get down on your knees. And turn your arse this way.

I won't, she says.

On your knees, Philida. Today you're going to pray before we leave this place.

I don't feel like praying, she says.

It is to say goodbye.

I do not need to say no goodbye. The Ouman must put down that belt, she says.

I won't.

Then I go back to the river, Philida says, aiming to turn away towards the fringe of the copse.

What about your child?

Give him back to me.

You'll have to come and get him first.

She shakes her head.

Get on your knees, *meid*, I order her.

Her lips are trembling. I can hear her breath come in sharp and shallow gasps. But she repeats: I won't.

Oh yes, you will, I tell her. I'm not waiting any longer. *Meid*.

I am not your *meid*, Ouman. Haven't been for a long time now.

I raise my free arm, now holding the belt. But then I stop and lower the arm again.

On your knees, Philida, I order her very quietly.

Why, Ouman?

The breeches lie crumpled at my feet. I kick them aside and say, Because you're going to leave us. After today I never want to see you again. This is the last time.

The Oubaas cannot do this, she objects. I lie with Frans now.

You got a bloody cheek, *meid*!

I will tell the Ouvrou Janna, she says.

For a moment I feel winded and cannot think of anything to say.

Frans lie with me, she repeats. I am his woman now. It's a bad thing the Ouman want to do in this bamboo place today.

What shit is this? I ask in a rage. You are no longer the Philida you used to be before you went to Stellenbosch.

My Ouma Nella tell me long ago what your father do to her, she says.

All I can say under my breath is, Bend over, Philida.

When this young woman bends over, it is different from when I lie with Janna. How shall I put it? The very first time I saw Janna it was clear, even at a distance, that she was a woman of substance. She was still a de Vos at the time, but that poor sod didn't last long. Janna is a woman straight from the Bible, great and wide. When she comes through the front door, and it is an almighty big door, she fills it from side to side. She can hit you with a fist so you feel like you've run into a stone wall. I know what I'm talking about. Janna knows no half measures, she always goes full out. And if the time is right and she is willing, which doesn't happen often, but when she's ready it's like an earthquake. I am small of stature, and with Janna, people say, I'm like a mouse on a sugarloaf, like a rowing boat on mighty waves. Janna is a terrible woman.

And Philida is everything that Janna is not. When she bends over in front of me, I feel my throat go dry. It is as if every word from that scene in Ezekiel suddenly seems to burst into flames before me. I see her and I feel like a horse or an ass again. As if the world has started spinning around me. For God knows how long I stand like this, with my bottom half bare and ridiculous. But nothing happens. I cannot do anything. Not with the thought of Janna which Philida has brought back into my mind. After a very long time she simply straightens up again and keeps her face turned away from me.

And now I want my child, she says.

I hand her the baby still swathed in his blanket. She lifts him up to her and clutches him against her breast. It makes a small whimpering sound, but then turns quiet again. By now I am crying in helpless rage.

After a very long time I stoop down to pull on my skin breeches and painfully slowly stumble away, cowering like a beaten dog.

Philida comes past me, without turning to look at me. I see the bamboos swaying in her wake, then closing behind her. And then she is gone.

Much later, as I stumble out of the copse I see Philida far ahead, on the riverbank, wading back into the shallow water of the river, her whole wet body glistening in the sun.

I hear the child starting to cry on the grassy bank. Philida wades out of the shallow river and goes to sit down beside him, picking him up. She doesn't even bother to put her clothes on again. From where I stand the child seems bigger and heavier than before, and it seems as if she is trying to smother him in the fullness of her breasts. She never even looks in my direction. Her body glistens. Not because of the sun on her wetness, but as if the light comes radiating from herself in that bright day.

Very slowly, I draw the *riem* of my breeches tightly around my body but without bothering to fasten it again. Keeping it hanging limply in one hand as I hold the breeches up with the other, I walk off back to the longhouse, feeling wilted and empty. Today, I know, today I'm an old man. Now I know what the LordGod must feel like some days when he looks down at his world and knows it's all been in vain, a bladdy failure. I look up and see the thin, tall palm trees swaying in a row in front of the house, even though I can feel no wind, not even a breeze. Climbing slowly up the rise to where the house stands waiting for me, I turn to look round again. Philida has gone back into the shallow river, splashing and splashing as if there isn't enough water to wash herself clean. As if she wants to scrub the very skin off her body.

IX

At the small green gate in the ring wall around the graveyard, halfway up the hill, I go inside. My generation has
not really taken root here yet. *I have been a stranger in a strange
land.* Oupa Andries died at seventy-one in the Caab and
that was where we buried him. I can remember how we
used to visit his grave every Sunday afternoon to leave some
flowers before we moved here to the farm. And Pa Johannes
will also be buried there, I suppose; he is already eighty.
Those of my own children who didn't make it were left in
the Caab. Pietertjie and Stefaansie and the little one without
a name. Here at Zandvliet little Woudrien is the only one
from my family to be buried in our graveyard. So far.

As I stand there among the graves of strangers – Du Toit,
Van Niekerk, Joubert, Hugo, several de Villiers, some people
who don't even have a name, leaving only the small mounds
of their graves behind – a shadow moves in between the
afternoon sun and me, and when I look up I see it is
Petronella. My mother. And she asks, Cornelis, what are
you doing here?

Nothing. Just standing.

Where you been?

That's not your business.

It is precisely my business, Cornelis. What were you
looking for down there among the bamboos?

I wasn't looking for anything.

Perhaps you weren't looking, but maybe you found something, she says, staring at me with that look I knew so well. The look that blames me for everything. What are you doing here among the graves? she asks.

I'm just looking at the place where I will come to rest one day. I and my children and my children's children.

I don't think you'll come to rest here. You got too many ants up your arse. And you don't even know the people who lie here.

There will be enough time later to get to know them. I'm slowly getting acclimatised. Look at the names on the stones.

There are many names here you don't know anything about and will never know. And here's lots of stones that are not even marked and still they're graves.

Like which ones?

There are people buried here – in this corner, in that one over there, everywhere – that go back hundreds and thousands of years.

What sorts of people?

My kind of people, says Old Petronella. Khoe people, Bushman people. Lots of them. More than you can even count.

Your people perhaps, I say. Certainly not mine.

People is people, and when they die they belong to everybody, she says. They're part of our blood, mine and Philida's.

That doesn't count and you know it.

It counts, Cornelis, and I know that too. And one day they'll stand up and come to ask from us what belongs to them.

There's nothing here that belongs to them.

What you think is theirs and what they know is theirs are two different things.

You talk too much, Petronella. You always come when I need you least.

No, Cornelis. I come when you most need me. Only you don't want to hear it. And what I say is what you *got* to hear.

There's nothing I got to hear, I grumble. But my eyes keep on wandering into the distance and of course she notices. Can there be anything anywhere she does not know about?

What have you done with Philida among the bamboos? she asks.

Nothing, I grunt, and try to move away, but she stops me.

I know what you wanted to do, Cornelis.

I didn't do anything, and that's the truth, I tell you. Now leave me alone, Ma.

I know about everything. She takes a knife from her pocket, a little peeling knife I gave her years ago. Very small but very sharp. Like a razor. She can probably see that I am trying to steal away again, but she blocks the way.

What's the matter with you today? I ask grumpily. I tell you I didn't do anything to that slave girl.

If you didn't do anything, it can only be because you cannot do anything any more and it won't be for lack of trying. She quietly starts sharpening the blade of the small knife on the palm of her hand: You seen how your workers press out the stone of an apricot if they want to dry it? Now you listen to me: You try to touch Philida again, and I'll get you by the balls and press them out, nice and whole and smooth. I'm not joking.

You're all out of sorts today, Ma Petronella, I snarl at her.

I'm just telling you so you can be warned, she continues. Very quietly, her voice pulls in, the way a cat draws in its nails. I'm going to press out your balls. I'm your mother. Do we two understand each other?

After a long time I say very quietly: I understand, Ma Petronella.

But this is something she has spoken about before, and I know she will do so again. In the daytime one can shake off these things like blackjacks from corduroy breeches. But in the night they come back to haunt me. Then I can see the people from those old graves rise up, struggling their way out of the ground, each one of them still covered with grass and dead ants and God knows what else in their hair and on their eyebrows and in their nostrils, and I see them coming on over mountains and dales, not in twos or threes or handfuls, but in their hundreds and thousands, from all the mountains and cliffs and across all the dusty plains and thickets and kloofs of the vast land, all the dead who can never lie still in their graves, but who go on living invisible among us, people who were born here and who died here and who will never leave us in peace. I don't want to know about them but I cannot ever shake them off or pretend they're not there. They throng around me and whisper to me and press against me until I cannot breathe any more. I no longer know what is happening inside my head.

Before I came to live at Zandvliet everything was going so well. Life seemed so ordered and predictable. I was a prosperous man. I had married well. My children were growing up to take my place after me. The wine trade flourished. I had twelve, fourteen, eighteen slaves, later thirty, forty, as the farm began to flourish. But today? The only thing that is accumulating is my debt. Ever since we came here, the price of wine started coming down, now it's falling every month. There's nothing one can rely on any more. I've had to start borrowing from neighbours and family and friends. Even from Old Petronella I had to borrow money. Three hundred and fifty rix-dollars. Twenty-five pounds in today's money. If it goes on like this I won't have a shard of pottery left to scratch my arse. And then? A few weeks ago I went to Kobus Coetzee's auction at Klapmuts. I saw the bailiff going from room to room with his papers in one hand, selling one thing after the other, with the crowd at his heels like a pack of hyenas or vultures around a carcass. Cupboards. Beds. Milk cans. Carpets. Wine barrels. Horses. Sheep. Tanned skins and thongs. My God, everything. I watch as they carried all of it out and put it into the rain, to be auctioned and sold and carted off. The poor old shit. And that evening I saw something like a vision – it wasn't a dream, I was wide awake, I saw it as in broad daylight – saw the vultures coming towards me, here at Zandvliet. Until there was nothing left to be scavenged. *A stranger among strangers*, as the Bible says. Is this what Grandpa Andries came here for, on that long sea journey from Woerden on the ship? To be buried here among dust and stones? Even in the cemetery those dark strangers are taking over everything. All one is left with in the end is one's own hole, the grave I dug to receive my bones one day. *Among strangers*. It is like a Last Judgement drawing closer. We try to keep it away, to forget about it. But all our efforts are just farts against the thunder.

I'm not growing any younger. Let us be totally frank: I'm getting old. One cannot see it in what one does but in what one can no longer do. Even something like bending over to tie your shoelaces when you get up in the morning. It's in your back, it's in your bones. I used to watch Pa Johannes as he grew older and I thought: No, the hell with it, I won't ever grow old like that. I dare not say this to anyone. Not even to Janna. Most especially not to Janna. She may be the only one who'd enjoy it. Then she needn't roll over in the night or the early morning if I feel the urge coming. There was a time when I never stopped feeling desire. Got it from the ancestors. Grandpa Andries with his thirteen children. Took whatever came his way, except for a wild hare – and that was only because the bloody thing was too quick for him. But I? Today? Slower and slower all the way.

Worst of all is to want to but no longer to be able to. There are nights when I lie panting with lust, but then I cannot. God is a bloody perverse kind of man. The desire he pours into one is the worst of all. He rides you bareback. And then he gives you this thing between your arsehole and your balls. An old man's gland, as Petronella calls it. I could understand if it gets you when you're old and decrepit. But not when you've still got a wildness inside you, if you can still feel desire. The only time when it works for me is when I see a young girl like Philida. Janna is useless when it comes to that. She's become an old dried-up cow that kicks you in the balls when you try to get some milk out of her. And she's the very last person I can talk to about it. All she would say is: Good. It's just what you deserve. It's the hand of God. And then I used to go to Old Petronella for help. There's nothing she doesn't know. Pity she is no longer as strong as in her younger days. But she can at least offer some remedies. Garlic cloves drawn on white dulcis was what she made me drink. Otherwise, honey and a pinch of saltpetre and some alum. It is useless for things like hanging or standing, but at least it eases the peeing, and that's already something. What does help to coax the old pole into a half-hearted standing, never for long, but in my state anything is better than nothing, is baking an ostrich egg on an anthill until it turns brown, then to grind it and pour boiling water on it. Or unburnt coffee beans drawn on boiling water. It's enough to help the old thing wriggle around a bit in the damp. Nothing like the grunting pleasure old Hamboud gets from her mud hole, but at least it stirs up a faint memory of what it used to be in its heyday. In the long run, I suppose, one simply has to learn to live with dry desire.

Those were the times when I understood Pa Johannes best. He often spoke to me when he felt the need to unburden. And in later years when his conscience gave him hell, then he would tell me about the weeks when Ma Magdalena was said to be ill, which meant that she denied him a place in her bed when he felt the need. Long periods, months, sometimes years. The only remedy, for he was a God-fearing man, was to ask for guidance from the Lord and to follow the example of other devout men from the Bible, like Father Abraham: so if his wife couldn't or wouldn't – and how can one ever know? – Pa Johannes availed himself of the services of a handmaid to assuage his need. Very special among them was Petronella, who in her youth had been a delight to behold and a woman who'd known all the secrets of the heart and the flesh. If I understood him correctly he would always begin by bidding Petronella to lie down, and then kneel between her legs to ask the Lord's blessing on what was about to happen, before lunging forward to end the prayer by adding the deed to the word. That may well be how I had also been made, like a couple of my brothers and sisters. We never even knew who they were, because his offspring with Petronella were always immediately claimed by the family and brought up by Ma Magdalena as her own. Petronella continued to nurse them all, she was blessed with abundant milk, but in the eyes of the world Ma Magdalena was the mother. That is how it was also entered into the books of the government as well as in Pa's Book. And to show my appreciation I arranged for Petronella's manumission in due course. A man must learn how and when to demonstrate his gratitude.

Compared to Pa Johannes, things went easier for me, because in the early years I never took no for an answer from Janna. But in later years she became more and more difficult, which was how I also discovered the meaning of futile desire. That's what the Lord gets for planting us in a fertile land like this, you might say in a garden rank with the fruits of good and evil, so it's no use for him to complain after the event. He ought to take his responsibility like a man.

All I'm asking is how I could be expected to keep my eyes and hands off a desirable young *meid* like Philida when I became smitten with dry desire? At such moments there is – sometimes – still a hint of something upstanding in my old body. When I can grab her or hurt her, when I can hit her and make her squirm or moan. A breath of dull life still glimmering in the burning, flaccid flesh. And that's about all it amounts to, except sometimes in my sleep. But even when I then wake up, it is usually too late, and I'm in time only to feel it shrink away from my grasp. It has really lost the ability to stand up properly. But it *remembers*. Oh my God, how it remembers. Old One-Eye forgets nothing. In its blue head memory lies embedded.

And that is when I need a remedy. What a terrifying, sordid, carnal creature a man is! In the fullness of his manhood he can do anything and everything, but he ends up sadly useless. And this, they say, is what it means to be created in the image of God. The same God who ordered Abraham to cut the throat of his own son. Perhaps, I sometimes imagine, that was the remedy that helped him stand up, right across the altar on which the child lay exposed.

And it just gets worse with all the worries I have to bear. About the wine and the vineyards, about the government that decides how much it will pay us for our harvest, less money every year. What will become of us? A Day of Judgement is already upon us. When I lie awake in the night, I can already imagine the worst happening. How I might be forced to look on – I with my dried-up member – to watch strangers trampling my home to grab everything I have accumulated in my life and carry it off from here, cart it away, all gone. Leaving only me and my naked desire before the eyes of a vengeful God. Cast out and outlawed, and filled with pain and drought and suffering.

And this is the time my own son, Frans, chooses to lie with Philida and engender a brood of children with her. What we need, I keep telling him, is money, not children. But does he pay any attention? He deserves to be punished. And today I felt the urge to go in unto her like the sons of God with the daughters of men in Genesis. For the first time in God knows how long I managed to get it standing. With the girl brought up by Petronella. The way Johannes Brink did earlier with my mother. Because they're slaves. The only thing we still have to cling to, is God. But he has also started to falter. He has turned his face away from us. All that will remain for us to trust, I think, is the land itself. And it is bound to find its own way of punishing us. Don't make a mistake. Ever since we arrived here everything has begun to go wrong. Perhaps it would have been better for us never to have been here. But if I no longer have that to believe in, what remains?

X

About a Gallows Rope and an Auction in the Bamboo Copse

Who still care about listening to the Ouman? It is my turn
to speak. Because it is terrible things that happen from the
day I go to Stellenbosch from Zandvliet until I come home
again and the randy old goat try to force me down on my
knees in that bamboo copse. As I stand there in the thick
shade, I think: JesusGod, this must be the very worst that
can happen to a woman. It may be even worse than getting
hanged. I cannot help thinking of the day he make those
two slave boys come from L'Ormarins to make them lie with
me on the flogging bench and he standing there with his
sjambok. On that day I want to die. And I with Frans's child
already inside me. Is there anything that can be as terrible
as that? And yet if you think of it, it is just part of the world
he live in. All those stories the old goat read us from his
damn Book, because he say it will do us good. But if you
ask me it is just to get him worked up so he can give it to
the Ounooi. That Bible is an evil book. Starting with Adam
in the Garden, baas and giver of names to every living and
creeping thing. But then Adam is not good enough for God,
so he send him Eve to make life easier. All he want is a
woman he could put his thing into, and it is the LordGod
who make her lie down and open her legs for him. And
look what happen afterwards. Lot and his two daughters.
Not one of them been with a man before, but think of their
father. He throw them out so that all the men outside can

take them in the street. And later those same daughters make him drunk so they can lie with him. And so it go on, with the woman Tamar and the man Juda, and the one called Onan who lie with his sister-in-law but then spill out his seed on the ground because he don't want to give her a child. All the way down to the good king David who get another man killed so he can have a go at his wife. A bloody heathen lot, which make me think twice about this LordGod himself. That's what the old goat make us listen to every night at prayers. And almost every time it is a woman who get it in her sticky parts.

So it go on, and now it look like my turn. There is no way I can get out of this. All I'm good for is to knit, but where does that take me? Everybody always say, You not just a farmyard girl, man, you a knitting girl. That's *something*. So I ask you: What is *something*? Can it help me when I get big with Frans's children inside me? Can it help me right in the beginning when I keep on telling Frans: All right, I lie with you, but then you must promise to buy my freedom? Can it help me the other day when the old goat want me to go down on my knees so he can get his snot sjambok into me?

I remember when Ouma Nella first teach me to knit. She just cast on the first row of stitches and show me in-over-through-and-off. That piece of knitting grow longer and longer, like a tongue, while Ouma Nella is busy somewhere else on the farm, so I just go on. The tongue get so long, after a while it push its way right over the doorstep, but still I keep on. Until Ouma Nella come back in the late afternoon and start laughing. I cannot see anything funny about it. Nobody ever show me how to cast off, only the in-over-through-and-off, and once I start on something I don't give up easily. But Ouma Nella is laughing so much she later start crying.

Why you laughing? I ask her.

Ooohoo! she laughing. My child, I can see you ending up on the gallows one day, I tell you. It looks like a gallows rope you're knitting there.

I nearly stop knitting right there. But after some time I start again, and after that Ouma Nella show me about casting off. I get fond of knitting. To make something with my own two hands and see it grow and take shape and turn into something that's different from what it was before. A length of wool that is teased out and spun and wound up into a ball. At first it's just wool, but then it change between your fingers and turn into something that can keep you warm in winter. It's like when you talking and you take a lot of words and put them together like loose stitches on a needle, and suddenly you find you saying something that wasn't there before. It's some sort of magic that happen in your mouth, just like between your fingers. You can say *cat*, or you can say *dog*, and then you can make the cat sit down or catch a butterfly, or you can make the dog bite, and then to stop biting, whatever. And you can say: *Look, there's a butterfly*, and suddenly the butterfly is there, even if there is no butterfly you can see anywhere. You just *make* it be there. You can make yourself butterflies in the longhouse, or in Ouma Nella's bedroom, or in the night, anywhere, any time. Or when the Ounooi is giving you hell, you can say, *There's a tick*, and then you can make that tick bite her just where and how and when you want to, and she won't even know why you laughing. She only itch. Or when the old goat thrash you, you can say: *Eina, it's sore!* But you can also choose to say: *No it don't hurt at all.* Or you can say: *I won't cry, even if he kill me.* And today I can say: *That blarry Oldman cannot hurt me and he won't ever try to lie with me again. And I won't ever call him Oubaas again.*

To tell the truth, I already forget about the day I knit the long wool tongue. Only remember it again on the day the old goat take us to the Caab to make us see how they hang that poor man Abraham and I pee myself. Not only because it is so terrible to see, although it is bad enough, but because I suddenly remember what Ouma Nella tell me about my knitting myself a rope for the gallows. Something I never-ever forget again. To carry my own death with me all the time and wherever I go. That must be why I keep knitting. Not to make that gallows story come true but to keep it out of the way.

This knitting been with me all the time. It start when Ouma Nella first tell me how to cast on the stitches, all the way to casting them off again. Then measuring to make sure the cardigan or the coat or whatever will fit properly. From the shoulder down to the starting row. Making sure it will fit properly – not too loose, not too tight. Getting to know all the different kinds of stitches. First garter stitch. Then cross stitch and blanket stitch and stem stitch. The whole lot of them. And not just one at a time. You learn to mix them together. Like you do with stocking stitch. Or with ribbing. Or with plain and purl. There's a time and a place for every kind. And you learn to knit them by turns, which I do most of the time. Until you reach the edge of the ribbing for the neck, to make sure it will fit properly. After some more time you learn about cables. One row of stitches folding over another, it can be up-and-down cables or thisway-and-thatway cables. For that, it's better to use thinner needles, it give you a tighter fit. You always use bamboo for needles, it work so much better. And there's lots of bamboo on the farm. I love going down to the bamboo copse to pick them. After a while Ouma Nella show me about binding and facing. Choosing the right stitches, usually with thinner wool. And, of course, all the time she teach me about correcting mistakes. In the beginning, when my fingers are still dumb, there are mistakes all the time, all the way, JesusGod! Dropped stitches, crooked or uneven rows, rows knitted too tightly or too loose. Picking up the dropped stitches. Knitting up where it start unravelling. It's like sleep, Ouma Nella always say. If you get too tired, your head unravel just like knitting. Then you need sleep to pick up the stitches and knit them up properly. After that, you learn about plaiting, and seams, and of course buttonholes. About gathering and ending off. So it go on, you always get new things to learn.

There come a time when I getting bored by knitting the same lot of stitches all the time. I begin to wonder what it will be like to try something totally new. Say a few stitches plain, then a few purl, a stocking stitch or two, a few garter stitches or something even more different, then knitting together a few, followed by crossing over some of the earlier ones, and repeating all of this for a few rows before moving on to something else again. Of course it mean planning very carefully and thinking ahead, otherwise it will all be a mess. You got to know how each row will go with the others around it, so each row got to be planned, then each group of rows, together and separate. In the beginning it make my head ache and my eyes burn, particularly in the evenings in the light of our lard candle. But I slowly find my way. Especially after I tell Ouma Nella about what I trying to do and she give me advice. First the two of us together, she and I, and later all by myself, I work and work to make my own patterns. A lot of trouble in the beginning. Even Ouma Nella keep saying I wasting my time and everybody else's, but I go on and on. For days, for weeks, even for months. Making plans, lying awake, thinking ahead, and then following my night-time thoughts in the daytime. Then my first jersey get done. Just a small one, to see what it can look like. And it look really pretty, if I say so myself. Ouma Nella say the same.

Now I want to go and show it to the Ounooi, I say. Ask her what she think.

Better not, say Ouma Nella. I don't trust that old cow.

She was right, of course. But I was too eager to show it to someone, and so instead of listening to Ouma Nella I take the jersey straight to the Ounooi.

She churning the butter when I get there, for that is something she always do herself, won't let any dirty hands spoil her new butter. If she don't keep her own fat hands on it, the butter turn out too hard or too runny, too salty or too insipid. Yes, she ask me, what you doing here? What do you want?

I just come to show the Ounooi something.

Well, show and be done, don't waste my time with your nonsense. What have you messed up this time?

It's a jersey I make for one of the children. For Alida or someone, I think.

She give it one look and ask, Who the hell told you to knit a jersey this time of the year?

Nobody tell me, Ounooi. I do it on my own and in my own time.

You're not supposed to have time of your own. Who taught you this?

Nobody, Ounooi.

And you think we got enough time in this house to waste on things like this?

I think it is a pretty jersey, Ounooi.

You listen to me, *meid*. You're not here to think. You're here to work and to do what we tell you.

Yes, Ounooi. But –

Don't talk back to me. And for all the time you've been wasting, bring me my *riem*.

But that's not fair, Ounooi. I just try to –

Just this or just that, it's all shit. Bring me that *riem*.

And then she beat me until I can no longer stand.

Not the end of it yet. Because after that I got to undo that whole piece of knitting in front of her eyes until there is nothing left of it. Nothing, I tell you. I just cry and cry. And that's something the Ounooi can't stand. So she beat me again. And she shout: For being so hard-headed and obstreperous you're not getting any food tonight. That'll bloody well teach you.

Luckily Ouma Nella was in her room to give me some bread and a mug of milk. But that night I cry myself to sleep. One of the very few times, for crying is something I do not *sommer* easily do.

But I do not stop knitting. Frans love watching me, and he like me to show him. I even show him to do some stitches himself. He don't do too badly. But what he like best is to play auction-auction with me. He first teach me, because he often go to the Caab with the Oldman so he learn everything about auctions. And when he come back home to Zandvliet again, he show me. Back to the bamboo copse. For whatever we want to do that is always the best place. Usually he is the auction man or the buyer, or both of them in turn. Then I am the slave that got to be auctioned. I got to take off my clothes and stand on a block, so all the buyers can have a good look at me. And Frans start talking in a high singing voice. *Mijne heeren.* Because there is usually only men at the auction. *Mijne heeren. Here we have a young slave girl. Take a look.* I got to open my mouth to show them my tongue, and my teeth. And my hands, and my feet. Then back to the hands to show the gentlemen all my fingers, one by one. That's when he start telling them about my knitting. All the clever things I can do with these thin fingers, he explain very proudly, all the things I can knit and sew. And how much a girl like me is worth to a farmer's wife, more than money or corals, he say. Whatever corals may be.

Once he is done with the fingers he can carry on with the auction. The part I don't like is when he want me to bend over to show my backside to the people so that he can show the men between my buttocks. And then to turn round so he can open me between his fingers.

Until I get fed up with the game and tell him to stop. One day I get off the block and I tell him straight, That's now enough. Now it's your turn to be the slave and I'll be the Baas. That I like. Off with your shirt. Down with your breeches. And move your arse, the Baas don't have time to waste.

Frans try to protest, so I whack him with the *kierie*. *Mijne heeren*. Take a good look at this fine young boy. His eyes. Those two eyes are so good, they can see a duiker three days away and they shine in the dark. He can see round a corner if there's any game coming. Now look at his ears. Let me tell you, *mijne heeren*, he can hear from a hundred paces away when a chameleon turn its left eye to you. Now watch closely. Those two arms may be thin, but they tough. Those legs are not exactly tree trunks, but they can run as fast as a *ribbok*, from one sunrise to the next. Look at his front. Look at his backside. Look at this mouthful of teeth. Those teeth can chew stones. I turn Frans round and round, I tell them to look, I show them everything. I pull his fingers apart. I show them his foot soles. I make him bend over. Take a close look, *mijne heeren*.

Then I show them his front again. By the time I come to his little thing, it already stand up like a stick. I do to him what we always do when we get together in the bamboo copse. Look again. This thing can shoot like an elephant gun. It's a bargain, *mijne heeren*, and the man that get him, he get more than he can see. For this boy-child is a clever little bastard. He can read and write. He can do anything you can think of. You won't get a better buy in this Caab of ours. Caab of Storms, Caab of Good Hope, Caab of Anything You Wish For in the wide world. His name is Francois Gerhard Jacob Brink, they call him Frans for short. Who will make me a bid?

All those auction games that go back over the years. But nowadays there is no time for games any more. The world now catch up with us. Today there is a very real thing waiting for us. When everything else is over and done with, this is what we got left: we're on the wagon on the road to the Caab, it's time we did something about leaving Zandvliet for good. Today the feet must be spared, so I can look in good form in case there's people interested in buying a slave girl. Just like Frans and I used to play, except there is no play-play today.

It is I myself who tell the Oldman it's now time for me to get moving. I must get away from here. Zandvliet got nothing for me any more. And I won't be sold like an ox or a goat inland and upcountry. The LordGod alone know what will happen to me upcountry, far away from everything, far from family and friends, far from myself. So if that is what it got to be, I rather find myself a new baas in the Caab.

All right then, say the Oldman. Get on the wagon.

XI

So we go the Caab. I and Willempie and also little Lena,
because I'm not leaving my children behind. And Ouma
Nella. Because she's coming too, she say.

We travel on the wagon with the leaguers of new wine,
for this time our feet must be spared. If I want work I got
to look fresh. It's like a big rock I carry with me from the
time we leave Zandvliet's farmyard and I see Frans among
all the other people waiting in the yard, so tall, with his
white hair, and so thin. Only Ounooi Janna isn't there, she's
too fat, may the Devil take her.

The children don't know what is going on, and at first
they enjoy the ride. But as it go on and on they get bored
and I can see the Oldman's arse is getting itchy. It's a long
thing, this trip, like that business with knitting the tongue
so long ago, but I can manage, don't worry, and by the third
day I can cast off. The Oldman first think we can stay over
with his brother, but the house is full with visitors and family
so he got to move in with people that used to be his neighbours, but Ouma Nella and me and the two children find
a place up against the Boere Plein where she still know some
of the slave people. She bring a letter from the Oldman
with her to make sure we won't get shit from anybody. But
even so it's not easy. Everybody turn away from us. There
is no work, one after the other tell us. Some of them set

their dogs on us, and at one place I get bitten on the calf. What make you think we need any more slaves? they ask. It's just trouble and problems and money in the water.

So it go on. Later on we find a woman who keep asking Ouma Nella question after question after question: can I knit this and that and the other? I can hear she know what she talking about, and she look like a decent kind of person. But then she say: One thing, I don't want a lot of screaming snot-nosed kids in my yard. You'll have to leave your children at home when you come to work here.

My home will be where I work, Nooi, I tell her. If my children can't come with me I can't come either.

Right there she lose her temper. You people always want all you can get, as if you're the Baas and we are the slaves. We give you a little finger and you grab us all the way to the *kieliebak*. I need a knitting girl, not a crowd of good-for-nothings that eat us out of hearth and home. You can go to hell.

The same thing happen at another house. After that it is no, no, no, all the way Ouma Nella and I go. Same story the next day. On the third day the Oldman tell Ouma Nella to her face: Look, this has now gone on for long enough, Petronella. It's time we get back to Zandvliet. I'm not a man that can just sit around waiting for things to happen and you know it.

Just give us one more day, Cornelis, she say, because that is what she call him when there is no one else around. That's all we asking.

Asking my arse, he say.

Nobody's arse, Ouma Nella tell him. If you want to get rid of the child, then you do it properly, otherwise you got me to deal with.

I think he know very well what she mean, and that make him shut up.

The next day Ouma Nella and I are out in the streets before the cocks have even begun to crow. And from then till nightfall we go up and down every single street in the Caab. Because Ouma decide it's the best way to do it, we start at the old stone castle on the beach. On the Parade right next to it everything is in commotion, even though it's still dark, because it's market. All night long farmers bring in heaps and mountains of fruit and vegetables, anything you can think of in heaps so big you have never even dreamed about. And it's not just fruit and vegetables, but everything that's made all over the whole wide world. It's bread and sugar and rice and coffee and spices from all the faraway Dutch places and even from a land they call America, with lucifers and carved wooden toys from Germany, and large and small karosses from upcountry, and all the wools and cloths and doeks and muslin you can dream of, and the fur of beavers, and yellow cotton, and all kinds of foodstuffs in huge bottles and cans and jugs, preserved and dried ginger, citrons and oranges, dates, litchis and tamarinds. And lots of things you don't see every day, like hops and agar-agar and smooth windowpanes and whale blubber and whale candles. Things that come by ship and got spoiled by the seawater and are now sold cheaply, and live animals nobody never set an eye on, and calves and lambs that come out badly, with five legs or three eyes or no eyes at all. There's even horses and cattle and sheep on the market. It look as if anybody can buy or sell anything in the whole world on this market.

I'd like to stay there for much longer, but Ouma Nella grab me by the hand and pull me along. On the corner of the Heerengracht and Strand Street she go to show me the shop of a man called George Greig, where one can buy chairs and tables and cupboards. And also materials and knitting and funeral clothes and umbrellas, peppermints and lovely stockings for women. Wherever we go Ouma Nella ask the people if they know anybody that want to buy a knitting girl? Or a slave woman for household work? Even outdoor work on a farm if it got to be? To everybody she tell how good I am, until I'm getting all shy and feel my whole face burning. But she keep on asking and enquiring. At last we move on down to the sea, to the place where the people go to empty their shit buckets, between the places they call the Amsterdam Battery and the Chavonnes Battery. It stink up to heaven, but Ouma say today I got to see all of it, so that I can know what kind of a place this Caab is if I really think of coming to work here.

Then we move on again to where we can see a ship coming in. The whole top of the ship, that Ouma Nella call the deck, is swarming with people. But they first got to wait, she say, until somebody can come from the land to inspect the ship's papers. And all the time as we stand there watching, small boats come rowing from the beach with baskets full of fresh fish and live crayfish and all kinds of fruit, all of it still shiny and smooth of freshness. And up on the high deck the ship's cook come out with a huge fire-pan full with glowing coals to cook the crayfish right there. The people on the ship are so hungry they grab the stuff straight from the coals. And the fruit and vegetables they want to gulp down without even chewing. It's because of all the months they been on that ship with only old rotten food or salty food to eat, Ouma Nella say, so they stuff themselves with anything that's fresh. And even while we still standing there on the beach with all the others she start shouting like a trumpet: Isn't there anybody up there looking for a slave girl? Her hands can take on anything. What about it, Mijnheer? Take a look, Juffrouw! But they don't seem to believe she mean it seriously.

· 108 ·

Just once a woman come to us from the side, in a nice striped dress and a large floppy hat on her tall hair, and she say to Ouma Nella: If the price is right, I shall buy the girl. Just like that.

And what do the Nooi think is the right price? asks Ouma Nella.

A hundred rix-dollars, say the woman.

Ouma Nella laugh from deep inside her guts and spit a slimy white gob right past the woman's face. Make it twelve hundred, she say, then we can talk.

You must be mad in your head, say the woman. I know what I'm talking about, I know all about slaves.

You don't know anything, Ouma Nella snap at her. You townsfolk know nothing about nothing.

I'm not from here, *meid*! the woman shout back. Do you see those mountains over there in the distance? I have a farm on the other side of them. And there's nothing you can tell me about slaves.

And what do the Nooi farm with? Ouma Nella press her.

Farm? jeer the fancy woman. It's a hell of a big farm I got there, my *meid*.

I'm not your *meid*, say Ouma Nella. I got my freedom.

Free or not free, you're a *meid* and you're stupid.

Well, so tell me then: what do the Nooi farm with?

I farm with sheep and cattle, and I farm with slaves.

And what does that mean?

It means, you stupid *meid*, just what I said. I farm with a lot of sheep, some cattle, but above all I farm with slaves. And then she tell us that her whole farm is full of slaves. Most of them women. Then, from time to time, she get a few men from England whose only work is to make children. They are her studs. For every baby that's born, she say, I get more money. So how about it? You must be too old for that, she tell Ouma Nella, but how about this girl of yours? She look young and strong to me, and ready to be plucked. I can see she's already got two children with her. If we start now, we can have another one by Christmas. And again next year. Before you know where we are, that farm will be covered in children. Each of them worth a good bag of money. Listen to me, *meid*: for every one this girl of yours breed, I pay her fourteen rix-dollars. Just a few years, and she'll be stinking rich, then she can buy her own freedom and retire in style. First she lie back and afterwards she sit back. What do you say?

Ouma Nella lift Willempie to her wide hip and she take my hand so quickly that it almost get lost in hers. Come on, Philida, she say. We don't belong here with the studcows.

The woman in the striped dress is still standing there, shouting a never-ending stream of curses in our direction until we are well out of the way. Up the incline, back towards those huge barracks which they say used to be a hospital, but now they use it to care for slave women that land in trouble with the court. And here, next to it and further down, is the small clearing with the gallows in the middle, the gallows where years ago the Oldman took us to the hanging of the poor skinny man that shat himself so badly that they got to hang him twice. And next to the gallows are the stakes where they tie up the people for flogging. That is where they also have the wheel on which arms and legs are broken with iron poles. When we get to it there is a man hanging limp over the wheel. They must have broken him yesterday already, I see, but he must have died soon afterwards and then they just left him there, because it's vultures wherever you look, squabbling and fighting among themselves for bits of flesh and making a racket like a bunch of drunken washerwomen, fluttering up from time to time to tackle one another in the air before they flap down again to go on eating. Willempie start crying because of the noise and I have to give him to Ouma Nella to take him away.

From there we go further. Through all the quarters where people live, the poor people and the ordinary working people and the free blacks, higher and higher along the mountain, past the woodcutters that come staggering downhill with huge bundles on their shoulders. But these people are much too poor for us, they cannot afford to keep slaves, I complain to Ouma Nella. I'm carrying Lena, Ouma Nella take care of Willempie. Even a baby grow heavy on a day like this. And I get tired of going from one house after the other, to the back door, asking if someone need a knitting girl. Or even an outside girl for the backyard.

The sun is almost down by the time we get to the Oranje Street, to a huge house where one can see that a lot of rooms have been added on over the years.

This is where we must ask, I tell Ouma Nella, because I think I remember the place from earlier days. These people must have lots of family, just look at all the rooms. Surely they must need a knitting girl.

They're not our kind of people, Philida, say Ouma Nella, taking my hand very firmly in hers. They breed like mice.

But they must be rich to have a house like that, Ouma. And look there at the side, that must be the slave quarters. I'm sure people like that will have place for me too. I don't take up much space.

I don't want you to work in a house like that, she say. They don't have proper manners.

How can Ouma say that? Do you know them then?

I know them. That is all she say, but from her voice I can tell she know more than she will talk about.

That make me go on nagging, like a fly that don't know when to stop. Until she get impatient and snap at me: Philida, I know what I'm saying. And it's not something I want you to hear.

Why mustn't I know, Ouma?

Because I say so.

That's not good enough for me, Ouma. I'm the one who got to find work. This is my life, Ouma Nella, not yours.

What make you think it isn't my life too? Her voice is getting angry. But then she put her hand on my shoulder and squeeze it so tight I can feel pee running down my knees. And through tight lips she say: All right. I shall tell you what I know. But not now. Later. This is not the right time.

How will I know when it is the right time, Ouma?

You will know. I'll tell you.

And that is that. The day grow old around us. And by the time the night come there is still nothing. It just feel as if I been walking a long uphill road, a road longer than the one that goes over the mountains to Stellenbosch, longer than to the Caab, a road as long as the whole world, longer than my life, and it feel as if I have now come to the last bend. But all the way there has been nothing. Just nothing. All the time, nothing. And now still nothing.

But I know it is not for nothing that this nothing look like nothing. Below all this nothing lies another world that you cannot see, but you know it is there. And it is full of the dead of years and years. All the children that died even before they were born, or when they were born, or after they were born, with crooked legs or no legs at all. With squinting eyes or blind eyes or bulging eyes, with holes in their palates, with bent-around arms or sideways necks, with hollow backs, with missing toes or fingers, all those that drowned, or died of measles or whooping cough or pocks or croup or fever, those that just died because they didn't feel like living in this place. All the slave children, all the children that were not born white and were a shame on their parents, the Baas people who won't live with that shame, a whole brood of ghost people that live just below the skin of the earth and now lie there waiting, or sit around quietly, or crawl about, waiting for the last trumpet that the Oldman always talk about, waiting to push the living aside to let them out, so that they are the only ones that are still there, a land and a world of the crippled and the maimed, the sick and the half-dead, the lame and the deaf, waiting for the Judgement. Why and for what? For what?

All Ouma Nella keep on saying is: It's the time that's wrong for us, Philida. And if the time is wrong, then everything will be wrong all the way to hell.

How can it be wrong for us, Ouma Nella?

It's because of all this talk about freeing the slaves, say Ouma Nella. Now nobody can pay for a slave and then be stuck with him, and all your money gone. Nowadays it's enough money for a whole farm.

All the way back to Zandvliet that is all we can talk about. The endless stories through so many years, spreading from farm to farm, about how we slaves will be freed. Yet nothing ever happens.

Remember what happened in '25? ask Ouma Nella. When some slaves far away in the Cold Bokkeveld got so sick and tired of all the stories of being freed that they rose up against their Baas? It was on a farm the people called Houd-den-Bek, which means Shut-Your-Trap, below the Skurweberge. There was a man with the name of Galant and his story is still living among our people. Nobody who is a slave will ever forget him. One day there was this story of the slaves going to be free, on a New Year's Day, I remember, and when that day came and went and nothing happened, Galant took his Baas's gun and shot the man dead. The farmer was called Nicolaas van der Merwe. And some of the slaves went with Galant. After they killed this Nicolaas and a few other people, the three gangleaders were caught and their heads were put up on poles in the Bokkeveld, and there came a kind of stormy silence to the land. I tell you it was a troubled time for the Bokkeveld, and everywhere. Many people remained angry and scared for a long while. But the one thing we all learned was never to believe these stories about freedom again. From then on we just stay put and keep our ears and eyes open, and wait for whatever may happen. It's the same today, my child. No use people get all worked up. What must happen will happen, and it's not for us to question the ways of the Lord or of all the old gods and things that live in this place.

I just sit there on the wagon beside Ouma Nella, and I listen to her stories. Not that I pay much attention, for my heart is heavy, as if there is a dead body I carry inside me. All the way home from the Caab to Zandvliet is like going to a funeral. I keep remembering how eager we all are about going to the Caab. Then everything is still alive in front of me, I am *mos* going to find a new baas, a new place to work, the whole world is going to become new. And now it is all closing up around me again. There is no more hope for me and Frans. They going to take me upcountry and sell me in the deep interior, that I know. Me and my children. Lena and Willempie. A place we don't know, in a land we don't know and don't want to know. Something is now gone for ever. Like Ouma Nella said. Gone to hell.

XII

About Origins and other philosophical Questions

Sitting on the slowly moving wagon like that and looking around at everything you used to think you know, it sometimes feels as if you don't know anything at all, and the whole world has become a strange place. You look at a flower, or a bee, or a butterfly, you see a small lizard scurrying over a rock, all of them born yesterday and dead tomorrow. And you think: I am no different from them. All of life caught in the sun of an afternoon. Flower, woman, butterfly, bee, lizard. And all of this because of Philida.

I went with her all the way to the Caab, on the wine wagon. And now coming back. And after this? On the road to the Caab she sat knitting most of the time, the way she usually does, with those clever, thin fingers she has, knitting and knitting. But on the way back she didn't knit any more. She just sat. With the stillness of a stone, a stone that tells you: it simply *is* there. It doesn't stir, but it isn't dead, deep inside it is a life you know nothing about, a thing like ice or fire, and which can burn you until there is nothing left of you at all.

I've known this child for ever. Philida who since her earliest days used to ask questions about everything in order to find out: Why is this like this? Why is that like this? Why is everything the way it is? Until she ended up by saying, It cannot always be like this, Ouma Nella. There must be something more. Something that is not like this.

And then she'd go on and on until I started wondering myself: Why is it like this?

From there it got more and more difficult. I remember the many many times she asked, when she was barely two hands high: Ouma Nella, where's my ma?

All I could say was: I don't know where she is. Nobody know.

And then: Where's my father?

I don't know, my child. Nobody know.

Why don't nobody know?

Because there are some people nobody know about.

There must be *somebody* who know. Ouma Nella must know because there is nothing she do not know.

There's nothing about this business that I know, I tell you.

And then, out of the blue, she would ask: Ouma Nella, where am I not?

I ask you.

Ouma Nella, where am I not?

But you're right here with me, Philida. So there's many places where you're not.

Tell me where those places are. I got to know. So I can go and look for myself.

Makes one feel quite upside down and inside out about not knowing the answer. *Ouma Nella, where am I not?*

Deep inside me I knew was the question I feared most of all, and I knew that Philida's questions would bring her back to this one: Ouma Nella, where do I come from?

I never wanted to go near that question. It's like a fruit. Like a peach or an apricot or a plum that is still green and that you must not try to press ripe. That just brings stomach ache and the squitters. I always managed to steer past it, but on that ride back to Zandvliet, after the emptiness of the Caab, I know the time for that question has come. I cannot dodge it any more.

So that is exactly what she asks: Ouma Nella got to tell me today, I got to *know*. Where do I come from?

For a long time I never told you, my child. Not because I did not know, but because you or I can do nothing about it. It just is what it is, and that's all.

So tell me, Ouma Nella.

For a while I just sit there, doing nothing, saying nothing.

She presses me on: Do I also come from a far place like Ouma Nella or Oompie Geert or Aia Kandas?

No, Philida. You come from the Caab. You were made right here.

I got to know, Ouma Nella.

That house we came past yesterday, in the Oranje Street, the one with the many rooms, where the Berrangés live. That is where you come from.

Is that where Frans wants to live, with a white wife?

It's not that he wants to live there, but his family is telling him so.

And is that the place, Ouma Nella? That big house?

That is the place, Philida. And that is why I don't want you to work there.

But now I got to know everything, Ouma Nella. I can't go on without knowing.

So it came that I told her. From very far back. Twenty-five years back. When I got to know the young girl Farieda that used to work for those people. A girl-woman, but not quite a woman yet. Just getting ripe, like a quince. I told you, man. Just a child still. Her mother came from Malabar, the people said. Came out on the ship, like I did from Java. It's not something I like to talk about. That time on the ship, all the rows of us in the stomach of the ship, with chains on our arms and legs, so you could never stand up, and barely sit or lie down, all those rows of people in the dark, stinking and smelling from all sides, vomit and shit and piss and sweat, day and night, but it all feels like night, just now and then a small bowl of soup, more water than soup, that you throw up again, almost immediately. And the ship that keeps on going up and down, up and down, some-times slowly and softly, but on other times badly, terribly, awfully, up like mountains, down like deep holes, so there's no more guts and stomach and stuff left inside you. No end to it, not ever, up and down all the time, all the time, in that night-time darkness, in that stink. Once a week or so, or less, or more, how can one tell?, it was only afterwards, when we could talk again, that we tried to figure it out, men came down to us with long whips and chased us up the smelly narrow stairs, not one of us could walk properly any more, we just struggled up the stairs, stumbled and struggled and fell and tried again, on all fours, and all the way the men laughed at us and beat us, until we got to the top where we nearly got blinded by the sun, where they upended buckets and buckets full of salt water over you until you thought you'd drown, and after some time, a timeless kind of time, they beat you back and chase you back and kick you back, down those stairs again, and back into the chains and then the night close down over you again. Until there no longer is anything like day or night left, just darkness and stinking, and then it is over.

So now they tell you we are at the place they call the Caab. The rest you know. About the auction, and the men who come to buy you and who first want to feel you and pinch you and poke at you, until someone buys you like a sheep or a goat or an iron hoop or a wine barrel or a pisspot or whatever. So, just as I came here, your mother Farieda also came. Somebody bought her, then somebody else bought her, then somebody else again, and that somebody else was called Daniel Fredrik, he was from the Berrangé family, and it's with one of his big brood of daughters, Maria Magdalena, that they say your itchy-arse Frans will now have to marry.

I could see that Philida wanted to say something, but I didn't give her a chance. I told her about Daniel Fredrik's brother, a man who was a dominee, that is a man of the spirit. But all that was needed was one look, and you could see he was a man of the flesh. Such big, sweaty hands and a face that said only one thing: Come here, little sister, and lie down, and let your bridegroom enter you with singing psalms and lots of prayers. It didn't take long before Farieda was swollen with child, even though our man of God was already a father of five children by that time, three of them slaves. Everybody said that with the help of the Lord he was going to turn the Caab into a white man's land. I had nothing to say about that, I don't move in between a man and the flies of his breeches. But Farieda was still a child like I said, and she just wanted to drown that baby in the shit bucket. So it was I who stopped her and took the little thing away from their house and gave her to a slave woman in the Bo-Caab whose little boy had just died after her Baas had beaten him to death for dropping a basket of figs in the dust. An eye for an eye and a child for a basket of figs.

And then, Ouma Nella?

That baby was you, Philida. I helped to bring you up

and later I took you in with me. So that is where you come from and how and why.

But what about my own mother, Ouma Nella? What about that Farieda?

Now she wants to know. This is her chance, isn't it? All these years I stayed away from that question, but now it can no longer wait. It's waited long enough and it is cooked and ready to serve up. Even so I still tried to duck away, talking about anything that came into my mind, blue almonds and everything. But in the end she cornered me and no longer allowed me to get away and said straight out: Ouma Nella, it is time to tell me.

Why go on asking, my child? All those things have been buried away far and deep and long ago.

I still got to know about my ma, Ouma Nella.

Ai, man. Is it really necessary?

I want to know and I *got* to know.

There came a silence that did not want to go away easily.

So tell me, Ouma Nella. About the woman that was my ma.

And so, at long last, yes, I told her.

She didn't live much longer, my child. You see, she tried to run away, *sommer* up into the mountain. In those days there were many slaves hiding away up there. The Berrangés sent a commando after her, they were already rich and important people and they could pay anybody to do what they asked. So Farieda was brought back. All I can tell you is that they didn't handle her softly. They knew a man who was a peeler.

What is a peeler, Ouma Nella?

Well, that's a man that peels off the foot soles of a runaway slave.

How do you mean 'peel', Ouma Nella?

Peel is peel, man. All you need is a nice sharp knife, then it peel away a foot sole as easy as any peach. Once you do that to a slave he is in no hurry to run away again.

But Farieda, Ouma?

Well, no matter how bad it was, I can tell you that Farieda tried again. But she was bleeding too much. So to those rich people she wasn't worth anything any more. They just let her bleed and so she died. I think it was better like that for her too. So you moved in with me and I brought you up. Later, when Cornelis bought me my freedom, you came with me and here we are still together.

This time Philida is silent for a hell of a long time, which is strange, for usually when we are together she never stops talking. She just sat there, staring out in front of her. Me too.

We rode on and on, through an empty world. No matter how many times in my life I came that way, on the wagon or on foot, there has always been a lot to see, but this time it is empty, there is nothing. There's nothing that looks as if it has anything to say to me. We come past places that do not have a name yet. We move through empty stretches where nothing grows, not even words. Even the sky is still. There's no clouds or birds coming past, no nothing. The land is holding its breath.

And so, I think, it may go on for ever.

But no matter what, we still have to go on, to get home. Cornelis is in too much of a hurry to get home. He drives the oxen until you can hear the breath whistling in their tight throats. It sounds like a death rattle. We must get home. Get home. Get home. But how can one say that home is what is waiting for us? Even if I have my own room, what does that mean? And for Philida it means even less. For all we know she may be gone one of these days, and no one will ever know where she ends up. And what will become of me then? All I have in this world is that small room. So many years and years. Before we came to Zandvliet there was only me at first. Then Philida and I together, far away from everybody else and the darkness of the world. Yet not so far away either. There are always people that come to knock on the outside door. Just to talk for a while, because I like company. Or to buy some wine, for Cornelis makes sure that I always have a small supply. It was part of the agreement when he bought my freedom and the room became mine.

Otherwise there are people who come to ask for help. They know I have a remedy for every complaint, so they come to look for that. When there's a knock deep in the night we know it must be one of those. Usually a man, for women don't walk about in the dark when the ghosts are loose in the yard. You can always be sure that if I open that door there's a man outside in the dark asking to come in. Summer or winter. Standing there with a thick blanket over his shoulders, white with frost or snow in the cold months. Sometimes not even a blanket. He'll be standing there with his clothes in shreds and tatters, and all he carries on his shoulders is the dark. He brings with him the glow of moonlight and the stars and the chirping of crickets and the squeaking of bats, he brings with him the cackling and the howls of jackals and the coughing of a leopard and the screech of a night owl and the moaning and chattering of ghosts, all of this he carries on his shoulders when he comes across the doorstep to ask for a whisper of ginger or camphor or dried garlic or burnt peach stones or man-root or nightshade or ground tortoiseshell or musk-cat skin or a pinch of filed tooth off a warthog, all the things you may need in the night when a child is dying or a woman goes into labour or a man is in need of love or a girl wants to make her man come back after he's run away with someone else or when a child has stomach ache or croup or fever or a burning this or an itchy that or anything we people have inherited since the beginning of the world. I am *mos* supposed to have a remedy for everything, and sometimes it seems to me I must be an ouma to the whole damn world.

That is the place I want to get back to. That is where my thoughts are holed up. It is the place where I belong.

And so we all come home again, in Zandvliet's farmyard, I with my load of half-breeds. There's my own child, Cornelis Brink, and then Philida, the daughter of Dominee Berrangé, and then the wagon drivers, Jannewarie and Apools, the offspring of one of the Boschendal de Villierses and two of his slave women, and the little wagon leader, who is the child of a Conradie with a Khoe woman from the Tanqua Karoo. I am the only one that wasn't kicked up from under a bush, although I must say that no one, not even I myself, will ever know what happened to my ma in Batavia before I landed on that ship. But why should I bother my head over that? I am me, Petronella, and I don't mess around with whatever lies on the other side of my thinking and my wondering. Although I do ask myself, when I look at this lot: What on earth will become of us in this godforsaken land? It is not just a matter of mothers and fathers. It starts with us, with those who don't want to know where they come from and where they fit in and who they are. Each one goes on looking for his own shadow that lies trampled into the dust and left to lie there. We have more than enough lost shadows among us.

The whole farmyard stands waiting for us when the wagon arrives. Not just the people – from the Ounooi Janna, as much of a misery and a turd as always, as thick as a badly stuffed sausage, down to everybody that works here, man and woman and child – but even the animals, the horses and mules and donkeys, the sheep and the few stuck-up cattle chewing their cuds, the muttering pigs, all except the filthy old fat sow Hamboud wallowing in her mud hole against the ring wall in a cloud of flies, grunting like Cornelis in the old days when he had his way with the Ounooi of an afternoon. There's the rowdy pack of dogs, and well out of the way, high on the wall, the cats, with Philida's Kleinkat, head up in the air, eyes half closed, looking sideways at the others and too proud to be reckoned with them. The poultry too, geese and ducks, the two turkeys. And somewhere out of the way, the noisy hen Zelda always cackling and gossiping about an egg laid by someone else. It's time somebody cut that good-for-nothing's sinewy throat. But I don't think anyone really cares, her meat must be too tough and stringy even for a hawk to be interested. And anyway, she smells too much of chickenshit and dishwater.

Behind all the animals and people in the yard I can make out other creatures too, among the trees, behind the bushes, in the kitchen garden, shadows moving behind windows and shutters or half-open doors, just to remind me that the ghosts are there too, we are closely watched all the time, and everybody is forever trying to find out: What now? What next?

XIII

*In which a worried Man concerns himself
with Dogs and Elephants*

So everything has now been arranged and decided. And
still there is a restlessness in me, precisely because there is
no turning back any longer. The day after tomorrow, well
before the sun comes out, we must set out to reach Worcester
in the district of Tulbagh in time for Wednesday. That, I
learned in the Caab, is when the next slave auction will be
held. God alone knows how it will go, because who in his
right mind will still want to buy slaves at a time like this?
Who still has money to spend on such a doubtful proposi-
tion? Here I've just been to the Caab, and what did I get
for my wine? Thirty-six rix-dollars a leaguer. A bloody
shame. Just more than half, I tell you, of what I got almost
ten years ago when I started farming on Zandvliet. In those
days we could reckon on fifty rix-dollars, give or take.
Perhaps a week earlier or later the price might have been
better. But it could also have been worse, because every
time it's different and you can never calculate in advance.
The one thing you can count on is that everything you buy
is getting more expensive. To transport that leaguer of wine
from the farm to the Caab costs almost twice of what it did
when I came here. How are we supposed to keep up? Unless
somebody can assure us that we'll make a profit by the
compensation the British government is supposed to pay
out next year when it's time for emancipation, as they call

it. But how can one trust the English? Up to now everything has just been covered by a bloody blanket of nice words and promises and lies.

You mustn't worry so much, Janna keeps telling me. But I tell her, I must worry, I'm a Brink. If I don't worry, what will happen to the world? She believes it will all work out for us. She comes from a family of de Wets where people always believed things will go right in the end, and if they don't then you beat or kick them right. I remember the warm feeling it gave me the very first time I saw her, she was still married to Wouter de Vos, but he didn't last long. Nobody could, with her. That body she had. Young. Eager. Solid. She could easily carry a *muid* bag of wheat on her shoulders to the barn. She could have smothered one between those two bosoms if you got so irresponsible as to push your face in between them. Long before we got married I already thought that would be the kind of death a man could wish for. She was a handful, everybody warned me. But I thought, what the hell, she was *two* handfuls. And for years I thought myself a happy man. Until the eating took over completely. I've never seen a human being that could polish a big plateful of food the way Janna could. What do I talk about a plateful? Bowls and buckets of the stuff. For a few years I could take it. It's true what they say about a fat woman: that thing may be narrow, but it's *deep*. That was before she grew all out of hand. In the beginning she could still be enjoyed from the side, in instalments. But I started worrying about the future. If that woman were to sit down on you, it occurred to me, she could kill a man in one sitting. There would be nothing left of you, not even a damp spot.

That was how Janna became a liability, no longer an asset. With all the other loads I already have to carry. And then the wine price jumping up and down all the time too, enough to make one dizzy, let alone bankrupt. And this whole business with the slaves.

Nobody can say for sure yet what will happen exactly in December of next year when the whole damn lot of them will be let loose on us. If you ask me, it will turn into a flood of vagrants washing over this Colony, worse than in '28 when that blasted Ordinance 50 gave the Hottentots a licence to roam and steal and kill to their filthy hearts' content. They say the slaves will remain booked in with us for four more years, but who says it's going to work out like that? The way I know them they'd rather kill us straight away with clubs and *kieries* and long stones and guns in our sleep. That's all they're used to. And that, after all the years we looked after them and cared for them like children. But now? Everything they've got in this world is what we gave them. I ask you: What's going to happen to us? What is a baas without a slave? Who will still respect us? And what about them, if they no longer have us to feed them and protect them and take care of them? And who will do the work? It was God himself who made them to be hewers of wood and carriers of water for us. That was written word for word in the Bible by God himself and that's why everything keeps going as it is: there are those who are made to be baas and others made to do the work. And even so it's still us who got to do most of the work, if you ask me. How would they know about digging and watering and pruning and harvesting and threshing if we were not there to tell them what to do and when to do it? What would that cheeky little slut Philida know about knitting if Janna hadn't shown her stitch by stitch? But it's not just about the work that I'm wondering and worrying. What I'd like to know is what will become of *them*? And what will then become of *us*? We all need one another. Is it not already too late to start wondering about it? Sometimes in a sleepless night I ask myself if it hasn't always been too late for us.

But again I say, it's not just about *us*. What will happen to that flood of slaves once they are unleashed on this land? They'll all die in a heap. It's us who kept them alive. Can a dog survive if there is no longer a baas to take care of him? And a slave is worse than a dog.

And is this the time to worry about such things? Are there no other, more important problems threatening us? I cannot allow my thoughts to run on side roads. A man that hunts an elephant cannot stop to throw stones.

XIV

Where Hell breaks loose in the Bamboo Copse

It was just after sunset that Pa came to talk to me where I was rinsing a few half-aum barrels before the next day's tasting of new wine for some customers expected from the Caab. I had no idea of what he'd got on his mind. All right, by this time we were more or less expecting what was going on in his thoughts, but not so soon. I believed it could wait for later, for a day in the distant future. But now, it seemed to me, everything had simply been decided behind my back and all the rest of us could do was agree.

The first thing he said, gruffly and quite out of the blue, was: Frans, you and I still have a chicken to pluck.

And what can that be, Pa?

That is when he came out with it: I'm off to Worcester tomorrow. There's an auction.

What kind of auction, Pa?

Slaves, of course, he said. What else?

I could feel everything drawing in around me like when a hoop is tightened round a barrel.

I still dared to ask: Is it about Philida, Pa?

Of course it's about Philida. What else?

All I could dumbly think of was: But it's too soon, Pa. The child is still too small.

Whose child?

Philida's child, Pa.

Why should a slave woman's child concern you?

I said nothing.

He pushed on: You mean your child too?

I still didn't answer.

When I was in the Caab, he said, the people were talking about this auction in Worcester. They even put it in the *Gazette*.

This is no time to buy or sell slaves, I told him. The market is gone down a big hole.

What choice do I have? he asked angrily. If Philida stays here there'll be no end to the shit. And it's all because of you. Because you can't control yourself.

I'm just following your own example, I told him, and I quickly stepped out of the way. I knew he could not move fast with that lame leg of his. He must have been aware of it too, because he made no attempt to block my way.

When he spoke again there was a whining tone in his voice: We're always on the losing side, Frans. Whether it's the government or God, no difference. He gave one of those deep sighs he seemed to draw from between his backbone and his gut. The people say, he went on, they say one day the LordGod said, Let there be light. And there was light. And then he said, Let there be people. And the whole world crawled with people. And then one day he spoke again and he said: Let there be Brinks. And then there was shit.

Now Pa is going too far, I said.

Says who? Have you ever seen the thing that happened to my Bible?

What thing are you talking about, Pa?

On the very last page, he said, after Revelations and the Scarlet Woman. On the empty page where I wrote down everything about our family. Ever since Oupa Andries stepped ashore here in the Caab. That was when the LordGod created the world as we know it today. Everything written down very carefully. Except for the bloody slave women that slipped in from time to time, of course, but they don't count. You know that. But now when I was in the Caab and I opened that last page one evening where I haven't looked for a long time, I saw with my own eyes that somebody spilled blue-black ink all over that page. As if he tried to cancel us from LordGod's own Book. Have you seen that?

That's not a page I ever look at, Pa.

Well, go and take a look, then you'll see for yourself. All of us blotted out from the Book. It's clear that the LordGod had nothing better to do, so he took it out on our family again.

He won't do a thing like that, Pa, I protested. That sounds like a human person did it.

Whatever, he said. I'm not saying God did it with his own hands. But he's a sly bastard if he feels like it. Then he gets the Devil or someone else to do his work for him, so nobody knows who to blame for it.

I could not resist the temptation to ask him: And who's to blame for Pa selling Philida now?

It's her own bloody fault, he hit back. After all the lies she told that man in Stellenbosch! All her doing. And yours. That is why she's got to be sold upcountry now. You heard all the things she said about us. Your ma cannot stand it any longer. And how do you think you'll ever get that Berrangé girl to marry you with Philida always underfoot?

Who says I still want to marry anybody?

He glared at me. What utter shit are you talking now, Frans?

Everything we discussed and talked about tells me I got no chance with her, I said.

You should have thought about all of that long ago. Now

it's time to get it arranged. The Berrangés are important people, we can't play the fool with them. And today we damn well need them, otherwise we've had it, jointly and severally.

What makes it different this time? I persisted.

That was when he put his big hand on my shoulder and he said: My son, it was only when I went to the Caab this time that it really hit me how bad it's going with us. Because of the wine price. Because of this whole slave business. I lie awake at night and behind my closed eyes I can see strangers trampling the house and the farmyard of Zandvliet to dust. Everybody coming here for our bankruptcy auction. That's a thing I'll never survive, Frans. It's just too much.

If that is how bad it is, I said, how can you stop it?

First of all we've got to get rid of Philida. She's making the water murky for all of us. That's why I've got to get on the road well before sunrise tomorrow morning so that we can get to Worcester in time. I hear that the prices in that part of the world are still better than in the Caab, but not for long.

Why can't we wait a little longer, Pa? I tried to hold him back.

Who is your *we*? he asked.

Pa?

Don't look at me like that, he said. You're not going with me. I won't allow you to bring even more shame on the family. It's not games we're playing, Frans, I tell you it's life or death.

But, Pa!

That's all I got to say. You have caused us enough trouble. Tomorrow when I take Philida to Worcester you will stay right here. And as soon as we get back, you better see to it that you get married to Maria Berrangé. I hope that is clear?

With this he stalked out.

For a long time I just stood there. Feeling as if he'd thrown a bucket full of cold water in my face. Or kicked me in the balls. This was much worse than the day I had to go to Stellenbosch to see the Protector about Philida. For the first time I now fully realised what was coming. That the two of us would never again go down to the bamboo copse together. That Philida would never set foot on Zandvliet again. Never. Not ever. No matter what I said or did, something was gone for ever. Between us, and for me. It was like a kind of dying.

I no longer even tried to think. All I could do was to get away from where I found myself and go to Old Petronella's room. I had to get to Philida. We had to talk.

I hurried straight to the inside door of the room and pushed it open without waiting.

Old Petronella was cooking at the hearth in the corner. Philida sat on a small red carpet on the smooth dung floor, the shiniest floor in the whole house, with Willempie on her breast and her Kleinkat on her lap. On the big bed Lena was playing with a little green elephant I'd carved for her long ago from a block of camphor wood.

What are you doing here? Old Petronella asked me straight, putting her hands on her wide hips to block my way. There's nothing here that belongs to you.

I've got to speak to Philida.

You got nothing to do with Philida. Let her be.

This is important business, Petronella.

Then Philida spoke up from the floor: You and I got nothing to talk about any more, Frans. I told you long ago.

But you don't know what is going to happen tomorrow, Philida!

I don't want to know nothing. You just get out of here.

That was when I hear Pa speaking right behind me: What are you doing here, Frans? Get out and move your arse!

I saw him standing there with a long *kierie* in his hand and I chose not to keep him waiting any longer.

Outside in the *voorhuis* I stopped to look around me, for now I really had no idea of what to do next. All I knew was that I *had* to speak to Philida before the sun came out in the morning. And just like a little while ago, it went through my mind over and over: Never again. Never again. Never the two of us together in the bamboo copse again.

That was when the thought formed in my head: No matter what I said, she wouldn't listen to me. It was over. For her there were only the children left, and the cat. It was useless to try and do anything about the children. But perhaps I could still reach her through Kleinkat. If Philida must leave for Worcester in the morning, she will never see that small cat again. And that was when the thought struck me.

Before I properly knew where I was going I was out of the longhouse. By that time dusk was already falling and I first stopped to clear my head. Then I turned back to the kitchen where I took a lantern from the shelf above the hearth, because I knew that in the copse it would be quite dark by now. In the first outroom in the backyard I found a small hatchet. Far away to the east the moon was already out. A deep orange yellow, and huge. It drifted up in the sky as if it were floating on dark water, so close that I felt I must duck. I made very sure no one could see me walking down from the longhouse. Once I was in the copse, I could light the lantern, nobody would see it from the house. And where I was walking right now I had no need of a lamp anyway, the moon was giving light enough, so strong that I could see a deep black shadow keeping pace with me to my left. It was both I and not I.

The copse is a very strange kind of place. As the bamboos close up behind me it is as if the whole everyday world around me fades away. Here it is as if I no longer know or recognise anything, and no one else knows about me any more. All that remains is *I*. Even my shadow has disappeared. In the pitch dark I can no longer see. I can only hear and smell. The heavy smell of the bamboos, a smell of distances and remoteness, of the sea, of darkness and strange animals. Of places where no one has ever been or knows about. When we were small Old Petronella used to tell us that these bamboos came from a place where she herself lived once, Java, and that they were brought here together with slaves and spices and herbs on ships, with stories of jealousy and rivalry and feuds and blood and murder and long knives. In a way all of that now lies soaked into the bamboos of this dark copse. It is a wood filled with life, and full of weird and terrible sounds, specially when the wind comes up, but even when everything is quiet, and in broad daylight. When I was a child those sounds used to scare me out of my wits: it sounded like the groaning and gnashing and whining and wailing of ghosts, people whose hands and feet were being sawn off with blunt knives, throats cut very slowly, a choking and rattling, a terrifying kind of world, very different from our own, and yet awfully close, much too close ever to allow one to breathe in peace. Even today, now that I know the sounds are only made by bamboo stalks and branches, it scares me, and at night it is even worse than in the daytime.

I strike a small flame from my tinderbox and light the oil lamp, and the wan light starts gnawing at the black trunks and stems, but it remains terrifying. And there is no more than a small yellow spot around me, which makes the surrounding night even more scary.

Our copse, Philida's copse and mine, since ever so long ago. For this is where we came to hide when she grew so terrified after the hanging in the Caab, that poor miserable bastard that they had to hang twice, when she started crying so badly and clung to me and we dropped down together on the cold damp black ground, and at first I didn't even know what was going on, it was the first time this had happened to me, and by the time it struck me I was already inside her and she was crying and talking to me, in my ear and in my face, and everything got wet with her spit and her tears. That first time, and then so many times afterwards. Always here among the bamboos and their groaning sounds and their stories about the sea and faraway lands. This is where our children were made. Willempie and Lena who will go with her to the auction tomorrow where they will be sold like skins and ostrich feathers and cattle. The children that she and I made together. Which makes my thoughts steal back to Little Frans, the one who was to bear my name. But we're not talking about him. What happened could not be helped, I swear to the LordGod. That was one of the occasions when I promised her: Philida, I swear to God, one day, as soon as I have the money, as soon as I can make a proper life of my own and Pa lies in his grave, I shall buy you your freedom. And the freedom of our children. Do you hear me? This I promise you. And I'm going to write this in Pa's big black book with our names. I promise and I swear.

But in the night, every night, it all comes back to me, together with the stories and the groaning and the moaning and the sighs of these bamboos. I am so very sorry, Philida.

I never wanted it to get as far as this. But how could I avoid it? What else could I possibly have done?

Time and time again we came back to this bamboo copse, she and I. I suppose tonight will be the last time I leave my footprints behind in this dark place. A testimony unto the LordGod. For tomorrow you are going away and I must remain behind on my own. If Pa and the LordGod will it, for I no longer have a say. One thing I can tell you: twice during these last few weeks I have walked out of the longhouse with Pa's hunting rifle in my hands. Once to the mountain, to the waterhole you went to show me long ago when we were still children, where the Water Women live. And once down to this very bamboo copse. I could not think of anything else I could possibly do. Somewhere, sooner or later, a man's footprints must disappear behind him. But I was too much of a coward. I couldn't. I'm so sorry, Philida. One day I suppose only this copse will know. This copse knows everything about us. Look at it in the meagre light of this lamp. Listen to it. Here the bamboos never stop rustling and whispering. Sometimes, when it is completely quiet everywhere else, it sounds like a storm wind in here. I've never liked wind much. The sun can blaze as madly as it wants to, but I can go with it and enjoy it. In the winter the snow may pile up all around us, but I like it. Every season, I feel, is good the way it is. The only thing I cannot bear is wind. It blows everything out of order in one's mind. I often argued with Philida, because she likes the wind, she says, specially here among the bamboos. It's their way of talking, she always says. Even then I tell her: Not in my ears. But she's got an answer for everything. And one day when I was complaining about the wind again, she said: No, man, Frans. Wind is good. That's how Ouma Nella taught me. It's the wind that teach the trees to dance. So how can I get angry with it? From then on I think I understand it better, even though I still wouldn't choose it myself. And perhaps she is right: nothing can be quite as magical as the wind in this bamboo copse. Listen to it. Lie on your back and listen to it. Feel it. Look at it. Smell it.

And there is one thing I shall never forget, no matter how old I get: I swear I was here one day, very long ago, when we were still small, when there were fireflies among the bamboos. Only that one night. I couldn't believe it. It was like magic. But I know I saw them. Nobody ever wanted to believe me. Except you. Because you always believed whatever I told you. If I close my eyes tonight, I still see them. The whole bamboo copse teeming with bright fireflies. It was a day when there was a big fight between Pa and me, something that happened almost all the bloody time, I could never do anything to his satisfaction. He always ranted that I was wasting time carving little things from wood when there was better work to do. And on that day he gave me a thrashing, said he'd wasted enough time talking, it was time I listened. He said I was worse than a slave, a damn disgrace to the Brink family, and on and on. My whole back was covered in blood. Even Ma went to talk to him, something she hardly ever dared to do, so he hit her too. I came here to hide away in the bamboo copse. Late in the afternoon I heard him calling in the backyard. He was looking for me now. And then other voices too. Ma, slaves, everybody. But nobody would find me here. I was the only one who knew about this hiding place. And Philida, of course, but no one else. And later, when they stopped searching and the voices fell silent, I stayed here. Swore I'd never go home again, nobody would again set eyes on me. In the end I must have fallen asleep. And when I woke up sometime in the deepest hollow of the night, the whole bamboo copse was twinkling with fireflies. At first I thought they were stars, I was wondering whether I'd come to heaven. Those fireflies. As if the whole wood was aflame with their tiny flickers. Embers, small specks of the firiest fire I'd ever seen. Never again in my life, nor any time before. But that night I saw it. And I still remember. Because I was here and I saw it.

Around me the leaves are rustling and whispering. The stems are scraping and grinding against each other, the whole night is filled with sound, the ghosts are everywhere, wherever the flickering light does not reach. The night is lukewarm with what is left of the day's heat, warmth curdled like dirty water in an old encrusted basin in which too many feet have been washed over too many years, but I cannot help a trembling moving into my arms and legs. It must be because the ghosts are running wild.

In a rush of panic I start hacking down bamboos for what I have to do. Nice thin ones, straight ones. From time to time I stop to make calculations. Until I have everything I need. Now the real work can begin. Even if it takes me all night till the coming of the dawn. Hacking and hacking away, wiping off the sweat, then hacking some more. I want to wear myself out, to get so tired that I can forget where I am and what is going to happen, forget about the ghosts that wander in the dark, hacking and hacking in a wood swarming with errant shapes and shadows, whining spectres. Ghosts with outstretched arms and long bony fingers that grab at me whenever I turn my head, wherever I'm not looking.

The light starts wheeling before my eyes, the stems become long thin skeletons, the leaves turn into avid whispering in a thousand voices, everything is infested with danger, the whole night is one endless nightmare. I find myself chopping faster and faster, and must keep ducking and jerking my hands away to avoid ripping off my own fingers.

And then something terrible happens. Afterwards I come to think that I must have kicked over the lamp, but when I first see it I have no inkling at all of how it happened. All of a sudden everything around me is just turning to fire. I smell the oil, I smell burning, and I see the flames, arms and fingers and shapes of fire, it's like something that Pa could read from the Bible, all those hissing and dancing tongues of fire, flickering and dancing as they try to grab me, to lick me up, to consume me as if I'm in the middle of hell itself and there's no chance of getting away, all those trunks of fire, branches of fire, ghosts of fire, devils of fire.

Who would have thought that a green bamboo copse could go up in flames like that? Almost in a single flash and whoosh of flame everything around me is transformed into fire. Yellow, orange, blood red, grey, pitch black. Bright, blazing, burning, translucent fire. In the first moment of shock I think: Tonight I'm going to be burnt to a cinder, it's like hell itself, the oven of Nebuchadnezzar. But after some time, which feels like a whole night, I find myself tumbling out of it. From the outside I can only stand staring at the flames. The Dwars River isn't far from here, but I have nothing to scoop up water with, only my two blackened hands, and the flames are too fierce to do anything. JesusLordGod, what do I do now? I can't even run back home to fetch Pa, he will kill me on the spot. Once, a long time ago, I saw the mountains in the distance burning, high up against the cliffs, near the shallow cave with the little dancing men and the elephants and the big elands and the praying mantis. It looks like what Pa read so many times about the Day of Judgement, the fire and brimstone, the weeping and gnashing of teeth. And in my madness I think: May the whole bloody Zandvliet burn to soot and ashes, let the Devil himself come down from heaven to take the lot of us away from here.

And it is only very much later that I come round again. I still cannot piece it together. All I know is that my throat, my chest, my whole body is burning as if I myself have been changed into flame, while in fact I am standing there shivering in a cold fever. All I can think is: I've got to get to Old Petronella, she will help me. There's no one else who can.

Without really knowing what I'm doing I burst back into the burning wood. And it's only some time afterwards that I find myself walking in the narrow white moon-road, back to the longhouse, with my heavy load of bamboos on my shoulders, churning up the dust, breathless and quite exhausted. And when at last I can think back, still later, I find I have no idea at all of what has happened or how it could have happened. Some time during the next day, after Pa and the others had already left for Worcester, when at last I could pull my thoughts together and start picking my way very carefully along the dusty path back to the river and the bamboo copse, I could find no more sign at all of the shock and confusion of the night before. Nothing. As if there had never been a fire. All I still knew, and still know today, is that the whole copse had gone up in flames in front of my eyes and that I myself had nearly burned to death.

I worked right through the night and only finished in the early dawn. It wasn't easy. I got so sleepy I could barely stay on my feet. What kept me awake was knowing that Philida would be leaving at first light. And God alone knew what would happen to her afterwards. Or to me, to all of us.

It was another of those mornings when the rooster was late with its crowing and Pa had to throw his alarm clock at the bird to wake him up and get the farmyard back to life. On such days, I knew, everybody had to pay for it. And I was still tying the last few slender bamboo stems into place when I heard the thunder and lightning breaking loose in Pa's bedroom. I began to work faster and faster. Should I finish too early, I might run into Pa, or Petronella could start shouting at me; if I took too long, everything would be lost. But in the end it just worked out. From the bridle room in the backyard I could follow the outside wall of the homestead to wait under Petronella's bedroom window.

As I knocked on her door I could see straight away that there was shit ahead.

Old Petronella opened the door and asked immediately: Well? What good-for-nothing business brings you here?

I brought something to give Philida for the road, Petronella.

What road? she flew at me. You want to tell me that you knew it all along?

I came to tell you last night but then we were interrupted by Pa.

And now you're here to enjoy our suffering, you little shit?

I'm sorry, Petronella. Honest to God, I did try to warn you, but it wasn't possible.

I cautiously moved out of the way so that I could see past her and get a glimpse of Philida. She was sitting on the bed with Willempie at her breast. Next to her I could see Lena, quiet and scared, staring as if she'd seen a ghost. On Philida's knees Kleinkat lay stretched out, purring as if there was nothing at all wrong in the world.

That gave me a chance to speak very quickly to Philida: I brought you something I made for you. It's for Kleinkat. So you can take her with you on the wagon if you want to.

There's nothing I want from you.

It seemed as if she was going to cry. But I couldn't be sure. And just then Willempie started screaming.

I worked right through the night, Philida.

I stepped quickly past old Petronella to put the cage on the floor, as close to her as I could risk it, and then very quickly stood back again.

What she said then I couldn't quite make out. Perhaps it was better not to hear it. But at that moment I heard something behind me and glanced up to see Ma in the passage behind me.

And what are you doing here, Frans? she asked.

I started saying: I just wanted – I. But then I decided rather to get out of her way. Still, there was something I wanted to tell her before she crushed me: I just brought Philida something, Ma. It's a long road.

You have a bloody cheek, Frans!

Just leave us alone, Ma. It's bad enough as it is.

Then I noticed Pa also coming down the passage and I had to run. But I did manage to get a last word in to Philida: I think I burnt down our bamboo wood, Philida.

There was no chance to say anything more. If only there was. But everything was over so suddenly. Nothing could be said or done, and that really was the worst of all. Perhaps we never stood a chance.

XV

Where are we going? When I ask, all I hear is: Upcountry. Upcountry. What the hell of a place is that? How far? How many days' travelling? How do one get there? I know we on our way to an auction, but will that be anything like the games Frans and I used to play? And what will become of me after that?

At daybreak, when the Ouman come to tell us, he must think that Ouma Nella will stay behind, that only the children and I are going. But she tell him very firmly, I'm going too, otherwise Philida stays right here.

The Ouman is furious, and soon the Ounooi come to join the talking, in that voice that sound like the cackling of a goose, but once Ouma Nella say No in that way she has, the no stay no. And so we get ready to go, before anybody say anything to me yet.

I keep on nagging her: I want to know how we going to get there, Ouma.

But all she say is: Man, if you don't know where you going, any road will bring you there.

But will I ever come back, Ouma Nella?

She just shrug her two shoulders. And she say: It don't matter how far a river run. It never forget where it come from. That is all that is important.

I say: I heard it's a dry place, Ouma, this Upcountry.

No matter if it's wet or dry, she grunt. As long as you

· 144 ·

keep a green branch in your heart, there will always be a bird that come to sing in it.

Just before we go off, while I'm still shivery with sadness and anger and the cool air of the morning, I get a thought in my head, and instead of climbing on the mule cart I first take my two children, Lena, who is two years old, and Willempie, the baby, and go to find Ounooi Janna in the longhouse. I am wearing the cast-off chintz dress I was given for New Year. We find her in the *voorhuis* drinking tea and eating rusks with crunching teeth, her big body folded into the couch like a *bulsak*. As I come in, with the baby on my hip and holding the girl by the hand, she half lift her huge body from the couch as if to have a go at me or to make room for a fart, but before she can speak I say very quietly: Ounooi, I just brought the children so they can say goodbye to their grandma. Because I don't suppose we'll see each other again very soon.

She open her mouth like a fish on dry ground, but for the moment she cannot get a sound out. Then she start trembling and drop her bowl and put her big soft hand on her chest where it keep hanging like a huge white spider. It take quite a while before she manage to say: Huh – And then once again: Huh . . .

Must be a stroke, I think. Because I seen this once before when the de Villiers Baas at Boschendal got a stroke and died right in front of us. But Ounooi Janna isn't dead yet. She support herself against the couch and say once more: Huh . . .

Just that, nothing more. So looking at the children I say: We also got to go and say goodbye to their father, Ounooi, before we get on the cart. We wish the Ounooi all the blessings of the LordGod.

When I look back for one last time from the broad front door, that beautiful door of orange-yellow yellowwood and almost black stinkwood, she still sitting there shaping with her small round mouth the sound: Huh. And that is how we take our leave, as the smart women of the Caab say.

This, I must say, make me feel a little bit better. Not yet fine, but better. And I think of something else Ouma Nella used to say to me and that help me to go on. It is this: It's no use crying in the rain, my child, because no one will see your tears.

And as it turn out, we travel most of that long road on the small blunt cart in the rain. Not hard, but all the time. Enough to make tears unnecessary.

Enough, too, to keep my shadow away from me. So far away that after some time I start thinking I must have left it behind at Zandvliet. As if I never had no shadow at all. The funny thing is that riding on the cart actually make everything easier. As if there is now nothing left to hold me back. Now I can go wherever I want to. Just on and on, wherever the wind take me. The same wind that Ouma Nella used to talk about when she speak about the San people that painted those cliffs on our mountain: the wind that bring stories from far away, and blow away your footprints until there is nothing left. It is scary, but in a way it also make it easier to breathe. For now you are free to go just where your own thoughts want to take you. Just go with it, then it happen all by itself. You fall like an apricot fall when it is ripe, you needn't resist. You just go. Easy as that. All the way to the Binneland, the Inland, where anything may happen. All that remain is the going itself. It's no trouble at all. As Ouma Nella says: Don't think you can climb two trees at the same time just because you got two legs.

And so I no longer try to resist. It feel like those last times when Frans and I were together: when I move the way he move, not against him, but along with him. As if we find ourselves inside a big, slow, steady wind, a wind that come and go like the sea. In and out. This way and that way. I am I and Frans is Frans, but together we're no longer two, only one, like the sea, like the wind. Then I know once more what I am and who I am, even though he now throw me away like a mealie cob that he wipe his arse with. Into the Binneland. Into the deepest inside of everything. Into myself. Where I can only be what I am. A duck cannot lay chicken eggs. It is what it is, it lay what it must lay. And it is good like that. I no longer want anything to be except what it is.

This is how it came that I just stop resisting. What use would it have been anyway? I just sit there staring as we drive away from the farmyard, that house of cats and ghosts, looking at all the farm animals that come to say goodbye, the two stupid donkeys, the rooster that never crow in time. The mad hen that cannot lay an egg of her own, but keep cackling to high heaven every time one of the other hens do it. The pigs, grunting and squealing around the dirty old sow. The cats that come running to say goodbye. And me sitting on the mule cart with Kleinkat purring quietly in the bamboo cage Frans made for her. Usually she cannot stand being shut up in a small place, but today she is behaving very well. As if she know exactly what is going on. Perhaps it's the way the cage is made. That man's clever hands will always amaze me. I don't want him to see me, so I refuse to look to where he stand, but I know very well he stand there watching us all the way. On the roof of the longhouse the pigeons sit cooing and kissing. And wild birds too, swallows and weaver birds and bead-eyes and *jakopewers* and mousebirds and bobtails and *bokmakieries* and *jangroentjies* and butcher birds and shrikes, many with names and even more that still wait to be named, also a couple of barn owls with wise and sleepy yellow eyes that blink now and then as if two handmade yellow curtains are drawn. All of Zandvliet is there, each kind in its place, only we going off: no longer here, not yet there. I and Kleinkat and the children, Ouma Nella and the goddamned Ouman who just sit there staring ahead of him and smoking his smelly old pipe, the pipe he always used to measure the floggings in the backyard. Past the small graveyard with its whitewashed walls where the dead lie waiting for the dark. Only my two children are not there, they were just buried in holes in the veld. Mamie, only a few months old. And KleinFrans of course, but we still not talking about him. Will there ever come a time when that will happen? He is dead, he is gone. And one day we shall all be gone for good. They here. I in that Binneland place, wherever that may be.

PART TWO
~
AUCTION

XVI

*In which the Reader is informed about the Slave Auction
in Worcester where Ouma Nella fends off a bothersome Bidder
until Cornelis Brink comes to her Rescue with a surprising
Announcement and the Business of the Day can resume*

The day is unbearably hot. Like a place from the Bible. Like
hell. Since well before sunrise the cicadas are shrilling with
such piercing loudness that it penetrates flesh and bone and
marrow and numbs one's ears. Friday 22 February 1833,
auction day in Worcester. In front of the huge new Drostdy
close to the church, the townsfolk are gathering on the
large open square, together with a number of farmers from
the district, and even from as far as the Bokkeveld and
Tulbagh where in the past they'd used the old Drostdy with
its tall pillars and high stoep for all the business that was
subsequently transferred to Worcester. In the environs of
the Caab people do not care much for auctions any more.
It is no longer profitable to sell slaves, since everybody
knows that emancipation is just round the corner and then,
no matter what kind of compensation the English are promising, it is widely believed your money will be lost. And to
buy is even worse. The only people still interested are the
elderly or widows or others in desperate need of cash who
have no choice but to buy or sell because for them there
is no other way out. But here in the interior the situation
is not so desperate, or not yet. The Caab is too remote to
be of much importance. The people live far apart, and

auctions are one of the few occasions when they still bother to get together, provided these can be combined with something like a funeral or *nagmaal*. Then one can bring one's hides and biltong and lard and chickens or ostrich eggs and sheep or pigs or *beskuit* or conserves or needlework or woodwork or tallow and dip candles to barter or sell, and exchange news and remedies. There are *knegte* that come to hire themselves out to the highest bidder, and itinerant teachers in search of work, and the occasional preacher who turns up to offer his services. More often than not an itinerant *smous* who has heard the news in time will turn up with ammunition and paraffin and salt and sugar and medicaments – balsam and white dulcis and green amara and red lavender and chest drops and essence of life, and purgatives – and bales of dress material of chintz or corduroy, or mirrors or tools or pieces of furniture or pins and needles and hairclips that may be of use to people far from the Caab. These are also occasions for baptisms and weddings and death notices. Many of the townspeople and also a crowd of farmers' wives will come to town with cakes and tarts and lemonade to exchange for the odd rix-dollar or half a crown or a bale of chintz. And through all this bustle the cicadas go on shrilling, and stray cats run wild and dogs fight and howl and bark and copulate and children cavort like mad creatures and a tame baboon may run amok or a pet meerkat may attack someone and get killed in return. Some of the farmers from the district make last-minute surreptitious visits to their carts and wagons to fetch bottles and jugs and pitchers to help business along. Cornelis Brink also collects a few flagons from his mule cart. He never goes on a journey without a decent supply. One cannot tell when it may come in profitable.

At last everybody can prepare for the day's serious

business to start. First there is a farmer, Maans Oosthuizen, from the farm Goedemoed, who has something to report to anyone within earshot. He's come in to town, he explains, to tell his story to the Commissioner, but everybody knows that His Worship tends to have problems over the weekend, which for His Worship usually begins on Friday, if not as early as Thursday. This means that Maans first has to locate a man who can replace the custodian of the law, because they have a busy day ahead and cannot proceed without some order and ceremony in their midst.

It takes a while to round up a small greyish man who is prepared to stand in for the magistrate, and at last Maans Oosthuizen can lunge into his narrative. The longer he speaks, the redder his face becomes as he relates the shit he's had with his Bushman Hottentot Kees who refused to listen to reason so that Maans was obliged to *klap* him. But then Kees jumped over a wall and came back with a bow and arrows and prepared to shoot left, right and especially centre. Whereupon Maans lost his temper and ordered two of his slaves to hold Kees down for a proper hiding with a new sjambok he wished to try out before the auction. Maans wasn't really angry, he explains, but a man cannot just allow God's water to spill freely into God's garden, so he did his Christian duty and applied some corrective treatment to Kees, not for too long, perhaps half an hour, but it could have been an hour, one cannot always keep an eye on the clock. And then the useless Kees just went and died on him. A real nuisance, just before the weekend, for how was he supposed to get his sheep into the kraal unaided?

At this stage the man who stands in for the Commissioner approaches. Very officiously he demands to know how many stripes Maans Oosthuizen has already given the late Kees. The law stipulates a maximum of thirty-nine. Maans is in a rage right there, his fleshy face like a large glowing coal. How the hell must he know? he asks. Who can bother to count so far? If he had to give an estimate he'd guess about thirty-nine stripes, no more. And immediately some of his friends and neighbours are prepared to testify that they've known Maans for many years, he will never hurt a man without reason, and anyway he can only count to thirty-nine.

Then we are agreed, says the small, greyish man who stands in for the Commissioner.

But at this point one of the slaves who were instructed to hold the late Kees down during the flogging intervenes to say no, *seur*, it was forty-four, he knows all about counting. And suddenly the second slave, a Hottentot called Snel, also speaks up to say no, he counted as far as two hundred and twelve. Many tempers are ablaze by now, because precious time is being lost. The man who stands in for the Commissioner says there is no way out, he will have to count the stripes himself. For the time being everybody moves from the square in a big throng to Maans Oosthuizen's town house two streets away. By the time they reach the backyard where the body lies, it is more a matter of guessing than counting, because most of the spectators have had time to take courage and refreshment from their wine flagons, which has affected either their eyesight, or their arithmetic, or both. Moreover there is little evidence one can rely on beyond any doubt, except for the marks on the body's back and buttocks and upper legs, and these are in such a mess that only the clearest stripes, those that broke the skin, can be readily distinguished. The rest forms too much of a criss-crossing jumble to be of any use. But at last, after numerous attempts, they all count loudly and in unison up to forty-three. Which is not all that far from thirty-nine, after all.

So, to avoid further delay, they may just as well agree on thirty-nine. The crowd breaks up briefly for some more serious rumination around the flagons and bottles, before all those gathered in the yard announce that they are prepared to agree on the figure of thirty-nine.

Just when everybody is finally ready to wind up the preliminary proceedings, a large man, allegedly from the Bokkeveld, approaches and pushes with his right foot against the deceased (the term introduced by the little man who stands in for the Commissioner), which brings to light more lashes on the front of Kees's dust-covered body. All the way from the shoulders down to the knees, not excepting the bloodied private parts. Let's make it seventy-two, as a fair estimate, says the surrogate Commissioner. In which case, we have a problem, gentlemen.

Yes, but, says the big man from the Bokkeveld. Yes. But. The law talks about the back and the buttocks and the upper legs, not a word about the stomach et cetera. Which means that any stripes on the front are irrelevant. So we can still agree on thirty-nine, and everybody should be satisfied.

Thus they reach agreement and the dead man is dragged off to where his wife and three small children are sitting at a distance in the sand, crying softly. Softly, because it is obvious that these farmers are in no mood for nonsense today.

Let us go back to the square then, announces the man who stands in for the Commissioner. We have a lot of work to get through. Whereupon everybody troops back from the town house to the town square, past the church to the front of the sober and imposing Drostdy, where they take up position to empty some more jugs and flagons in celebration of a job well done.

At last the auction can begin. The first few persons offered for sale do not resemble the slaves Philida and Old Petronella are used to. These look more like dusty Bushmen rounded up in the veld in a far place and dragged here yesterday or early this morning, presumably tethered to the horse of a Baas. There are four women with bulging stomachs like calabashes, and elongated breasts, and altogether seventeen or eighteen children in tow, some still infants at the breast. It is the mighty man from the Bokkeveld who has brought them for sale. After taking another swig from his wine jug he casually flicks his long sjambok around the group by way of timely warning.

This lot, he says, I brought from the other side of the Cedarberg after they came to steal sheep from my farm.

Nobody enquires for particulars about the how and when and where and why, not even the miserable greyish man who stands in for the Commissioner. They need labourers and one of these days they'll be without slaves. If these creatures can be booked into service straight away, they can at least see one through a few more years.

Against the law, Old Petronella hisses in Philida's ear from behind.

You shut up! Cornelis snaps at her. If you're looking for trouble today, just you try to take on this little runt that stands in for the Commissioner.

There were twenty-four of the vermin, says the big man from the Bokkeveld. But some of them were too weak for the long walk, so I had to discard them along the way.

How are you selling them? somebody asks from the crowd. One by one or the whole lot together?

Take your pick, says the man from the Bokkeveld. As long as we don't have to stand in this ungodly sun all day.

A long argument ensues. Then some of the bigger children are sold in ones or twos or threes. Two of the women are allotted to a buyer from Paarl, the other two separately, one with two small children, the second on her own, the rest of the children in a group. The prices remain pretty low. Nobody wants to venture too much on a bunch of good-for-nothings that probably won't last a month.

This is followed by some commotion as a man comes pushing through the crowd with another Khoe woman and three children. Somebody recognises them as the wife and children of the dead Hottentot, Kees. The man who pushes them to the auction table is none other than Maans Oosthuizen, who caused the first interruption of the day.

I reckon we can *maar* finish this business right here, he says, his face an even deeper red than before. Get these things off my hands too, and the sooner the better.

A bid of three hundred rix-dollars for mother and children is on the point of being knocked down when someone else pitches in with a hundred for the oldest boy, who must be about ten years old. He should be quite useful around the house by now.

The greyish man who stands in for the Commissioner asks cautiously whether it isn't against the law for families to be broken up in this manner.

That law is made for slaves, a large woman with a split palate corrects him and he almost chokes as he tries to scuttle out of her way, and these are just *Boesmans*.

The information is accepted with acclaim and the transaction is clinched.

The mother and her two youngest children are dragged off, not without crying and scuffling, and it takes two of the heftiest farmers with sjamboks to return them to order. After that the eldest boy, still sobbing and with his small face smeared with snot, is loaded into a horse carriage and the farmer and his thickset wife drive off with him.

A few more indentured Hottentots are brought in one by one. This goes relatively fast. Only one of them, a little stick insect of a man with a white-grey head, who says his name is Ben Goliath, threatens to cause a disturbance. When he was a child, he protests, his Baas told him he would be booked in until he turned twenty-one, to pay off his father's debt. Today that Baas, who was only a beardless boy at the time, already lies in his grave, a grandfather with many offspring, yet here he, Ben Goliath, is still around on the farm. It is time they let him go, he pleads, surely his father's debt must have been settled very long ago.

For how long were you indentured? asks the man who stands in for the magistrate.

Very long, says the spindly little creature.

How many years?

How must I know? says the Hottentot. Nobody ever told me to count. But it must be a very long time.

Come and tell me when you turn twenty-one, then I'll let you go, says the man who stands in for the Commissioner. Who will make me an offer?

A hundred and fifty rix-dollars, shouts a bidder, and Ben Goliath gets a new baas. For another twenty-one years.

At this moment the real Commissioner makes his appearance, a deeply tanned man in a starched uniform and with a sharply pointed Adam's apple. He is welcomed with loud applause and the greyish man who stood in for him hurries away in the direction of the nearest wine wagon.

A couple of slaves approach from the front stoep of the Drostdy with a long sturdy table between them. This is set up in front of the crowd. Almost immediately it is shifted again so that a red carpet can be spread open in the dust where the table is to be positioned, several bulky chairs are brought and arranged in a row, after which the Commissioner and his assistants take their seats on top. In front of the Commissioner a pile of heavy, leather-bound books are placed, followed by a stoneware jug on a tray. At last the auction proper can begin. A swarm of gnats is whirling around the jug and in the heat a heady smell of young wine envelops the crowd.

Inevitably the spectators soon start getting rowdy and the Commissioner has to make a serious effort to ensure that the proceedings can unfold in a more orderly manner.

The first slaves brought to the table and instructed to clamber on it are a family – father from Macassar, mother from Java, three children whose ages are given as fourteen, eleven and eight. Comments and remarks are shouted from all sides, and very soon all three children are crying. The two oldest ones are girls, the youngest a cross-eyed boy. Their Baas, Petrus Jacobus Conradie from a farm near Gouda, feels obliged to belabour them with his sjambok before the noise subsides. By now, both Baas and family look rather the worse for wear. The farmer is as skinny as a biltong, with somewhat bulging eyes that sit very close together in a bony, sunburnt face with a stark white forehead above the line of his hat. Some of the bystanders start scurrying out of the way of his two long knobbly feet that give off an ungodly smell which sends both humans and dogs scampering out of reach. He remains surrounded by a cloud of flies.

The bidding starts slowly, but then the drink takes over and the procedure moves more smoothly until at last the whole family goes for four thousand two hundred rix-dollars. The only disturbance is caused by one of the bidders who pushes through to the very front line, presses himself right up against the table, where he demands that the older girl first open her mouth so that he can study her teeth. It takes a long argument and a resounding slap from the Baas before she complies. After that she grows even more obstreperous, when the bidder instructs her to lower the top of her dress so that he can see more of her. The Commissioner, recently promoted to his rank after years as a field cornet in the district, and who presides *ex officio* as auctioneer with the help of a long-winded interpreter, asks rather reluctantly whether this is strictly necessary. Of course it is, insists the prospective buyer, identified as one Stephanus Gotlieb Maree. He explains that he wants to use her for breeding purposes, so it is obvious that he must make very sure she is properly equipped for the task. The girl tries to resist and only after the dress has been practically torn from her can the auction proceed. A few of the women in the crowd are now mumbling in tones of sullen annoyance, but the men are growing more and more vociferous before at last everybody calms down and the child is silenced with a blow to the face.

Now comes Philida's turn. With her cat in its bamboo cage, the baby in an *abbadoek* on her back and the small girl held by the hand, she takes her place on the heavy table. Her eyes are fixed on a spot in the distance as she stares up towards the remotest blue mountains, a blue that almost disappears in space, like ink spilled on a page in a big book with names inscribed in the hand of a Cornelis Brink.

Afterwards she tells Ouma Petronella how it felt, and in this way her story spreads through the Brink family. It was, she recounts with a shrug, as if she wasn't there at all, as if it was a story told by someone else. As if she stayed behind when the mule cart rode away from Zandvliet. She saw everything – Cornelis Brink and the driver, and Ouma Petronella, herself with the two children and the cat in the cage made by Francois. She saw herself on the cart, for more than two full days, but at the same time she could look at everything from a distance. The whole road with its many curves and bends, the mountains with their tall cliffs and boulders and ridges, the high and slowly wheeling bateleur eagles, the watercourses, the little waterfall that had dried up in the hot summer, a troop of baboons right against the road just after the first of Paarl's huge round boulders, followed by other troops, as well as by many more mountains and plains, a few fords, and at last Worcester with its few dusty streets and its large Drostdy. She was there, and at the same time she wasn't. I felt, she explains, like a ghost trying to get out of a mirror. From there her thoughts ran far and wide. Hadn't it always been like that, she wondered, as if she'd never really been exactly where she was? Except on a very few occasions, and those were times she could remember more clearly than others. For instance, there was the day she had gone on the wagon to the Caab to see the skinny slave hanged – and what made that even worse was that she wasn't only there to see what was happening to the skinny man, but she could see at the same time how she changed places with the man, felt how it was to be hanged, the first time when the rope broke, and later all the way to the end, even feeling the life spurting out of her, everything. And back at Zandvliet afterwards, that first time with Frans in the bamboo copse. And also, months later, the day KleinFrans was born, and what happened then. Still later, there was little Mamie's birth, and Lena's, and finally Willempie's. On those occasions, yes, she was there. And at a few other times when she didn't really want to be there at all, like when the Ouman wanted her to go down on her knees in the bamboo copse. And now this time, on the long road to Worcester, to the open space in front of the Drostdy. She can remember everything, but still it doesn't feel as if she really was there. Somebody else must have seen it and turned it into a story one could choose to believe or not. A story is after all a story, it all depends on who tells it.

The Commissioner with the tanned face proceeds with the auction. As the wine spreads through his body, he speaks faster and faster. He is not one of the new lot appointed by the government in England, all of them retired military men who don't take nonsense from anybody, but a farmer from this rude frontier district. When he remembers about it, he instructs a pale grumpy official beside him to translate the proceedings from Dutch into English, but for long periods he forgets, and nobody dares to interrupt. Not that it matters much, for the audience is used to the ritual and the men put in their bids quite haphazardly, as they are wont to do.

Right at the beginning there is one bidder who starts making a nuisance of himself. He pushes through the crowd to the front, up against the solid table, with a long *kierie* in his hand. This *kierie*, it seems, is not meant as a walking stick. In his small bullet head he clearly has other thoughts. His name, Philida learns from Ouma Petronella afterwards, is Magiel Christoffel Botma, but he is known to most only by his initials, Emcee. A few minutes after the bidding has started, he puts the *kierie* in between Philida's ankles and starts pushing up the seam of her long dress. She takes a step back without shifting her eyes from the mountains in the distance. The man leans forward to stay close to her and proceeds to inspect her with the *kierie* once again, now between her knees. A few of the other spectators are sniggering by now, prodding one another in the ribs, as their comments become more and more voluble. After a while the Commissioner becomes aware of the rumpus and looks up. His slightly bulging eyes flutter furiously.

Silence! he thunders from his chair. Stop this commotion!

It sounds like an order to attack. Magiel Christoffel Botma starts violently, drops his *kierie* and bends over to pick it up; as he rises to his feet, breathing heavily, the back of his head slams against the edge of the table. From his mouth slithers a blob of spittle.

The Commissioner puts out an arm to protect his pile of books. What are you doing, you clumsy lout? he thunders again.

He just wanted to make sure the *meid*'s legs meet somewhere, somebody explains, collapsing with laughter. A man's got to make sure before he buys.

The crowd jeers and jitters.

Stand back! the Commissioner orders in a stentorian voice.

Staan troei! the interpreter translates unnecessarily.

One hundred pounds, the Commissioner starts again. Do I hear anybody say a hundred and ten?

One thousand four hundred rix-dollars, the interpreter translates. And hurry up, His Worship does not have all day.

Philida keeps staring into the farthest distance and pretends to know nothing. She is no longer here.

But by now Magiel Christoffel Botma is quite steamed up and not in a mood to take any more shit from an Englishman. He returns to the table and clasps the edge in his two hands. It looks as if he is aiming to move closer to Philida. A new commotion begins. Several people are urging him on, a few others want to intervene. The table begins to wobble.

At this stage Philida can take no more and stomps on the man's fingers.

That is the moment when Ouma Petronella slides from the mule cart and moves in closer. You leave her alone, *Duusman!* she shouts at him from behind.

He looks round, staggering on unsteady legs and clearly loses all control when he sees who is talking.

Shut up, blarry *meid!* he says, raising his long *kierie* in warning.

She is not your *meid*, you turd! Cornelis Brink joins the fray. He may be a small man, but he is evidently ready to fight. Before anybody quite knows what is going on, the whole situation threatens to get out of hand. Cornelis grabs the thin man by a bony shoulder and angrily shoves him aside.

Why are you getting so worked up over a damn *meid?* whines Magiel, suddenly tearful as he tries to scuttle out of sight.

Cornelis pulls him back so fast that the spindly man gasps for breath.

She's nobody's *meid*, warns Cornelis, bottle in hand, swaying on his legs and sounding for all the world like a growling dog. She's nobody's *meid*, you hear me? And once again he enunciates every word separately and very clearly: She is my mother.

Suddenly it is deadly quiet on the dusty square in front of the Drostdy.

Ouma Petronella lifts her head. I am a free woman, she says with tight lips, putting a hand into her dress to pull out a sheet of paper with an embossed red seal on it: I can say what I want. Now you shut your mouth or I'll do it for you.

The crowd is humming and rumbling like a bees' nest, but nobody dares to come any closer. His face by now the colour of an overripe fig, the Commissioner wipes his cheeks with a very big white kerchief. Let us proceed, he orders. It sounds like a command to a firing squad.

Magiel Christoffel Botma quickly slithers out of the way, enraged, and deflated, and broken, and sorry for himself, all at the same time, but too scared to open his mouth again.

The bidding resumes, in fits and starts at first, but gradually gaining assurance and speed. Nobody dares to bother Philida again. Cornelis Brink returns heavily to his seat on the mule cart. Philida remains standing on the long table with the thick legs. The baby on her back, Lena squatting next to her, playing with a small wooden horse Frans once made for her. All the words and sounds sweep past Philida's ears, but she doesn't hear anything, nor see anything, just keeps staring into the distance, towards the farthest mountains. By this time nobody knows any longer what has happened to Magiel Christoffel Botma. (It will be late evening before, having drunk himself into oblivion, he will come home, stumble over the dog at the front door and into the passage, kick his wife and children, and tumble on his bed, snoring to make the yellowwood eaves shudder.)

For a while the auction proceeds in its prescribed manner. As usual, there are a few people taking part for only a little while before they drop out. But three or four of them persist for longer. One, a Doctor Atherstone from Grahamstown in the Eastern Cape, joins in the bidding several times. It seems as if something about Philida has attracted his attention. Once he turns to the man next to him and says out loud: Have you seen that one's eyes? Pure obsidian.

What is obsidian? asks his neighbour.

Don't you know? demands the doctor somewhat haughtily, stroking his well-trimmed beard. It's a very special gemstone. Pitch black.

One cannot see in Philida's face that she has heard the exchange. But she has. And she doesn't forget a thing like that very easily.

Soon afterwards the doctor loses interest, which leaves only a single bidder. At one hundred and twenty-three pounds two shillings and sixpence the bid on Philida and her children is clinched and a somewhat breathless man called Bernabé Jan Gerhard de la Bat, who has arrived almost too late for the auction, takes possession of his new slaves. The formal announcement is read out by the Commissioner-Auctioneer in halting English, lengthily translated into High Dutch by his interpreter, then written down in the thick auction book, and signed with a flourish by the Commissioner's quill, steel nibs not having found their way to an outpost like Worcester yet, and blotted with fine sand from a silver bowl. Afterwards slaves approach to carry off the table and clean up the square. Two of them collect the cow dung and horse turds on the square in front of the Drostdy in buckets. (They should have scooped up old Emcee as well, somebody remarks in passing. He belongs with all the other shit.) The people decamp in small groups.

It is time for Ouma Petronella and Cornelis Brink to travel over the mountains and the more distant plains, for their few days on the road back to Zandvliet. But just before they can get the mules moving, Ouma Petronella comes back to Philida for one last time to hug her and her children against her ample body.

You better hurry back home now, Ouma Nella, whispers the young woman. I can see the Ouman's arse is on fire.

You must watch out and take care of yourself, says Ouma Petronella. Remember, if you don't do that I shall find out and come and give you hell in your sleep.

· 166 ·

Philida shrugs her narrow shoulders. It's getting late, she says. You got a long way to go.

How will you ever manage on your own? asks Ouma Petronella, suddenly tearful.

You teach me *mos*, Ouma Nella, Philida says quietly. And she smiles, a small and crooked movement of her lips. But then she adds with surprising firmness: Remember one thing, I now learn to say *No*.

Once again Ouma Petronella presses Philida against her. Then she climbs on to the cart and the axles groan under her weight.

XVII

Something has been bothering Philida ever since the day
of the auction, something she remarked as an undertone to
the tumult around the scene at the long table, which
remained with her after the disturbance caused by Emcee
Botma had subsided and the crestfallen man with his long
cane had slunk away. And she realises that it has not been
her imagination when three or four days later a well-dressed
Khoe man in a tall hat arrives at the home of Meester de
la Bat in the Church Street with a message for the slave
woman Philida of the Caab from the Commissioner to
summon her to the Drostdy without delay.

Shall I go with you? asks Bernabé de la Bat who has just
come home from his office. Perhaps it's something I can
help you with.

No, Meester, says Philida. But she can feel a heavy lump
in her stomach, as if she's had too many green apricots to eat.

It turns out that it is the Commissioner himself who wants
to speak to her, the man with the long, tanned faced who
had been in charge on the day of the auction at the Drostdy.
When she arrives, he is seated behind a wide desk covered
by a slew of untidy papers.

Without beating around the bush he asks her: What do
you know about the commotion we had at the Drostdy on
the day you were brought to the auction?

Meester? she asks. She has decided that in future, for safety's sake, this is how she will address all the important men of the Colony.

That man made a nuisance of himself, she says.

He is a leading farmer in our district, says the Commissioner. You are a slave. I got the impression that you didn't know your place.

I always know my place, Meester, Philida says quietly. It is a slave's place. That man was the one who was looking for trouble.

How was he looking for trouble?

He put that stick of his under my dress, Meester, says Philida. Where in that mess of papers and books on your table does it say that he got the right to do such things with me?

You are a slave, the man says again. But this time he makes it sound more like a remark than an accusation.

I know I am a slave, Meester, says Philida. But I am not *his* slave. What do your big books say about that?

She feels the heaviness around her beginning to ease a little bit. And she goes on: If that is what the law say he can do, then the law must be wrong.

To her surprise she sees the hint of a smile in his pale round eyes.

And suppose I tell you that this is how it is?

Philida is quiet for a moment. She lifts her head to look him in the eyes and says: Then I must say No to the Meester and his law.

I see, grunts the Commissioner, and he starts shuffling his papers like a hen trying to make a nest.

So what is the Meester now telling me to do? Philida dares to ask after a few moments.

The tanned man does not look at her. What I say, he says,

is that it was a public auction. You did not have the right to interfere and step on the man's fingers. You disturbed the peace and that is against the law. Only now does he look up, and he places his two farmer's hands on the papers in front of him. Then he adds: But between you and me, I would have done the same if I were you. And if anybody does a thing like that again in my presence, he will rue the day. For much too long have we shown a lack of respect for the law in this land. The Meester gets up behind the big desk and his hands start shuffling and ordering all the papers again. Half raising his head he adds: It goes for that unruly man. A brief silence, before he pulls a straight face and says: And of course it goes for you too.

Thank you, Meester, says Philida with an equally straight face. And if Meester want me to, I can come here one day to put all these messy papers straight on your desk. This is really looking very untidy.

I shall appreciate it, says the Civil Commissioner. Can you start next week?

Philida nods, turns round and quietly walks from the office into the startling white light of the summer's day.

XVIII

*Which informs the Reader about the Changes in
Philida's Lifestyle after her Arrival in Worcester and about
Newcomers to her Acquaintance, notably a Man who is
set to play a major Role in her Life, and a Ghost from the
Past whose Legacy haunts the inland Districts*

The first weeks after she arrives in Worcester, Philida has
enough opportunity to study the house and its occupants.
It is very different from Zandvliet. After the longhouse she
was used to, Master de la Bat's house is quite squat, although
it is bigger than most of the other homes in the little *dorp*.
There is no gable. But the walls are high for shade in summer,
and the ceilings are made of rushes. There is a *voorhuis* to
the right when one enters, two smallish bedrooms left, and
a kitchen and pantry at the back. In the backyard are a few
barns, a dairy, a wine cellar and three outrooms for servants.
At the moment the one in the middle is filled with mealie
bags, chests and barrels; to the left there is one for the slave
Labyn from Batavia, who does carpentry and sometimes
works for other people too; in the third, slightly bigger
outroom, the housemaid Delphina sleeps and that is where
Philida and her children also move in.

In the beginning she feels constantly ill at ease. She knows
exactly why. It is because her shadow has not come with
her. Somewhere in the clouds and misty rain on the long
road between Zandvliet and this new town on this side of
the mountains the sun got lost, and when she arrived here

and the sun heated up again, there were shadows once more, but not the sun she was used to. Especially in the evenings she felt the need to crawl in with her own shadow, to find a space for it to lie behind her back, but it wasn't the one she was looking for. There was no chance to fit in properly any more.

She just has to get used to it. But getting used to a place doesn't mean that you have found the place that is really yours. This was what she felt at the auction: that something had moved in between what she knew and what was foreign to her.

It isn't that she feels dissatisfied or unhappy. In many ways this is a better place than Zandvliet. Easier, even friendlier. This Nooi isn't always picking on her, she never orders one to undo a piece of knitting, never comes with a *riem* or a switch. Meester Bernabé de la Bat isn't moody or difficult. After the pesky Brinks he not only leaves her in peace but tries in his own way to make her feel at home.

Good in his own way, yes. Meester Bernabé de la Bat is not a man of many words, nor a tall man with a short fuse. Actually one never knows what is going on in his head. A long head, his hair combed flat on his scalp, his eyes behind the thick glasses always rather worried, almost apprehensive, as if he never feels sure that someone is going to scold him or find him ridiculous. An important man, Philida heard from Delphina. So important, one may get the idea that he thinks from her knees up a woman's legs are joined together. The first lawyer this town has ever known, they say. Lawyer? That, says Delphina, a small quick girl, bright as a mouse, means a man who knows the law, to whom you can go if you have problems. But not like a father or an older brother; even to his two children he is always aloof and rather distant, not a man for jokes or games, as serious as a secretary bird, with the same stiff steps as if he is always worried that he may tread on shit.

This man is married to one Anna Catherina Hugo, a quiet person, like a duck that got chased from her nest too quickly, but a member of one of the top families at the Caab, as Delphina can tell. At the time Philida arrives, they have two small pale boys, three years and one year old, with another one pushing up a molehill from inside.

From Delphina Philida often asks advice when she is not quite sure what to do. Delphina is a bit older than she, people say that in her young days she had a hard time with a baas at the Caab. Three of them, actually, because the man and his two sons were bothered by their pricks and were always ready with a *riem* if you hesitated to lie down with them, and it was just as well that their seed didn't take on her, as she always sought timely advice from other slave women to get rid of their leftovers if she began to swell. But Delphina isn't much of a talker. If she has to sweep a floor, she will sweep; if she has to wash up plates, she washes up plates; and if she is ordered to bathe the two pale boys in the zinc bath she bathes the boys in the zinc bath; nothing can ever upset her routine and she doesn't like loose talk. Her small tight body warns you at first glance to let her be. Only once she's learned to trust you, her tongue loosens up.

As a result Labyn is the one Philida usually comes to talk to. He could have been her father, the father she has never known, and with him she feels safe. A peaceful man who takes his time with everything, and is always to be found with his calabash pipe in his mouth. Where he plucks the leaves to smoke, Philida never discovers; and when she asks him, he just looks at her with a small, pursed smile and gives no answer, but they are sweet-smelling leaves and that is another reason why she likes to go and sit with him when she has no work to do or when her knitting doesn't need close attention.

To see him working on a piece of wood gives one a special deep pleasure inside. He must be, she often thinks, like the father of Jesus, the only other carpenter she has heard of. He has a deep kind of *respect* for wood, each piece is different, each one he comes to know intimately. Yellowwood, young and creamy white, or older, a deep yellow like butter, later even darker, like burnt sugar; the heavy stinkwood with its fine grain that comes alive under your fingers, camphor wood that sets free its smell when you saw or shave it; wild olive with its stains and curves; *kiaat* from Batavia, walnut, cedarwood, cherrywood, iron-wood, wood for chairs or benches or tables, wood for wagon wheels or yokes or yoke-pins, wood for a *jonkmanskas* or an armoire, wood for hedgepoles, wood you can feel or judge with your fingers or the inside of your wrists or with your cheeks, wood with which you can have long conversations. With wood, she discovers from Labyn, it is like talking to family: Do you by chance know this one or that one? Isn't he an uncle or a cousin or a grandchild of so-and-so? His mother must have been a de Villiers girl, or a Basson or a de Wet, married to a Pieterse or a Swanepoel, one of the step-aunts must have been a Lamprecht or a van der Merwe, his great-grandfather came from Borneo on a three-master. And then there is wood for coffins. Those are Labyn's special love, and each coffin becomes a cherished chest in which he himself would love to spend the rest of his days when there are no more days to spend.

One late evening when neither of them can sleep, they lie talking for hours on their palliasses of straw or rags in the heavy dark still fragrant with the early evening's candlewax, Delphina tells her that in his youth Labyn had a young wife, Lavinia, whom he loved very dearly. But she was impossibly beautiful and the white men of the Caab wouldn't leave her in peace. From the smart houses in the Heerengracht or Oranjezicht, or from the taverns, from the workmen's houses on Caledon Square or closer to the beach, or from the Rondebosch to the far side of the mountain or at Hout Bay, or even from the deep interior when the men came to the Caab to buy and sell, from high and mighty lords to scruffy looters or ruffians and drunkards. In the Lodge on the Heerengracht, just this side of the old Company Gardens, she always had strings of visitors. She tried her best to ward them off, but for how long could a slave girl say no? What she did was to tell them she was already married, and she didn't lie with any other man because her husband was a real devil who readily ran amok and he'd already throttled three or four people with his bare hands. If they wanted to know more about this husband or if they threatened to kill her when she refused to talk, she started telling them that the man was Labyn, who'd come with her from Batavia, thinking that this would put an end to it. But what they did then was to round up five or six of their mates to catch Labyn on the Boereplein late one Saturday night and beat him senseless and cut off his balls. The same five or six men who'd attacked Labyn lay in wait for her at the women's washing place up against the Table Mountain and did terrible things to her and then just left her lying there, where some predator got hold of what was left of her in the night and finished her off.

In the end Labyn survived, but he was no longer what he'd been before, and in the end his Baas sold him upcountry, and that was how he came to Bernabé de la Bat, far from the Caab, far from Lavinia, and all he had left was his carpentry, and his coffins remained much sought after. What also drew people to him was his storytelling. Which, more than anything else, was what caught Philida's interest. And of course the fact that the two children, even the baby, so soon became infatuated with him while he became an oupa for them. Stories she'd known since childhood were retold by him, the one about the Water Women, the one about the snake with the shiny stone on his forehead, the one about the woman who had an eye on her big toe, the one about the Ouman with fire in his arsehole; and also a whole bagful of others. Some he'd brought from Batavia, others he'd picked up on the ship during the sea voyage. Still others the wind had blown to him in this Colony. A number of them he'd probably made up. His stories were put together the way he made furniture from wood, furniture to which he became so attached that he found it almost unbearable to sell it, and even then it would be only when there was really no other way out.

One night just a short while after Philida arrived in the village, Meester Bernabé de la Bat comes to the room of the women slaves to tell them they have to get up very early the next morning, he is taking Philida to the Bokkeveld. For what? He has to visit one of the farms and wants to use the opportunity to show her something important.

For a moment she feels annoyed. Meester de la Bat may not be a Brink, but they are both white and neither of them ever says anything he doesn't want to say. She can feel her lips twitching, but says nothing.

And what about the children? she asks after a while.

They can come along, he says.

But when she discusses it with Delphina later, the woman says, Don't worry, it's easier for the children to stay behind. She has an idea of what is coming. It's something he does with all his slaves. She, Delphina, will look after the little ones. It will be better for them to be here, rather than go all the way to the Bokkeveld. So early the next morning Philida goes off with Labyn and Meester de la Bat.

It is a terribly long way, and on the Cape cart it is a rough ride, but Labyn is a capable driver. They have to go past many places. The Sand River and the Wabooms River and Romans River. Then Vaalvlei and De Liefde and Waveren and Vredeoes and Skoonvlei and Welgemeend, then past Welkom and Visgat and Bokveldskloof and Vaalbult and Kolen River, afterwards Groenfontein and De Hoek and Wadrif, to Op-die-Berg and Remhoogte and Wyekloof; apart from all the fountains: Merriesfontein and Koperfontein and Gansfontein and Kleinfontein and Doornfontein.

By the time the day starts to draw its ears up into its neck as the sun grows red with weariness and shame, Meester de la Bat at long last orders Labyn to rein in the horses at a farm where he has to deliver some court papers, and there they are invited to stay for the night – the Meester in the house with the farmer and his family, Labyn and Philida in an empty stable outside in the yard. Without Willempie, Philida's breasts are painful but there happens to be a slave woman who has twin babies and can do with some milk, so Philida can provide some relief.

Very early the next morning they set out again, and on the way back, just where the road narrows to leave the Bokkeveld, they stop at a strange thing which they'd passed the previous afternoon when everybody was too tired to pay attention. But this time they stop to have a proper inspection. At first Philida thinks it must be a scarecrow, like the thing they used to put up in the vineyards at Zandvliet to scare off the flocks of birds that fed on the bunches of grapes in the early summer.

Except this is not a scarecrow.

The three of them get off to follow the Meester for a closer look. It is a long iron pole, painted red, with something stuck on top.

Only when they come right up to it Philida can make out what it is: a human skull, dirty and dilapidated, with very little of it left. A tuft of hair here and there on the bare white bone. Two hollows of eye sockets staring into nothingness.

And this? asks Philida, when it looks as if no one else is going to speak.

This, says Meester de la Bat, this is the Galant some people in the Bokkeveld still have nightmares about.

I think I hear about him from Ouma Nella, says Philida.

That is possible, says the Meester. Galant was a slave here. He did terrible things.

Is this the Galant that make a rebellion against the farmers of the Bokkeveld?

He was a very famous man, says old Labyn quietly, almost reverentially. Everybody in this Colony knows about him.

Meester de la Bat clears his throat. Today most people have forgotten about him, he says sternly. And well they should. But about seven years ago he conducted a reign of terror in these parts.

What's he doing here? asks Philida. And what are *we* doing here?

I wanted you to come and see. As I just said, this Galant led a slave rebellion against the white people some years back. He and his followers killed three of them. Then they were caught and taken to the Caab to appear in court, and brought back here to be executed. Two were hanged, and their heads were stuck on poles here in the Bokkeveld, for all to see what happens when slaves try to rise up against their lawful masters. They were left here – one in this place, the other one at the far end of the Bokkeveld, to be consumed by time and the birds of heaven.

Is this really necessary? asks Philida.

Is what necessary?

Everything. The hanging. Putting the heads on the poles. And travelling all day yesterday and today just so that we can come and look at this thing.

This one, says Meester de la Bat, this one was the gang leader, Galant. And as you can see, he is still here.

Again Labyn speaks: Is this so that the people can see or to make them angry?

Labyn, says Meester de la Bat.

I'm just asking, Baas, says Labyn.

Meester de la Bat gathers up the long flaps of his black coat and struts off with his stiff secretary-bird steps, back to the cart.

What about the others? asks Philida behind him.

The white man stops to look back. Which others?

The ones that wasn't hanged. You say there was others.

Yes, there were others that were also punished. I told you there was another one that was put up at the top corner of the Bokkeveld. And a third one who was hanged but his head wasn't put up on a pole. And then five more. They were tied to the gallows when the three leaders were hanged. Afterwards they were taken to a stake where they were flogged and branded. And then they were locked up in the jail behind the Drostdy in Worcester for hard labour, three for life, and two others – their names were Achilles and Ontong – for fifteen years.

So they must still be there, says Philida.

They must be there, says the Meester. And I'm sure they'll be there for a long time still.

He suddenly seems to be in a hurry. Come, he says. It is time to go back.

Wrapped in her own thoughts, Philida wonders: Those five. Perhaps they were the ones who cleaned up the Drostdy square on the day of the auction, and swept up the cowpats and the turds. But if you really think about it, nothing has been cleared up at all.

The sun is sinking. Against the blood red of the scarecrow pole one can see the dirty white skull, looking out across the empty world with its empty eyes. As if he is anxious to take everything in. From here, for all one can tell, all the way to the Caab. To the sea, to the other side of the sea. To all the places in the world where there are still slaves and people who know about slaves. Those eye hollows, Philida thinks, they miss nothing, they won't ever miss anything, they're too big, too empty. Eye hollows that stare through day and night. Eye holes that *know* and that will never stop knowing.

Thank you that Meester came to show me again, Labyn says demurely next to her. This truly was a great man, I heard a lot about him and I'm glad every time I can see him. To Philida he says: Maybe we can look up the other five in the Drostdy sometime. He turns back to the scarecrow and makes a small bow in his direction. Good day, Galant.

Philida sits unmoving in her corner of the cart. What she thinks is: How little remains of a man. A sliver of bone. Two hollows for eyes. But as long as they still can look, perhaps nothing has been in vain. This man Galant was here, and now we came all this way, a whole day, to get here to him. Perhaps, in a way, it was worthwhile after all. It's too early to be sure. But will we ever know?

And without meaning to, she can hear her own voice

speaking quietly into the wind, a wind which after the oven-hot day suddenly comes blowing ice cold against her face. Good day, Galant, she says. And deep inside her head, without knowing exactly what it is she is thinking, conscious only of Labyn's comforting arm around her, she murmurs: Yes, it was good to see you.

But the day is far from over. Somewhere along the road they have to outspan and spend the night in the veld before they can drive on the next day, all the way through the long emptiness, back to Worcester, back to home.

XIX

*In which Labyn reveals himself as a
Storyteller of Note and introduces Philida to a holy Man
who will be with her for the rest of her Life*

After that ride to the Bokkeveld Philida starts spending
more and more of her free time with Labyn. There are
often only the two of them, usually at his workshop where
the wood smells settle in one's nose. But the children loved
being there too. For Lena there is always some little wooden
thing to play with, while Willempie is usually happy to lie
on the floor on a *kaross*, playing with his toes, or otherwise
in an *abbadoek* on Labyn's back. Many times Kleinkat comes
to play with small cut-offs or tools, with a mouse or a
butterfly she has caught outside, or with the fantasy friends
she finds everywhere. To Labyn's great pleasure she is
particularly partial to olive wood, and can spend hours in
his workroom, playing in wood shavings, or rubbing herself
luxuriously against newly sawn olive boards. Otherwise,
she simply sits and cleans or preens herself, one hind leg
stretched out past her head, or with her pink nose under
her tail to reach her little arsehole. That is to say, until the
day she disappears.

The great sadness comes soon after they went to the
Bokkeveld, and nobody can find out why or how. It takes
days before they realise what has happened, because at first
Philida thinks she has just hidden somewhere in the house
or in the yard, there are so many hiding places or spots to

play in. But after Labyn has once asked, What's become of that little cat? Philida starts getting worried. Everybody is questioned, but no one has seen her. Not even Meester de la Bat, and everyone knows that his writing desk is the spot where Kleinkat prefers to nest among the papers.

Apart from her children it is about the only thing Philida still has with her that came from Zandvliet. If she wasn't so busy she might have tried to ask permission to walk back along the road to look for Kleinkat. But even though it is midsummer, Nooi Anna has decided that she has to start her knitting for the winter early, because in these parts the cold comes with a vengeance and it comes early. So Philida has to swallow her sadness. Which isn't easy, and many times, especially at night when the children are asleep, it creeps up on her like a searing pain inside, as if the skin has been chafed away to expose the tender flesh underneath.

All that helps to ease the hurt, is to keep herself busy with her knitting. Or to spend more time with Labyn. And one hot day Philida once again sits knitting on the bench near the door of the carpentry shop where he works. Lena is playing with small cut-off blocks on the floor. To one side Willempie lies fast asleep. The workroom smells of fresh sawdust.

Labyn is talking non-stop as he usually does when she is around. All the shit we got in this Colony, he tells her, comes from the Christian people. He is planing a long yellowwood plank for a table. Every now and then he stops for a while to lift it up and aim with one eye along the side to make sure it is completely straight.

You and me sitting here, working and working all the time, while the white people are sitting on their backsides in the sun or in the shade as the case may be, he says, it all comes from that Jesus of theirs. It is his fault. So I think it's time for you to come over to the Slamse like me.

But I don't understand about the Slamse, says Philida. At Zandvliet the Ounooi always say one must stay away from them, with that lot you'll go straight to hell.

Did that Ounooi of yours ever say anything you could believe?

No, you're right, Labyn. But what can I do? That's how I was brought up.

Brought up for the fire that will burn you one day. My Slamse people are not like that. With us there is no baas or slave. We're all the same. Just people. And it goes very far back, hundreds of years, to a man called Muhammad where it all began.

I don't know him, says Philida. What must I do so that he can help me?

This is where it begins: with the stories. Labyn tells her about the Year of the Elephant, when a man called Abdallah went into a woman, Amina. And when she fell pregnant, there came a voice, saying, You're expecting a child that will be the Lord of all his people, and when he is born, you must call him Muhammad.

Philida immediately likes this, because she knows it must be the Elephant Trail along which she walked to Stellenbosch on that long-ago day to take her complaint against Francois Brink to the Slave Protector. And then the other Elephant Trail on which she travelled together with Ouma Nella and Ouman Cornelis here to Worcester. So if there is talk about elephants, she opens her ears.

Well, in that same year, Labyn tells her, a Christian man called Abraha came from a far place with a herd of elephants to attack the town of Mecca where there stood a pitch-black church.

Abraham? asks Philida with a small frown between her pitch-black eyes. Was that the Abraham of the Bible?

No, man, this one was just Abraha. Not ham.

Sounds a bit blunt to me, says Philida.

You want to listen or you want to argue? asks Labyn.

I'm listening.

All right then. We still talking about the elephants that stormed the church. The name of that church was Ka'aba, and the enemies that came with the elephants through the desert, that was the Christian people of those days, they wanted to break down the black church to build their own church. But just when the elephants came there, a big thing happened. The LordGod, who was the Baas of every man and woman and child, they called him Al-lah, he sent a huge flock of birds, each one with a stone in its beak, and they started dropping stones on the elephants. There were so many of them, the sky was black from one side to the other. And the elephants got scared and turned round and ran back into the desert, and so the beautiful black church was saved. That's the Ka'aba. And that was where Muhammad's mother Amina brought him up until he was nice big boy.

Now you must listen: One day when he was looking after a flock of sheep in the desert, two strange men in white clothes came to him with a big golden bowl full of white snow. And they pushed Muhammad down on the ground and took out his heart and washed it with the snow.

That must have been blarry sore, says Philida.

Not at all, says Labyn. He did not feel a thing. He just lay there watching how they took out his heart and pressed it until a small drop of pitch-black blood came out, and then they carefully put it back in his chest, and the next thing Muhammad knew was that the two men disappeared right in front of his eyes. But from that moment everybody knew this young boy Muhammad, who was then nine years old, wasn't just any ordinary boy. He was very special, and everybody respected him.

One day he met a very rich widow, Khadija, who was forty years old at the time, she could have been his mother, and she sent him into the desert with a herd of camels to go and buy and sell in another land, its name was Syria. And when Muhammad came home and Khadija saw how much money he made, she said she would marry him straight away. After some time they had a whole house full of children, and that was how Al-lah decided he was now ready to go with Muhammad.

Not long after that Muhammad came to a high mountain, Mount Hira, as high as the Brandwag Mountain here behind our Worcester, and Al-lah said to him, Speak! And ever since then Muhammad has been speaking to his people. He speaks to the poor, he speaks to the slaves, he speaks to the old people and to the sick, he speaks to everybody that is in trouble and that suffers and that is hurt and that needs help. That is why I tell you, Philida, Muhammad is our man, he's our Lord. They always say to us that the Lord looks after us, but that is not what happens. The LordGod looks after the white people, not us. Almost the first thing Muhammad did after the Lord Al-lah spoke to him, was to free his slave Zaid. For him there wasn't a place for slaves in the world any more.

But here at the Caab they also talking about freeing us, protested Philida.

Some of them talk like that, I know, but not all, says Labyn and he slams his beautifully cut plank on the working bench so that the sawdust is sent flying in all directions and Willempie wakes up and starts screaming. Philida has to calm down the child before Labyn can go on: You hear for yourself what the Baas is saying, don't you? Always grumbling and complaining and threatening. This thing I must first see with my own eyes before I believe it. Even if they free us, we'll still stay booked in with them for years. Muhammad said nothing about booking in. All he said to Zaid was: Now you're free. You can go where you want to. And that is what he wants for all of us. Now that is why I'm saying: He's the man I stand with.

And where do all this come from? asks Philida. Does Muhammad also speak in a thick book like the Ouman's LordGod?

Yes, he speaks in a thick book just like that. Only, it isn't called Bible, its name is Koran.

Philida grins. *Korhaan* is a funny name. It's a bird like a bustard, isn't it? Why would the LordGod want to have a book like that?

I suppose it is because you can say it flies in its own way, says Labyn. It puts wings in your head. Once you read what it says you won't think it's funny any more.

She sniffs. And how and where did *you* learn to read, if I may ask, Labyn?

I shall teach you, he says.

You?! Where did you ever learn?

I learned, I tell you, he says. I even went to school, before they sold me to a white man called Oubaas Harman Venter. Now that was a good man. He would have bought my freedom too, only he died of a bad pain in his chest and then I had to go and stand on the block in Stellenbosch.

She remains silent for a long time before she asks, Will you really teach me to read, Labyn?

My word is the word of a Slams, he says. Not the word of a Christian man that lies and cheats. If I promise something it is promised.

And from that day Philida's life is no longer what it was. Together with all her knitting and her other work, she is also the *minnemoer* of the de la Bat family, which means that she must look after the children, and these are a dirty lot that sometimes have to change clothes two or three times a day. The easiest way is to bring them up with her own Lena and Willempie. Feeding or bathing or putting to bed four children is not much more trouble than two. And when Anna de la Bat discovers how easily Philida handles it, she more and more often leaves her Gerard and Josef with the others.

On Mondays, Philida goes to the Drostdy to tidy up the Commissioner's office as they agreed after the auction. On most other days, when Philida isn't busy with knitting or caring for the de la Bat brood and her own, one can find her behind the big house in the carpentry shed with Labyn. Sometimes she is just listening to his stories, more often than not about Muhammad, but mostly she is sitting beside him at the long workbench learning to read and write. He himself can write so beautifully that it looks like print in a book. That must be because he first learned to read and write Arabic script, which taught him to form his letters very precisely. She cannot understand how on earth he could have learned to tame two languages so different from one another, but when she asks about it, he usually just shrugs and grins.

Most human languages are easy, he tries to explain. The really difficult one is the language of wood. And he offers to teach her that too, but at the same time he insists that she can only start learning after she has mastered the reading and writing of ordinary language.

Word for word he teaches her. Many times she feels like giving up, because it is so difficult. But she has always been a determined and even hard-headed person. Once she has set her mind on something, it isn't easy to make her waver. And, slowly but very surely, she starts shaping her letters and building her words, until the miracle happens and she can write the words she pronounces on the slate with the pencil Labyn has given her. Many nights she remains sitting on her heap of straw writing out her words. The children soon learn that when Philida is writing, she is not to be bothered, because if you keep on nagging you'll get clouted.

After a month or two she goes to Labyn to ask, Can you show me how to write Frans Brink's name?

Why do you want to know? he asks, annoyed. From what you've told me that man is a *skelm*.

Just show me.

That's not a name you need to worry about, Philida. Forget about him. Shake him off.

No, I got to learn. If I can write his name, I can send him to hell. Otherwise he'll keep on haunting me.

Labyn tries to argue, but he has already learned that Philida does not give anyone a chance to talk back. And so she learns to write:

FRANS BRINK

From there she can move on. She doesn't try to explain to herself why it's so important to write that name. But gradually she realises that by writing the name on a slate or a piece of paper, as on the last page of a Bible, she can get a kind of hold on Frans. She writes his name, and then she's got him. Caught, as in a fist, and that is where she wants him. That is how writing works. Going a little step further and doing a little bit more every day.

But a bit of writing and a bit of reading isn't all she does with Labyn. When they have done that for the day he can start talking and Philida listens. Stories, mostly. About

Muhammad and his wife Khadija. After the death of his uncle Abu Talib who always protected him against his enemies, and when Khadija also died, Muhammad felt like a thin little tree trying to remain standing against all the winds of the world.

Then a new woman came into his life, the pretty young girl-child A'isha, the daughter of a very important man, Abu Bakr. When Muhammad first met her she was only nine years old. But that didn't bother him, because they fell in love and soon they got engaged.

That's just plain stupid, says Philida.

No it isn't, says Labyn. Look, they were engaged but all that meant was that once she was grown up they could start thinking of lying together. Until that day came, they just didn't.

I'd like to see the man who can do that, says Philida.

Well, I can tell you that Muhammad respected her, Labyn says curtly. Whether you believe me or not, that was how it was. A'isha was still a child, but they were together and they believed that one day it would get better. Wherever Muhammad went, A'isha went with him. He brought her up the way he wanted and slowly she turned into a woman. But then there came trouble. Because one day when she was again with him on a raid against his enemies, she slipped from her carry-chair to go and pee, and when she wanted to go back, she found that she'd lost a beautiful necklace he'd given her. That was proper shit, you can believe me. She started looking for it, everywhere, everywhere, but that necklace was not to be found, and when in the end she came back, the whole caravan had left.

It was only the next day that the men discovered the lovely A'isha was gone. You can imagine how upset they were. But while everybody was still hunting here and there and everywhere to find Muhammad's beloved wife, they suddenly saw a cloud of dust coming towards them from the desert, and when it came closer they saw it actually was A'isha on a camel, together with a young Arab man with whom she'd grown up, a man with the beautiful long name of Safwan ibn al-Mu'attal. They heard that he'd found her in the desert wandering around on her own looking for Muhammad. Even though she was wearing her black veil, because by then Muhammad had seen to it that all women wore veils, Safwan immediately recognised her. As was expected of a shy and decent woman, A'isha didn't want to talk to him at first, but she did get on the camel with him and galloped through the night until at last they got to Muhammad in the morning.

The problem was that people then started gossiping. You know what people are like. Especially when there's a beautiful young woman in the story. Muhammad had no idea of what to do. He started behaving in a very cool and angry way to her. And when the stories did not stop, he went to her and told her, Look, I want you to go and tell Al-lah you're sorry, then I'll forgive you and everything will be all right again.

But A'isha was furious, and she said to Muhammad, I swear to heaven I shall never tell Al-lah that I'm sorry for the thing you are accusing me of. And she turned round and ran out of Muhammad's house in the city of Medina at the time, and went back to her mother, the way women do.

You can just imagine how everybody then started gossiping. Poor Muhammad was shattered. He went to all his friends and followers and asked them, How come that everybody is saying such awful things about me and my family?

Secretly, the people were all thinking that A'isha must be

guilty. Such a beautiful young woman always gets the blame. But in order to get into Muhammad's good books, they all pretended to think that this A'isha was a very decent and chaste person. There was only one man, Alí, who kept on saying that whether A'isha was guilty or innocent, Muhammad had to divorce her, because the story was too harmful to let it pass. A'isha's father Abu Bakr was furious, but it didn't seem as if he could make any difference.

That was when Al-lah decided the story had now gone far enough. So he appeared to Muhammad and showed him a revelation that confirmed A'isha was innocent. Muhammad was in the seventh heaven. He immediately ran to A'isha to tell her: Rejoice, A'isha! Al-lah himself has just revealed to me that you are innocent. All of that is to his greatest honour, don't you think?

So what did A'isha do? As we know, she was a woman who never allowed others to tell her what to do. And she pulled herself up and answered him like a slap in the face: Yes! she said. Perhaps it is to Al-lah's honour. But it is to your dishonour!

But at least that was the end of the whole nasty business.

This story, like so many others, Labyn told to Philida while he was sawing and planing and hammering, making his benches and tables and chairs and shelves and coffins.

But it was more than just stories. People say that Labyn also recited verses and passages from the Koran to Philida – he had a very deep, beautiful voice and she could never stop listening when he spoke, and he also taught her to recite verses from the Koran herself. Slowly, slowly, Philida became a new person.

Sometimes she could listen for hours to Labyn's voice when he read or recited to her, because she couldn't get enough of his deep voice – how it got wild and violent like the sea when there is a storm coming up and churning up the waves, and how it grew quiet like when the wind dies down in the vineyards and only a few leaves go on rustling. With his voice he could do anything, specially when she closed her eyes: words of anger, and of caressing, and of dancing, usually preceded by those special words that used to resound in her ears:

In the name of Al-lah, the Compassionate, the Merciful! Bismillah! Al-Rahman, Al-Rakim!

Then it would be like a flood and a thunderstorm breaking over her:

When the sky is rent asunder; when the stars scatter and the oceans roll together; when the graves are hurled about; each soul shall know what it has done and what it has failed to do.

Oh man! What evil has enticed you from your gracious Lord who created you, gave you an upright form, and well-proportioned you? In whatever shape he could have surely moulded you according to his will.

Yes, you deny the Last Judgement. Yet there are guardians watching over you, noble recorders who know of all your actions.

The righteous shall surely dwell in bliss. But the wicked shall burn in Hell-fire upon the Judgement Day: they shall not escape.

Would that you knew what the Day of Judgement is! Oh, would that you knew what the Day of Judgement is! It is the day when every soul will stand alone and Al-lah will reign supreme . . .

Often Labyn asks her to listen and pay attention, and then he reads to her about Al-lah and the Prophet who always comforts the weak and the oppressed and cares for them: then it is as if all Labyn's words are really meant for *her*. Because Al-lah, he assures her over and over, does not talk only to the Baas and his people like the LordGod, but to all who suffer, with the slaves and the slave women. Because remember, the first thing Muhammad did was to free his slave Zaid, and then he made sure that all the slaves of his friends were also freed. And with each one he sets free, he is really telling us that this is how all people should live. And he calls them by name: first of all, the orphans and the vagrants and the beggars and the slaves and the poor. It means that each single person in his loneliness is really all the people in the whole world.

That was why we laid it down for the Israelites that whoever killed a human being, should be looked upon as if he killed all mankind; and that whosoever saved a human life should be regarded as though he had saved all mankind.

Philida doesn't understand everything Labyn is trying to explain to her. But from what he says she can feel that for her Al-lah is the man she wants to be the Lord of all. He can understand. He can read one's heart, he made everything and understands why everything is the way it is.

Hear what the Koran says, Labyn continues: *He created the heavens and the earth to manifest the truth and fashioned you into a comely shape. To him you shall all return. He knows what the heavens and the earth contain. He knows all that you hide and all that you reveal. He knows your innermost thoughts. In six days we created the heavens and the earth and all that lies between them; nor were we ever wearied.*

But still she had some problems with him. If he is so powerful and so caring, Philida wants to know, then why does he make it so hard for us? He could have made life easy, finished and *klaar.*

Labyn shakes his head and his eyes are full of laughter. Al-lah puts to the proof those he loves, he explains. The Koran says, *Do men think that once they say: We are believers, they will not be left alone and not be tried with affliction?*

Then you better tell Al-lah when you see him again, Philida berates him, that it's a bad thing he is doing there.

Al-lah knows who speak the truth and those who lie, answers Labyn.

That's not good enough for me, Philida tells him. If he really knows everything, he should know better how to deal with us. No wonder there are so few people who are willing to believe in him.

One cannot speak to Al-lah just when you feel like it, Labyn warns her.

I'll wait until I see him, then I'll tell him myself, Philida says firmly.

You needn't tell him anything, Labyn answers. All you need to do is to keep your ears and eyes open. There are signs everywhere. Listen to what he says: *Surely in the heavens and on the earth there are signs for the faithful; in your own creation, and in the beasts that are scattered far and near, signs for true believers; in the alternation of night and day, in the sustenance that Al-lah sends down from heaven with which he revives the earth after its death, and in the marshalling of the winds, signs for men of understanding.* And then Al-lah speaks to us in the Koran and in our hearts, and that is all we need.

How can I ever be sure it's Al-lah or Muhammad that speaks to us? Philida prods him. That's what the Ouman's Bible also kept on saying. But how do we know? Who must I believe? They both say the same nice things and the same angry things.

It's not a matter of nice or angry, says Labyn. Al-lah himself tells us that the Koran is there to warn us, to warn the living and to judge the unbelievers. He is there to show us the way. For those who believe and do good works, he gives a good reward, it's all streams of water and green fields. And those who say there is no life after this one, he will punish.

I don't believe a man who always just promises or warns or punishes, says Philida. That sounds too much like the Ouman of Zandvliet.

It's not for you to believe or not to believe, says Labyn.

The Koran doesn't order you this way or that way. He tells you how it is and from then on you got to decide for yourself. This is what the Koran says: *It is for you to believe in it or to deny it.*

Ja, snorts Philida. It's easy for him to talk, man. But I tell you, if you just put a foot wrong he'll *klap* you.

You first think about it carefully, says Labyn. The Koran says, *Do not treat men with scorn, nor walk proudly on the earth. Al-lah does not love the arrogant and the vainglorious. Rather let your gait be modest and your voice low: the harshest voice is the braying of an ass.*

That I know damn well, says Philida. Nobody on Zandvliet could make such a bladdy noise as those two donkeys of the Ouman.

All I can say to you again, says Labyn, is that Al-lah gave us his book of wisdom and that he taught us what we didn't know before. And he is with us wherever we are. *We are closer to him than the vein of his neck.*

I'll knit you a jersey for the winter, Philida says with a small smile. Then you'll find out what is closest to you.

She stands with a frown between those black eyes. Labyn keeps looking at her without speaking, but for some time she remains silent. Until he decides to prod her again.

What's the matter with you? he asks. I can see there's something like muddy water dammed up in you.

It's not so bad, says Philida. It's just that it feels to me as if this Al-lah of yours speaks too much like the LordGod of the white people. They talk to people of far places and other countries. But we are from this place, Labyn. How can we know that it's meant for us too?

Don't you know about Sheik Yusuf then? he asks.

Who and what is Sheik Yusuf? she asks suspiciously.

That is when he tells her about the man who came to the Caab more than a hundred years ago, a rich and important man from Java, who started preaching to the slaves and the poor people over here. The Baas people in Java became scared that he was going to cause trouble there, that's why they sent him on a ship to the Caab with his wives and his children and some other people too. Because just like our Muhammad he also had a house full of wives. Here at the Caab he died and they put him to rest in a *kramat*. If we ever go there I shall show you. So you see, Sheik Yusuf belongs to this land too, not just to far places, and he left his words for all of us.

Hm, Philida says. That does sound a bit better, I must say. You can tell Al-lah from me that I shall think about it.

I think Muhammad would have liked you, says Labyn with a click of his tongue. For all you know he might have taken you for a wife.

I'm not there just for the taking, says Philida. I make one mistake with that and it won't happen again.

XX

*In which the Story moves back to Zandvliet
and the constant Tension between Francois and Old Cornelis
until an unforeseen yet unavoidable Event interrupts
the Course of all the Lives drawn into it*

Weeks after Philida left, Kleinkat unexpectedly came back
to Zandvliet, her little feet in a sorry state, her fur knotted,
and missing in patches. She'd always been smaller than other
cats, but now she was barely the shadow of a cat. The
curious thing was to see how her return disturbed Frans.
Considering how he used to react to cats, how he drowned
the rest of Langkat's litter, it is difficult to understand how
he could have been thrown so completely off balance by
this new event. Janna was on the warpath immediately.

This cat, she rants, this cat is going to infect all of us
with diseases. What can you expect of something that *meid*
brought here to the farm?

Philida didn't bring her here, Ma, Francois protests, much
angrier than he usually speaks to his mother. I gave her to
Philida and she's going to stay right here. You should be
sorry for the poor thing.

If she puts her feet in this house I shall personally get
rid of her.

Just you try and we shall see.

What shall we see?

You get rid of her, you get rid of me. And then who will
marry that Berrangé girl?

That draws Cornelis into the argument very quickly: *You* will marry, he says.

Who says I'll even like her if I get to know her? I heard she's a real vixen.

That's just hearsay, Frans. You don't really know her yourself. I tell you, she's our salvation.

It's unfair, the way you and Ma are trying to force me. It's the rest of my life that is at stake and all you care for is the money.

Cornelis explodes. For God's sake, man, don't you understand anything? If you and Maria Berrangé don't get married, we'll be bankrupt.

And whose fault will that be, Pa? Not mine.

Don't talk to your father like that, Frans, Janna scolds him. She forces the almighty joint of flesh that is her body in between them. You got to show respect before the LordGod.

Don't try to force me, Ma. Look, I really want to help you if it comes to the worst. But then you mustn't make it impossible for me. He turns back to his mother to warn her. And don't you dare to lay a finger on this cat. She is mine.

She belongs to Philida, not to you. Used to belong. And that is bad enough.

What is Philida's is mine.

Why do you keep on about Philida all the time? storms Cornelis. She's a slave, can't you get that into your blockhead? She's a slave and she's long gone. For us she does not exist any more.

For me she does, says Frans, so quietly that Cornelis cannot help falling silent to stare intently at him. When he speaks again, it is in a changed, strained voice. What's the matter with you, Frans? What did you really want from Philida?

What I wanted from Philida was what I want from a woman who is my wife, says Frans in a steely, faraway voice.

You can't mean what you're saying.

I just wanted her to be with me, says Frans. Not because of the children or because of the law or because of needing her to help out on the farm or because of anything else. But because of *her*. To me, Philida is not like just any other woman. I know her ever since she looked after me when I was a baby. I know her and she knows me. Can't you understand that? I need her. And now it may be too late. Because I betrayed her.

I'm afraid it is indeed too late, says Cornelis without looking at him. You'll just have to believe that. It is too late, for you and for all of us.

That is something I cannot accept, Pa. Now Frans is pleading from deep inside his guts: I *got* to try again. Please, Pa. I just *got* to. And you must give me that chance.

Cornelis shakes his head very slowly. I'm sorry, he says. That is something we cannot undo.

I won't accept that, Pa.

Very suddenly Cornelis cannot take it any more: I said what I got to say and that is now the end of it. Do you understand me? That is that. Finished and *klaar*.

For me it isn't, Pa, and it never will be.

Frans, you're not too old to get properly thrashed, Cornelis warns him.

Just you try!

Cornelis pulls back his shoulders and stares at him. He smothers a half-formed growl deep in his throat and turns away. Let me get out of this place before I strangle somebody, he mutters.

This is only the first of several quarrels. The words spoken or shouted at Zandvliet in these days are not what one would expect of good Christians. And it gets worse. But Kleinkat stays. Soon she starts catching mice again, and puts on some weight, and her brindled coat becomes smoother and glossier. But Francois continues to sulk. One can see plainly that there is thunder brooding in his head, but he refuses to speak to them.

The stories that have been doing the rounds become darker and gloomier. Strangers make their appearance on the farm, from Stellenbosch, and even from the Caab. With each visit Cornelis Brink's smouldering temper gets closer to the surface. And then, one day, it breaks loose. Everybody starts talking openly about it. Among the neighbours, in the district, among the slaves, wherever you turn: Cornelis Brink is bankrupt. He has to sell out. There will be an auction and he will be stripped as bare as the day he was born.

On 5 and 6 March of that Year of Our Lord 1834 Mijnheer Johannes Marcus Knoop makes his appearance at Zandvliet to draw up an inventory of every man and mouse and turd and slave and sickle, every wagon and wine barrel, every table and drawer, every chamber pot and bottle of muscadel, every cupboard and coffin, every featherbed and fishbone, every spoon and knife and fork, every shirt and hairpin, every cotton-reel and calabash in the longhouse and in the yard and in every distant corner of the farm, signed at the bottom, ready for the death blow.

And four months later, on 7 and 8 and 9 July, the inventory is followed by the auction itself, the whole farmyard churned to dust under the feet of buyers and would-be buyers, the curious and the know-alls and the know-nothings and the bastards and the *moerneukers* who have turned up to relish the downfall of someone else.

The one person who is not prepared to face the shame

and tries to stay out of sight of the snoopers, is Janna Brink. She would have preferred to withdraw to her bed with a blinding headache, but nowhere is there any hiding place to be found: everything has to remain accessible to the public which moves in a solemn procession from *voorhuis* to passage, from stoep to kitchen, from room to room on the heels of the chubby auctioneer. The only meagre refuge she can find in the throng is in Ouma Petronella's room, in her bed, under the *bulsak*. For Ouma Petronella is *mos* a free woman, not a member of the family, most certainly not a slave, and consequently not involved in the auction. And here Ounooi Janna herself, as she will repeat afterwards, over and over, to whoever is prepared to listen, or not to listen, as the case may be, is able to withdraw into a sanctuary out of sight and hearing of the vultures. A disgrace to God and man. This is what comes from marrying a Brink. This she will never be able to wash from her hands, this taste of gall and vinegar she will never get rinsed from her mouth. For her, the worst is not the inventory and the selling and the bidding and the carting away of every possession. No, the worst by far is the exposing of everything that has been hers and her family's, the denuding and baring and stripping away of all protection, leaving one naked in front of the full congregation so that they can stare through you like looking through a windowpane covered in dust and dead flies, or right into you as into a cracked mirror, unwrapping and laying bare every hole and gap and hollow. And the slaves gazing and staring with just as much glee. The slaves who are to be sold later in the day with the rest of the household belongings, the cows and sheep and pigs and beds and spittoons and chamber pots, but who are now free to stare as if they don't care a damn. As if, to tell the truth, they are thoroughly relishing what they are gawking at so fearlessly and blatantly.

And Cornelis Brink stands gawping with them. He will not miss anything. It is, he keeps thinking, like a rotten tooth you are worrying with a sharpened needle, worrying and worrying, and the more it hurts the more you feel compelled to persist. The children who have turned up with mothers and fathers and brothers and sisters, keep to one side and pretend to be playing. But Cornelis himself keeps up with the auctioneer every goddamn step of the way, his cold pipe clenched between his blunted teeth, his eyes glaring ahead as if he is seeing nothing and nobody. But God knows, he sees everything. He *wants* to see it all. What is curious is that it feels as if he is both there and not there at all. As if every minute thing that happens, even the most fleeting and insignificant, he sees double. With his eyes he sees everything that takes place within his field of vision – every plate and cup and feather-duster and broom that is carried off – and with another, secret eye deep inside him he sees something like a vision, as if he is staring into the most distant future, and this eye sees not only his own possessions that are carried off, but a whole country with all the people inside it. He sees the vast plains stretching out from horizon to horizon, and the unbreakable chains of mountains stretched across them, and people trying to find under an empty sky some hiding place which they cannot reach. He stands staring at the slaves who are also standing and staring, and he can almost hear what they are thinking: Our turn will come. *Duusmanne*, our turn is coming. All that is yours will be carried away, to hell and gone, into the farthest distance, into nothingness, until no speck or smudge of you remains, not even a cloud as big as a man's hand. Nobody will ever know that you have been here once. This is our Day of Judgement. You never wanted to admit it. You tried to hide it behind your vineyards and fields and manors and town houses and village squares. Your Drostdys and cellars and Company gardens and cobbled streets, your Constantias and Meerlusts and Zandvliets. But today all of this is turning transparent like an autumn leaf through which you stare to see the fine network of veins between yourself and the world out there, and now you can discover how all of it is teetering into nothingness, how all of it is already beginning to fall apart like an old wine vat crumbling to dust, while the heathens and savages are closing in from all sides, the living and the dead, all those already exterminated from this land, all those we *thought* exterminated, and who are now returning like dust-devils across a dusty plain.

In the footsteps of the auctioneer. The man with the wad of papers in his blunt hands with the tufts of reddish and pale hairs on the backs of the fingers. From room to room. Without skipping or omitting or avoiding anything. Until there is nothing left to skip any more.

In the *voorhuis* where the grandfather clock stands ticking and ticking, and where the four tables and the fourteen *riempie* chairs are displayed, and the barometer on the far wall, and the mirror in its heavy frame, and the tea table against the wall loaded with cups and plates, and the two spittoons, one white, one blue delft. In the bedroom on the right, another long mirror, and a large brass bedstead with a *bulsak* and drapes of glazed chintz and a bolster, and a narrow bed for when another child is born, and yet another table, this one with six chairs with horsehair cushions, and six spittoons and six footstools with fire-pans for the winter months. Then the bedroom on the left: a stinkwood bed again with drapes of glazed chintz, a bolster and four pillows and a blanket, another mirror and a small bed and a table and an enormous brass teapot. Followed by another bedroom, with a huge wardrobe in which a grown-up person can easily hide away, and an escritoire and a chest with six drawers, and six pictures on the walls. The *Broad and Narrow Ways*. Jesus with his curly beard, a row of blue Dutch windmills. And much, much more, too much to register. And all the chamber pots, enough for pissing through nights and days until the second coming of the Lord. And things and things and more things. All of it written down on Mijnheer Knoop's list, for better or for worse, everything called by its own inevitable name, from Bible to commode.

And then the pantry, where Philida used to come as a child with her Ouma Nella, she was never allowed in there on her own, there must have been too much she could damage or break. This is the room that smells best, even though Mijnheer Knoop's list says nothing about the scents. The shutters before the tall window are always half closed, which keeps the air inside cool and dusty, so it makes one notice the other smells more strongly. Camphor and dried peaches and raisins, and beeswax and honey, and ground coffee, and bags of tea dried in the outdoor oven and thrashed in the attic, there are rows of drying biltong, and green figs preserved in large round copper basins, and sugar brought from the Caab, and rolled tobacco and *beskuit* and *moskonfyt*, there are containers of paraffin and piles of blue soap and yellow soap boiled in big round cauldrons in the yard, and lemons and quinces and dried apricots, and flour and bran in wooden boxes, and breadloaves as hard as stone, and bags of *beskuit* with raisins and aniseed, and cloves and cinnamon sticks and nutmeg and water candles and wax candles, there are sweet-smelling things from all the far places in the whole world. And there is a deep shelf with crockery, 12 beer mugs, 12 wine glasses, 4 earthenware carafes, another 4 glass carafes, 9 glasses, a liqueur shelf with 4 bottles, another 18 empty bottles, 10 ceramic pots, another 19 earthenware pots, 12 white dishes, 2 white soup tureens, 16 silver spoons. Then 4 more large silver spoons, a silver serving spoon, 4 brass candleholders, 5 copper candleholders, 2 flat brass candleholders, 1 food warmer, 2 snuffers with long handles and 1 snuffing bowl, 1 teapot, 1 oil stand, 6 jam jars, 12 small cups and saucers, 12 cups, 1 old tin kettle, 24 knives, 24 forks, 15 bowls, 2 baking pans, 2 shelves. Another food warmer. And 4 coffins, in sizes from large to small, polished with beeswax and honey, the inside upholstered with silk and chintz and decorated with bows, dressed up for a good long sleep, and temporarily filled with sweet-smelling dried peaches and apricots and quinces.

Next, the kitchen: 1 table, 1 flour chest, 1 shelf, 1 butter pail, 3 buckets, 2 barrels, 1 water jug, 1 churn, 2 small butter vats, 7 iron pots, 4 chairs, 1 hearth chain, 1 water kettle, 1 copper colander, 1 fire iron, 1 three-legged pot, 2 iron forks, 1 skimming spoon, 1 small hatchet, 1 axe. This is without counting the storeroom next door, with 46 earthenware pots of various sizes, 42 bowls, 6 soup plates, 1 candle box, 1 barrel, 1 bread knife, 1 large chest, 1 old chest, 1 shelf, 4 chamber pots, 5 trays, 2 pitchers and ewers, 3 flat irons, 1 soup ladle, 1 bridle, 1 chicken coop, 1 slaughtering table, 1 small barrel with copper hoops, 1 large tea can, 3 flagons, 6 bags, 2 old frames, a bushel and its box, 4 flour chests, 3 flour pitchers, 1 vat, 1 long plaited sjambok.

Up in the attic there is more waiting: 1 tea jug, 1 kettle, 3 jugs, 6 bags, 2 old frames, 1 bushel, 4 flour chests, 3 flour jugs, 1 barrel. And more and more and still more, as if there will never be an end of it.

And this is only the longhouse. What about outside? The 8 stable horses, the 6 saddle horses, the 40 draught oxen for the wine wagons, the 7 pigs, 4 black and 3 white, old

Hamboud the fattest and filthiest of them all and always grunting or squealing for more and never satisfied, the 2 headstrong mules, the coop with chickens, among them the useless hen that never lays an egg but makes more noise than 7 others, the 2 ox carts, the 2 Cape carts, the mule cart and the mule wagon, the plough and 2 ploughshares, the yokes and yoke-pins and thongs, 2 wine racks, 6 picks, 18 spades, 14 sickles, 8 pruning shears, the chest with assorted tools, 1 handsaw, 1 flourmill, a heap of old iron, a heap of wood, 8 scaffoldings, a heap of bamboo, 2 window frames and 1 door frame, 1 gate, 2 windows, firewood and assorted wood.

Down in the cellar: 10 leaguers, 2 fermentation vats containing 6 leaguers each, 14 stuck-vats (5 leaguers each), 2 leaguer barrels, 2 half-aums, 1 small barrel, 2 vinegar barrels with some vinegar in them, 2 funnels, 7 buckets, 1 threshing vat and 1 catchment vat with their stands, 6 broad barrels, 1 set of scales with its weights, 3 ladders, 10 bushel baskets, 2 copper potstills, 2 wagons loaded with hides.

Only one room in the house – when you come in at the front door, then left, past the *voorhuis*, to the very end – remains untouched with all its furniture. For this is where Ouma Petronella lives, where Philida used to live with her: because Ouma Petronella has announced very calmly that she is a free woman and that none of her belongings may be touched, she is not for sale. One day, when everything else has been cleared up, she will come back, she and her people, like the little bushes of the Karoo, like the sands of Zandvliet or the sea, and claim whatever used to be theirs, for ever and ever, amen.

While all this is happening, Cornelis stands looking at what is his, what was his, everything he no longer knows and which no longer knows him, and which will be blown away by the wind. Rooted to the spot, shocked and dazed, he remains staring while the auctioneer is calculating the sum total of his life, while the neighbours are watching and relishing what they see, and while the slaves are thinking: one day, one day.

Yes, let us not forget about the slaves.

There is Moses of the Caab.

There is Cupido of the Caab.

And look, Joab of the Caab.

Willem of the Caab.

Adriaan of the Caab.

Aleksander of Mozambique.

Adonis of Mozambique.

Moses of Mozambique.

Apollis of Mozambique.

Maart of Mozambique.

Slembang of Batavia.

November of Batavia.

One slave woman named Maria of the Caab and her two children, Regina and September.

Julenda of the Caab with her children, Rachel, Labina, Barend, Willem, Morné, Kaming and Gabriel of the Caab.

Sara of the Caab.

The list can keep one busy for a long time. But sooner or later it comes to an end. And when it is all over, there stands Cornelis Brink, behind the house at the empty wine cellar, thinking: So much, indeed. But when it has all been cleared away? What remains? What remains? Is this all that can be written up and said about my life? A double bed, some empty wine barrels, a plaited sjambok.

How disposable a man remains at the end of it all, once everything has been added up and subtracted and calculated.

Zandvliet, he will think, Zandvliet. What used to be everything, has turned to nothing. Dust unto dust. As if a Bible has been upended and emptied over it all, shaking out all the words over it like salt from a cellar.

Over and over: What remains? How does one make the sum of a human being? Dear LordGod. The old preacher may well repeat it all:

In the day when the keepers of the house shall tremble, and the strong men shall bow themselves, and the grinders cease because they are few, and those that look out of the windows be darkened; also when they shall be afraid of that which is high, and fears shall be in the way, and the almond tree shall flourish, and the grasshopper shall be a burden, and desire shall fail: because man goeth to his long home, and the mourners go about the streets: or ever the silver cord be loosed, or the golden bowl be broken, or the pitcher be broken at the fountain or the wheel be broken at the cistern. Then shall the dust return to the earth as it was and the spirit shall return unto God who gave it. Vanity of vanities, saith the preacher; all is vanity.

XXI

*Where a sudden Trip undertaken by Cornelis
to the Caab results in an entirely new set of Consequences for
the Inhabitants of Zandvliet, while a Visit by Francois to
Worcester closes down other Prospects*

Francois was devastated by the auction at Zandvliet. Over the preceding months his father had constantly complained about the deterioration of his financial position, but no one could believe that matters were really so dire. The first arrival of Mijnheer Knoop, the bailiff of the court, on the farm in March that year, to draw up the inventory, caught all of them unawares. And that was only the beginning, for on two more occasions the bailiff returned to complete his task, accompanied by an assistant and a helper. Then in early July, as we know, came the auction itself, with the whole farm trampled to dust by the crowd that came swarming through home and farmyard to gawk at everything, turning over plates and spoons to assess them from close by, and upending chairs to make sure the *riempies* were firmly crossed and tied, and defiling it all with their clumsy calloused hands and leering eyes.

Once everything was over and the homestead was left behind like a ruin that had died before its time and the family remained in the hollow rooms like after a funeral and gazed about them as if they no longer knew one another nor really wanted to, the worst was to come. Everybody was waiting, but they weren't sure what it was they were waiting for. Probably the wagons that had to arrive from somewhere to cart everything away. Where to? Nobody really knew or in fact cared.

It was in those days that Cornelis saddled his black horse and rode from the farm in a cloud of dust. At first no one knew where he was going to, or why.

In the end, as far as we can recover it all today, it was Janna who confided in her oldest daughter, Maria Elisabet, and after that the news was out.

But the why was still unclear. And following whose tracks? Nobody could tell for sure, and they were all too scared to ask. It was Alida, the youngest, who dared to utter what none of the others could or would.

He's gone for good. Perhaps we'll never see him again.

But no. Five days later Cornelis was back, his horse exhausted, and lame in one hind leg. On any other occasion Janna would have given him total hell, but this time not even she dared to ask or comment.

Nobody spoke.

Cornelis gazed at all of them in turn where they stood waiting in the *voorhuis* as if all this had been arranged beforehand, and then went to the old Dutch armoire to pour himself a *sopie* of sweet wine in a delicate VOC glass, the wine everybody used to assure him tasted better than Constantia, though changing their verdict once his back was turned. He emptied the glass in one draught and went to pour another. This one he finished at his maddening leisure.

Still nobody spoke.

He poured the third glass and returned very slowly to where they were all still waiting in silence.

Only then he said, I went to the Caab.

Still no sound.

I went to see Berrangé.

Berrangé? asked Janna, her voice quite unsuited to her bulk.

Daniel Fredrik Berrangé, said Cornelis. The man who knows the law better than anyone else in this godforsaken place. He turned to look Francois full in the face. Adding calmly, as if it was a discovery: I'm talking about Maria Magdalena's father.

Still not a word from the gathered family.

Now I know everything, said Cornelis Brink. Everything that happened at the auction, and why it happened.

They all start talking at the same time. All of them dumbfounded, he can see. The news must be too much to bear. Worst of all for Janna. The shame, she stammers at long last, in a low voice, the shame of it. That I, a de Wet, have to see a day like this. It will be the death of me. My heart cannot stand this. The shame. And I, born a de Wet.

You've been a Brink for years, Cornelis lashes out at her. I wouldn't be so sure about your de Wet father if I were you. He was a man with a reputation as long as his cock.

My poor dead father, she sobs. In case you don't know it, he was one of the most devout Christians among the pioneers of this Caab.

Of course. And the one thing they all had in common was the sowing of wild oats.

Cornelis!

And even more important, my dear wife, he goes on, is that he himself may have been a wild oat.

I shall not survive this, she gasps.

Oh, you will, you will, he assures her. Wild oats grow in all kinds of soil.

My late husband Wouter de Vos would have skinned you alive to hear you slander me like this! He was not a man that would have sold his wife's earthly possessions to a lot of strangers and heathens.

What about the children you brought with you? he asks. If I hadn't saved them they would all have gone straight to hell. And look how well I've married them off. You can thank the Lord that I gave you an honourable name and a roof over your head and a broad couch for your backside. When I married you, you were like a precious piece of porcelain on a high shelf. But look at you now!

Janna gasps for breath and starts crying like a biblical deluge in the wintertime.

It is not about Johannes or Francois or KleinCornelis or Daniel or Maria Elisabet or Lodewyk Johannes or Alida, or any of slaves who stand listening at every door and window of the *voorhuis*, but everything gathered inside the large woman over years and years of long dry summers and long wet winters, and now at last needs space to explode, like the bloated belly of a cow that has eaten too much green lucerne.

Among all the others it is Francois on whom Janna's eyes suddenly alight. And what about you? she screams. It's all your fault. It's you who started consorting with that *naaimandjie* Philida. If it hadn't been for you, we would all have been living together happily and like good Christians. Aren't you ashamed, Frans? Do you have no respect left in your sinful body? *Godverdomme*, don't you have any shame?

Her weeping starts whirling upwards out of her chest like a huge bird – like a crow or a hadeda or a duckostrich-pheasant that no human eye has seen or heard before, and it flaps higher, through the ceiling of rushes and the thatched roof, through everything built by human hands, to come tumbling and flapping back only much, much later, to collapse on the floor in a flutter of blood and gastric juices and feathers. In a shuddering wail all her pent-up breath escapes from her convulsing body: Francoooooooooooois!

For a long time it is deathly quiet in the *voorhuis*. From outside, far in the distance, one can still hear a few guinea-fowl clicking in the dark, and a pigeon flying up, and an owl announcing untimely death.

Can I make Ma some coffee? Alida asks in a weepy voice. Or some sugar water?

Nothing for me, thank you, Janna whispers.

Anybody else? pleads Alida. Perhaps Pa?

Everybody has suddenly become unbearably polite.

Boetie Francois?

Yes, thank you. Black. And strong.

Alida scuttles past on dirty bare feet.

From there we must imagine the rest:

Now where were we? asks Cornelis, avoiding their eyes.

With the decent man, Wouter de Vos, suggests Frans.

No, says Cornelis. Before that.

With the auction, says Frans.

Hmm. Cornelis clears his throat. Well, does anybody else want to say something about the auction?

All I'd like to know, says Frans, is: what happens now?

They all look at Cornelis, father of a multitude.

Nothing happens now, says Cornelis.

How can Pa say that? Weren't you at the auction?

I wish I wasn't, says Cornelis very calmly. It was like a Day of Judgement for us all. But nothing needs to happen now.

How can you – Once again, they all start speaking together.

I told you I went to see Berrangé, says Cornelis. From him I heard what I myself was too upset to see. Didn't you notice who bought all our stuff at the auction?

· 214 ·

What are you trying to say? We were all here, were we not?

But didn't you notice that all our stuff, everything here at Zandvliet, everything in our house at the Caab, everything we possess on God's earth, was bought by our own family, or family-in-law, or neighbours and close friends? We have lost nothing. They are taking care of our possessions until such time as we can buy everything back again. Through the infinite mercy of God, our Father, Son and Holy Ghost. And of Daniel Fredrik Berrangé who has arranged it all.

For the time being not one of the children can manage to utter a word. It sounds too much like some made-up story told by someone who is trying to dish out comfort.

There are conditions, of course, Cornelis resumes. He looks at Francois: And these depend on Francois Gerhard Jacob. He allows time for the words to sink in, like when they are irrigating the vineyard. Then he continues: With the Berrangés to protect us, we can pay off our debt and buy ourselves out when the time is right. We can start again and go on as before. It will mean a lot of hard work, but I have never been scared of hard work. And for this farm I'm prepared to put in whatever is expected of us. With the help of my family, every one of you.

He turns back to Francois: As soon as the debt has been paid, you will bed and marry Maria Magdalena Berrangé. Not a day earlier, nor – God help me – a day later. So be it. Frans, bring the Bible.

What he reads, once they are settled round the massive dining table – with all the slaves squeezed in with their backs against the inside wall – is no doubt predictable: Cornelis's favourite chapter from Genesis about Jacob and Isaac and the ram on the mountain.

This is how God is putting us to the test today, Father Cornelis expresses his considered opinion. Let it never be said of us that we haven't done our share.

The very next morning, we now know, Cornelis set to work – urging on everybody else to do the same – and got going as if he had a devil clawing to his back. He spoke about new plantings, particularly of red grapes, as soon as the season arrived, and clearing and preparing the vineyards in anticipation. From almost everybody he knew in the area, he started negotiating new loans for vats and barrels of all descriptions. And old loans that had been taken up years ago, were renewed and extended with promises enough to bring music to the very ears of Satan. Only Ouma Petronella, from whom he'd borrowed money as far back as '24, when he first bought Zandvliet, refused to extend his debt of three hundred and fifty rix-dollars.

It's because of Philida, she told him to his face. You treated her badly and I won't let you shake it off like a burr in your clothes. It's your own grandchildren you sold with her. God will come back to ask you for them one day. One way or another, it doesn't matter. I know him, and he will.

It was between her and Frans, Cornelis answered. I can't interfere in their affairs.

But I can interfere in yours, she told him. And I promise you, I'll follow you all the way to the gallows if I have to, and you'll pay for it.

He even started working on two new gables for the front of the longhouse.

In those same days Frans also got exceptionally busy, driven by something, like that devil between his father's shoulder blades, but in a different way. He started building a new bamboo cage. Much like the previous time, he cut and prepared the bamboos in the night, but this time he set to work slowly and methodically. Everything has to be just right. A bit bigger than the last cage he built for Kleinkat, but more manageable, more comfortable, neatly finished off, nowhere rough or uneven. Room for a sand tray, a food bowl, a small *bakkie* for water. A soft blanket. And nobody is told what he is working on. To Ouma Petronella he says what it is, only because it is impossible to keep anything from her, but not before the very last moment, the day before he leaves.

Very early that morning he sets out, the first hour or so very cautiously and slowly, so that his parents won't suspect anything. Old Petronella has to be warned, in case anybody asks her, just to say he went off, she isn't sure where to, but most likely to the Caab, presumably to visit Maria Magdalena Berrangé.

You sure you doing the right thing? she asks Francois, but he refuses to discuss it. Of course it's the right thing. What else can he do? It's for Philida, it's for his children. He realises what he has done only now that she is gone and all he knows is that it must be put right.

The whole long journey one can think of as a route of psalms and hymns, over hills and dales, under a sun that scorches like hell itself. But it doesn't bother him. And he doesn't want to think either. Neither of what is past, nor of that gone; nor of what may still be ahead, because there is no way of imagining anything in advance. All he does know is that if it fails, if Philida cannot come back with him, he won't come back either. Then he'll simply gallop away, as far from the Caab as possible, over mountains and rivers, perhaps to a distant place about which, over the years, he has heard rumours, a place that sounds as if someone has remembered it from a dream, the Gariep. In the Caab, from as far back as he can recall, when he was no more than a boy, there have always been stories about the Gariep. About all the runaways that gathered across its muddy red waters, beyond the whole of the known world. Runaways, murderers, slaves, good-for-nothings, vagrants, adventurers, dreamers, young men in search of wild dreams, old men grown grey from too many years and too many mirages, too many improbable stories. A place that has by now become a kind of Paradise in his imagination, like the one Adam and Eve were once expelled from. He knows only too well what people say, that one cannot step further than your legs are long. But for once he is sure his legs are long enough. And he will take it slowly. Until one day he reaches that distant Gariep. A place for anyone who has grown tired of a world where everything is known and predictable. A place like the stories Philida used to tell when he was almost too young to understand. Gariep. Yes. Gariep. A name like a rising sun, like an unexpected shower in a dry landscape, the promise of a rainbow. He. He and Philida and their children. And nobody else. Not a father with a sore back and a mother as big as a packing shed and a crowd of brothers and sisters and bothersome ghosts. Gariep.

So he rides to the rhythm of his thoughts. Forces himself a few times to stop so that the horse can have a rest and take water. Almost too impatient to wait. But he has to think about coming back. Either coming back or going on to the Gariep. But then with Philida.

But even in his thoughts he knows it is too extravagant to be true. He remembers the last few times he saw her. What she said. Most especially what she did *not* say.

But if he doesn't do it he will never know. And he's got to try, at the very least. Otherwise he will be even worse than she has always said he is.

What will he say if she allows him to speak? Something like this? — Just give me a chance to explain, Philida. Please listen. Please, I do not want to waste your time. But let me look at you. Try to remember the bamboo copse. That first time and all the other times. I know it is asking a lot. After what I've done. But just give me a chance. For God's sake!

His head churning with thoughts, after a difficult night of rest in the mountains, Francois covers the last stretch of road where the mountains open on a long plain that stretches out pale yellow and rough in the summer sun, broken here and there by small clumps of trees. And the many blues of new row upon row of mountains in the distance.

The cluster of white houses of the village opens up ahead of him like a picture book, surrounding the large white structures of church and Drostdy on the clearing in the centre.

He reins in the horse. Large white saltpetre stains are visible on his trembling, shiny flanks. Reaching a small group of people — they must be slaves, they're all barefoot — Francois brings the horse to a standstill.

I'm looking for Meester de la Bat's house, he shouts at the group.

All the people point in the same direction, close by.

Jesus! he hears a sharp voice exclaim behind him. That man must be mad in his head. Did you see he got a cat with him?

Minutes later he reaches the house. A middle-aged coloured slave with slightly oriental eyes approaches from the backyard to help him outspan.

Is Meester de la Bat here?

The man points to the back. He's at work now, but if the Baas waits for a while he'll be back.

I'm really looking for Philida, he says. She works here.

Why didn't you say so? asks the slave.

I first wanted to greet the people.

She's also a people, the pale brown slave says cheekily.

Francois tightens his grip on his crop, but changes his mind. He's not looking for trouble.

I'll go find out if she can come, says the slave, not subserviently at all.

Two, three minutes later she stands before him, her eyes screwed up against the sun. Those eyes of obsidian.

The woman stands waiting in silence. She is wearing an old bluish dress which hangs down to her feet. Her dusty bare feet. Francois fleetingly remembers what they felt like in his hands, so many years ago. Beyond the orchards and the vineyards, along the Dwars River. But it feels like something that must have happened in somebody else's life.

Philida? he asks hesitantly.

My JesusGod! he hears her exclaim against the sun. She approaches very suddenly. But it is not to come to him: it is the bamboo cage on the horse she has noticed. And she calls shrilly: My *Kleinkat!*

Before he can intervene she stands with the cage in her hands and squats down on her haunches, making small sounds deep in her throat. And the cat replies. Philida puts out her hands and starts tugging at the thong that keeps the gate shut.

Watch out! he cries. If she gets out she'll be gone for ever.

But it is already too late. The little gate is wide open. Kleinkat darts out. But this time she isn't trying to get away. Deep into Philida's arms she crawls, purring and chirping like a small nightbird. She wriggles into the woman's embrace, and Philida wriggles back, pressing the cat against her, turning her upside down to push her face into the grey-and-white belly.

She still just as small as ever, coos Philida. And just as pretty. Oh my God. Has my Kleinkat come back to its Ounooi?

It takes a long time before she can sit back and glance up, quickly and almost furtively, towards Francois, once again into the sun.

I knew she wanted to be back with you, he says, happy and embarrassed at the same time. I *had* to bring her.

Now Philida's body becomes more rigid. With the cat pressed against her chest, she draws back, out of reach.

Why did you do it? she asks. What you doing here?

I came to find you, he says openly. Both of us missed you.

We got nothing for you here, she says tonelessly.

But, Philida –

You want to buy me back with the cat, says the slave woman. We don't want you here.

But I had to bring Kleinkat back to you.

Kleinkat is one thing. You are something else.

Philida, please understand!

I understand blarry well, she says. If you tell me *Come*, you want me to come. If you tell me to scoot, I got to go. How many more times do you want me to do that?

That's not what I came for, he says wretchedly.

What is it then? You want to push your thing into me? Philida gets up from the ground, the cat still pressed against her.

Or is it your old pa that needs me again?

Philida, no, please! He looks around, not knowing which way to go.

Without warning Philida bends over and pushes the little cat back into the cage, then ties up the thong again.

Take the cat, she says. Go back to Zandvliet where you come from. You not wanted here.

But *you're* the one I want! he pleads.

You had time enough to say that. Now that time is past. Go home.

Round the corner of the house he sees two children approaching. Two small fair heads. Both with dirty bare feet. The little girl is skipping ahead, her long dress billowing. Behind her follows a baby on all fours, covered from head to toe in red dust, his small bottom bare. A boy, no doubt about that.

For some time Francois cannot find anything to say. Then he ventures hoarsely, Our children have grown –

No, says Philida. They're mine. They don't know nothing about you and they don't want to know.

I've come all this way from Zandvliet! My backside is raw. But it was all I could do.

For what? she asks, still closed and resentful.

I told you: I had to come and see you. We didn't have time to talk properly when my father took you.

We got nothing more to talk about.

I brought you something.

She shakes her head. I don't want anything more from you. And I got nothing to say to you.

Wait and take a look first.

I don't want to see nothing and I don't want to hear nothing. She prepares to turn away.

Philida, it's time for you to come back. Back to us. I am the children's father.

Now you expect me to come back? After everything you done? After everything you made *me* do?

We can forget about that and start again.

How does one start again after a thing like that? Until the end of my days I'll carry this thing with me like a half-chewed lump of meat in my guts.

I'll help you. We *can* start again. Even my pa is going to start again after what happened, after the auction.

I'm not talking about selling and throwing away, Frans. That is bad enough, but in a way I can still understand it, because you are white. But the thing you made *me* do I shall never understand and never forget.

I didn't make you do anything you didn't want to do, and you know that bloody well. We had good times together.

It was good to *naai*, she says. So good I could see your eyes turn up. But when you saw I had a child in me, what then?

What else could we do? Pa . . . and Ma –

To hell with your pa and ma, man. What you made me do was more than anyone got a right to do.

You chose to do it.

Chose? To choose something you got to be free to choose or not to choose. What did I have? I was a slave. *Your* blarry slave. It was you who wanted to go and drown that child the way you used to with kittens. And when I tried to stop you –

I had to stop *you*, goddammit! And from that day you can say I never really lived again. I was dead. I walk about like one of the *Vaalvoete*, the Shadow People, I no longer leave footprints when I walk.

After a long time he says, Do you think you were the only one who found it difficult? What about me?

You?! Philida gives an ugly laugh. Nothing can ever make up for what you did to me. Life is not long enough for that.

That is all over and done, Philida. We must now move on from there.

After what you did there is nothing more anybody can do, Frans. So just please let me be. And never come back here.

She bends over and sweeps up the two children from the ground, then walks off with them to the house without looking back.

Francois remains staring after her. Once the back door has closed behind her, he leans forward and slowly picks up the bamboo cage again and goes to his horse.

As he rides out of the yard, Meester de la Bat comes walking through the small gate. As usual, he is wearing his black suit and the tall hat on his head. He stretches out a hand in greeting, but quickly drops it again as the man on horseback nearly crushes him against the wall. De la Bat keeps staring after him before he shakes his head and walks on towards the house.

In the *voorhuis* he meets Philida who is standing with one child on the hip and the baby at her breast, as if she is not quite sure about what to do next.

Who was the man who left in such a hurry? asks Meester de la Bat, still nonplussed.

She does not look at him. Don't know, Meester, she mumbles. I have no idea. He just come here to ask for the road to the Bokkeveld, but he don't really know where he's going to.

Meester de la Bat sniffs and moves on to the main bedroom.

Philida goes round the house towards Labyn's workroom. Just as well she did not stay behind to look after the stranger and see what happened: how he rode on, out of the village, and how, once out of sight, without reining in his horse or even slowing down, he hurled away the small cage with the cat inside into the bushes next to the road.

XXII

*An Account of another unforeseen Visitor
arriving at the de la Bat Household in Worcester, where he
encounters a Philida he has very clearly not expected*

Just under two months later, they received another visit,
this time even more unexpected than when Francois showed
up. Because on this occasion it turns out to be, of all people,
Cornelis Brink. We do know that very soon after Francois's
visit he ran into Daniel Fredrik Berrangé in Stellenbosch,
when Cornelis went to deliver a stuckvat to someone in the
district; Berrangé had come to discuss with the Slave
Protector the punishment of a slave for his cheekiness: with
the emancipation of the slaves at hand it was getting impossible to keep many of them under control. They met in the
home of a mutual friend in the Church Street, enjoyed a
few glasses of wine together, and used the opportunity to
exchange some thoughts on the prospects of their children,
Francois Gerhard Jacob and Maria Magdalena. For Cornelis
it would no doubt have come as a shock to learn that Maria
had already heard about Francois's visit to Worcester, news
had an amazing way of travelling through the Colony. The
story had undergone quite a transformation in the process
and the impression was created that the young Brink had
secretly tried to look up his old love.

Impossible, Cornelis retorted in indignation. I know my
son, and I know your Maria is the only woman he ever
thinks about. That slave *meid* has never meant anything to

him. He was just a boy with red shins when the thing started and you know how we all were when we were young and didn't know any better.

That is not my understanding of the matter, Berrangé replied. According to me – he and his family were still very Dutch in their habits and ways of thinking, and in most discussions he would invariably open his argument with *According to me* – Francois is still infatuated with that slave girl Philida and barely even notices any other female around. And rumour has it the two already have a barnful of offspring. What father of a nubile daughter could stomach a thing like that?

Slander! Cornelis shouted. You know how envy and jealousy get out of hand in this Caab of ours. The moment the children get married and settle down, all the stories will be forgotten. That's what happened to you and me too.

For you perhaps, Berrangé replied haughtily. In my case such lies were never spread. I have always been most scrupulous in my behaviour.

Before they knew where they were it was a full-fledged quarrel. Cornelis could already see all the arrangements made in the wake of the auction blowing up in their faces. No wonder he now decided it was his turn to go to Worcester. But it was not just a matter of saddling his horse and galloping off. Cornelis was a busy man, especially with all the new schemes he had set in motion after the auction, and there were many decisions to be taken.

But at last, in the dark predawn of a Wednesday morning, Cornelis sets off, once again in the mule cart, driven by one of his skilled slaves, Slembang of Batavia. The road is long, as always, and there is enough, too much, to think about. Perhaps he's acted too hastily, he thinks. But what was there he could really have done about the case? Philida has been sold upcountry. Francois is at Zandvliet. Maria Magdalena is in the Caab with her parents. And God alone knows what will happen next.

His head feels thick to bursting with thoughts, but it makes no difference to the tightness inside him. Shouldn't he just turn back? But whatever may lie ahead, returning to Zandvliet can only make it worse. He spurs on the mules. As far as Paarl the road is relatively easy. But beyond, where one has to pick one's way through Du Toit's Kloof down to the Breede Valley, one has to be very careful, past old Schonfeld's tollgate and the Clay Hole where Cornelis is forced to get off several times to help the mules. Even then it's hair-raising and more than once the wheels of the cart very nearly slide over the edge into the abyss.

In Worcester, where he arrives the next day, he is announced very politely at Meester de la Bat's office in the Drostdy. The tall thin man with the pointed Adam's apple, who now looks even more like a scarecrow, welcomes him at the door with outstretched hand.

Mijnheer Brink, he says. A pleasure and a privilege. To what do I owe the honour of your visit?

I have an important matter to discuss with the slave girl Philida, says Cornelis, feeling terribly ill at ease in the man's company. His whole prepared speech has dried up in his parched mouth.

I hope it isn't illness or death? asks Bernabé de la Bat.

No, no. It is much more serious.

Then it must be very bad. Shall I accompany you to my house?

Over the last stretch Cornelis feels as if he is on his way to his own funeral.

At Meester de la Bat's house the homeowner invites him to sit in the *voorhuis*; his wife appears to greet the visitor, half suspicious, half inquisitive, and quickly leaves again to fetch tea in spite of his protests – these people prefer tea to the potent bitter root brew that here in the interior passes for coffee – to hear Cornelis's unexpected story.

By the time she returns with the tray Meester de la Bat has already enquired about the business that has made him come so far.

Actually, he has come to see Philida, Cornelis explains again, embarrassed. He starts in a very long-winded way as is his wont, by asking about the slave woman's health.

For that, says de la Bat, you should ask my wife. It is for her that I bought the *meid*.

We don't have any complaints, Anna Catherina says laconically. Nor does she have any, I should think. She is the best knitting girl I have ever had. Nowadays she is giving rather a lot of time to knitting the baby's and children's clothes, but that doesn't interfere much with her other work, so I'm not complaining.

This Philida, says the Meester, is doing such good work that we have started hiring her out to other people too. In that way she earns a few pennies which she can put away for next year, when the slaves are freed. We don't want her to end up on the street.

That won't happen anyway, says Cornelis. If I got it right, the slaves will stay booked in for another four years.

Exactly, confirms de la Bat. But one has to make provision, not so? Otherwise they end up with nothing, and you can imagine for yourself what will happen in the Colony after that. He gets up. But let me go and call her, Mijnheer Brink, then you can speak to her yourself.

A few minutes later Philida returns to the *voorhuis* with a half-finished piece of multicoloured knitted baby clothing hanging from two ivory needles in her hands. She is wearing a faded green dress, a doek and a red-chequered shawl over her shoulders. From her doek protrudes a fringe of her dark hair. And of course she is barefoot, as behoves a slave.

She looks flustered. And before she has crossed the threshold she asks, What's the matter? What has happened?

Nothing has happened, says Cornelis curtly. I've come about what may still be happening.

What is that?

It looks as if my son Francois may not get married after all.

Philida draws in her breath deeply and very slowly. Then she asks, What's that got to do with me?

If he doesn't marry Maria Magdalena Berrangé we'll all be down the drain. His face flushes a very deep red. And then it'll be all your fault, Philida.

You come all this way from Zandvliet to tell me that?

It's very serious, Philida. You've got to come back to Zandvliet with me. You've got to talk some sense into Frans. He will listen to you if you tell it to him yourself. Afterwards I'll bring you back here again. Or if you prefer, I can buy you back.

That is not what he has meant to say. But now that it has come so far there is no turning back.

You must be mad in your head, she says very quickly.

Philida, please think about it. You don't know what you're holding in your hands today. It's all our lives. We've made a hell of a mistake, man. You must go with me and help me to make Frans understand reason.

You know it's not about Frans. It's not even about the Berrangés. It's all about yourself. You want to make me kneel in the bamboo copse again, and that I'm not doing. Not for you and not for nobody. They say that next year in December I'll be free. But here inside me I'm already free.

It's no longer for you to say do this or do that. You understand that, Oubaas?!

Please, Philida. For God's sake, please!

What use will my talking be? she asks shrilly. It's you, the white people, who tell us what to do. But now we saying no.

I'm talking to you about my whole family, Philida. About our future. So it's about your own future too. I'll make it worth your while, I promise you, I swear.

That's what Frans also said to me when he tried to make me lie with him the first time. *I shall make it worthwhile for you, Philida. I shall make you free.*

Don't you understand? he asks in a rage.

No, I don't understand. I understand nothing about you people. When you want to use me, I got to kneel before you. But today your balls are hanging in the sand, so now suddenly you want me to help you?

The words break out of her: I swear to you today, Ouman, I swear to Al-lah!

You swear to what? He gawks at her. For a long time he cannot utter a word. At long last he manages to force it through clenched lips: I can see what is happening here. You've landed among the heathens here. Look, I want to bring you back home so that you can live among Christian people the way you were used to, the way we brought you up. We want to save your soul!

Why you suddenly care about my soul? Here in this place I got to know Labyn. He taught me different.

Who is this Labyn?

He is a slave like me. But on the first of December next year we shall both be free, that is what he tell me.

What shit are you talking, Philida? What kind of a man is that Labyn? What kind of a weed in our garden?

Labyn is a Slams. I am with the Slamse now.

Cornelis gasps for breath. Philida, you got mixed up with the Slamse now? That will take you straight to hell.

I will rather burn in hell than sit in your *voorhuis* again with my back to the wall when you open your big black book in the evening to read all the names and things. And as soon as you finish reading it's back to the bamboos and you know it. You know that book better than the bamboo place. What you don't know is that the Slamse people got their own Book. His name is Korhaan. And he don't talk to white people and shit. He talk to *us*.

I don't know what to say to you any more, Philida.

Then don't say it. I hear and see enough of you Christian lot. I got nothing more to do with you.

Does Meester de la Bat know about this shit you're talking?

I don't care if he know or not. My shit is my own and my soul is my own.

Somewhere along the road you lost your way.

Look here, Ouman. She holds up her hand when he tries to interrupt. Look here, she says again. I'm not clever like you. Right now I'm just learning from Labyn. I still got a lot to learn. But all I know is that I want to be with the Slamse, that's where I belong. You Christians treat me like dirt.

Cornelis shakes his head. I told you I don't understand you any more. Philida.

You never understand me, Ouman. It always just been you, you, you.

A strange wailing sound slides into his voice. Today I'm on my knees before you, Philida.

You used to make me kneel on mine. Now it's your turn, Ouman.

This is when he surprises her. Slowly and laboriously he

· 231 ·

goes down on his knees, breathing heavily through his mouth. Philida, look at me! What must become of me!

She does not even try to answer. With the half-knitted baby cardigan in her hands — in many colours, red and white and yellow and green and blue — she turns round and goes to the kitchen.

Cornelis slouches back to the front stoep, where he finds de la Bat.

I'd better be going again, he says. That one won't understand reason.

You cannot go back like that, Oom! protests Meester de la Bat. You're no longer a young man. At least stay over for the night. Things may look better in the morning.

Cornelis still considers for a while before he reluctantly decides to accept the invitation. But he withdraws quickly into the bedroom assigned to him, keeping the shutters closed, and only ventures outside in the late afternoon again — just in time to see Philida coming past. It doesn't look as if she has noticed him. Perhaps she doesn't want to.

At the back of the house she goes to Labyn's workroom. He's busy with his wood. Today, as so often in recent weeks, it is a coffin. Smooth pale panels, with fine stinkwood struts in between. Too beautiful, really, to be buried in the earth.

He glances up and goes on with his work.

Who was that man? he asks when she says nothing.

He used to be my Baas, says Philida. It's he who bring me to the auction.

There's many people who churn up a lot of dust these days coming after you.

They want me to go back.

And?

I'm staying right here. This is my place now.

What did he say about that?

· 232 ·

Said I must move back to live with Christian people.

Labyn sniffs, but says nothing.

I tell him I'm with the Slamse people now. That's what I decided. I want you to tell Al-lah that when you see him again.

Inshallah, says Labyn and goes on smoothing one of the darker struts between the pale panels.

Another silence. At the best of times Labyn doesn't say much.

Now you got to help me, says Philida. I want to know more about this Islam of yours. I want to know what I'm doing here with you.

He gives a crooked smile, but she can see his eyes shining. I shall tell you everything I know, he promises. The Koran says, *Some of us are Muslims and some are wrongdoers. Those that embraced Islam pursue the right path; but those that do wrong shall become the fuel of hell.*

And as always, these first words open the roads to more. It is as if the smooth dark wood in his hands brings to life something inside him. He says: *Consider the water which you drink. Was it you that poured it from the cloud or we? If We pleased We could have turned it bitter. Why then do you not give thanks?* Always remember this, Philida: *Indeed, Al-lah does not need you, but you need him. If you give no heed, he will replace you by others different from you.* Whatever happens, remember what I tell you: *Your God is one God. There is no God but him. He is the Compassionate, the Merciful.*

And then he says: If you wish, we can start with your lessons again tonight.

XXIII

*In which two more Visits to the de la Bats
in Worcester are narrated, both of which will have long-term
Consequences for Everybody involved*

Around the time of that unexpected visit two more visitors turn up at the de la Bats' home in the Church Street in Worcester. On both occasions the visitors come to stay. The first, quite out of the blue, only a few days after Francois Brink rode off, is Kleinkat.

She looks a bit dishevelled, somewhat rough at the edges, rather thin and clearly hungry, but her paws do not look worn. Because this occurs quite soon after Francois's departure, the de la Bats come to the conclusion that the cat must have run away very soon after she'd left Worcester. Philida, who has had a very good look at her and discovered that her face around the mouth looks chafed and bloody, concludes that she must have struggled pretty fiercely to get out of the bamboo cage and most probably chewed her way through the thin slats. But she was not badly hurt. The only thing that rather surprises Philida, even though it is also cause for relief, is that she hasn't chosen to escape to Zandvliet like the previous time, but decided to take the short cut to Worcester. Presumably Kleinkat has decided, after all her tribulations, that her real home is with Philida after all. And the slave woman welcomes the cat like a prodigal child from the Bible. She caresses her behind the ears and smells her feet and rubs her cheeks against the little pointed face and kisses her on the nose. And Kleinkat chirrups like a bird and quietly revels in Philida's caresses as if her whole small life has briefly become concentrated on this moment of warmth and safety and pure bliss.

Philida has a bad fright on the day Cornelis comes to visit, for her first thought is that he has come to claim the cat again. But she quickly realises that something so ordinary would never have upset the old man so much. Even so, as a precaution she locks up the cat in the room she shares with Delphina and keeps her there for a few days. But she soon finds that there is no need to get so upset, and from then on she does not worry about Kleinkat any more, and she and Delphina, and the children, become inseparable from the cat.

The second visitor is of an entirely different kind. His name is Floris and it turns out that he is a slave who previously belonged to Meester de la Bat, a man of forty or thereabouts, who absconded from Worcester about a year before and, when he couldn't be found again, was completely written off by the de la Bat family. He has now unexpectedly decided to come back of his own accord.

It is late on a Wednesday afternoon, when the sun is already sinking, that he turns up at the back gate to the property, a greyish man covered by what seems like weeks of dust, wearing a cap of dassie skins with a sprig of rosemary on top, a long buttonless shirt and a chameleon on his right shoulder. He is clearly exhausted and grey with hunger, yet there is an irrepressible spring in his step. When Delphina comes from the back door to offer him a bowl of water, he starts gulping it down like a horse. Afterwards he goes into the kitchen uninvited – which makes Philida realise that he is familiar with the place, that he belongs there – and dunks his whole head into the washing barrel, keeping it under water for so long that Philida begins to fear that he may never come up for air again, then shakes off the excess water like a frisky dog with an exuberant shout: Yooohooo!

The noise attracts the two bull mastiffs from the *voorhuis*, and they tumble over each other to get to him first, and for a moment Philida, not knowing how they will react to a stranger, fears that they may tear him to shreds right there.

Labyn! she shouts. Here's trouble! Come and help!

Labyn jumps up from his workbench where he is putting together a delicate table standing like a small steenbok on tall thin legs. But to Philida's amazement he gives a broad grin, like a rising sun. She sees the two large dogs charging towards the visitor in a tumult of barking and taking a flying leap at him. Instinctively she closes her eyes. But when she dares to look again, she sees the stranger on his knees, exuberantly fondling the dogs as they both dance around him to lick his face from all sides.

Just then Meester de la Bat makes his appearance like a large black bat with folded wings.

He stops on the threshold. Floris . . .? he asks.

Meester, he says, here I am. I been walking all over the place and now I got home again. You can go and fetch the *riem* and give me a proper hiding because I got a lot to talk about. But we can only talk after you beat the shit out of me.

This leads to a long discussion, as Meester de la Bat is thrown quite off balance by Floris's return, but the runaway insists he can only talk after all the formalities have been complied with – and that will only be possible once he has had his prescribed punishment. In the past this used to be completely in the hands of the Baas, but ever since the English took over there has been a rule and a regulation for every damn thing.

We can talk about it tomorrow, says Meester de la Bat.

If it's all the same to Meester, I'd rather get it over and done with straight away, says Floris, meek but adamant.

All right, then come with me, says de la Bat with a sigh. I don't like it but the law is the law.

Is what I also say, Floris agrees.

They go round the house in the direction of Labyn's workroom at the back, followed by the others. Labyn and Floris move the heavy workbench into the backyard. Only now does Philida realise that the workbench is also the flogging bench and that all the brown stains on the surface must be old blood. Low down on each of the massive legs are rusty iron rings to which Meester de la Bat and Labyn are now preparing to attach Floris with thongs from the stable.

Lie down, orders Meester de la Bat. Floris removes the chameleon from his right shoulder, and stands looking around him for a moment.

You come and take this, he tells Philida. Will you keep him for me?

Won't the thing bite? she asks hesitantly.

No, he's used to people, man. Just hold him gently so that you don't scare him.

She gingerly takes the chameleon from him, still not quite reassured. So far, she has cautiously kept away from the little creature because of Ouma Nella's persistent warnings over the years: You better watch your step with this thing, my child, he brings death with him.

Philida stands a few steps aside. Lena approaches with

great caution to see better, but keeps ready to scamper off as the chameleon turns his big eyes in her direction.

Delphina helps Floris to take off his long loose shirt. Then the breeches that reach down to his knees. His entire back and lean buttocks bear the dark criss-cross marks of old floggings. It is clearly not the first time Floris has had a run-in with the law. He tries to find a comfortable position on the flogging bench, on his stomach, letting his arms hang down the sides of the heavy bench. Meester de la Bat goes down on his heels to attach the wrists to the rings on the side. As he struggles laboriously his pale face flushes a deep red from the effort. Once he is satisfied that the arms are firmly attached, Meester de la Bat gets up again to take the two remaining thongs from Labyn. Floris's thin ankles barely reach the foot end of the bench.

Help me, orders the Meester as he passes one thong up to Labyn while he pulls the second one tight around Floris's left ankle, closest to him. Now tie it properly, he orders.

But Labyn turns out to be very reluctant. He makes no attempt to come closer and take the thong.

Meester de la Bat looks at him with a frown. What's up with you now? he asks irritably.

I am sorry, Meester, Labyn says with tight lips. But I cannot help you with this thing. Floris and I come a long way together. He is my friend and I am his.

And if I order you to beat him?

Labyn shakes his head. Then I shall have to say no to the Meester. That is not my work.

You are a slave, Labyn. You will do what I tell you to do.

Not if Meester asks me to beat him.

Labyn?!

I think it is against the law nowadays, Labyn says quietly.

In this place *I* am the law, says the Meester through his teeth. You are a slave like Floris.

In a month, in a few months, we shall both be free.

Until that time you will do what I say.

I am sorry, Meester, Labyn says very calmly. I told you: not if you ask me to beat him.

Floris ran away, the Meester says curtly. A year ago he absconded from Worcester. The law is very strict about desertion.

He came back of his own free will.

He stayed away for a full year.

That doesn't make a difference. Now he is here.

Do as I tell you, Labyn!

Al-lah will hear about this, says Labyn, more to himself than to the Meester, and very calmly and politely.

What do you say?

I'm just saying about Al-lah, Meester. He sees everything and he knows everything and he will not like this.

I have the LordGod on my side! shouts Meester de la Bat, more furiously than anyone has ever heard him. Some of the children who are watching from a distance with wide eyes, start crying.

Then bring your LordGod, Meester, says Labyn. I shall call Al-lah. They can fight it out. In his quiet way Labyn adds, He is the God of all the slaves and all the oppressed people in this land, so I already know who will win.

Now you are looking for trouble! snarls the Meester.

Conceived and born in sin, Meester, says Labyn. Made like that and left like that. All of us, Baas and slave.

Meester de la Bat mumbles something, but no one can make out what it is. After a moment he marches back to the house in a military manner. But at the back door he looks round: You can lie and wait here, he tells Floris. I shall come back when it suits me. He firmly pulls the door to after him.

For some time no one says a word. It is as if they're all waiting for him to come back, but the door remains closed.

I think we got a long night ahead, Delphina says at last.

Then why don't we just sit and make ourselves comfortable? asks Labyn.

What do I do with the chameleon? asks Philida.

Just keep him with you, says Floris from the flogging bench without turning his head. Find a place to sit so long.

Now it is in Al-lah's hands, Labyn says, resigned to his fate.

Philida comes to put a hand on Floris's bare shoulder. Can I bring you some water? I can see you brought a big tiredness with you.

Yes, thank you, he says. That will help.

They make themselves comfortable around the flogging bench.

Delphina was clearly right. It is going to be a long night. As the sun goes down in a big show of red, the huge moon appears in the east, like a cow bladder bleeding against the sky. The air smells of khaki weeds and bruised grass. The first stars appear. The night spreads itself in all directions.

In the beginning there isn't much talk, but as it grows darker the words find their way more easily.

You must tell us about the Gariep, says Labyn.

That Gariep is a different kind of place, begins Floris with a small grey chuckle. You won't think there can be so many people living on an open plain. And of all sorts too, from the preachers and baptisers of Al-lah and the LordGod to runaways and murderers and robbers, everybody. There are deserters and free people among them, black and brown and yellow and white, all the colours under the sun and moon and stars, and in a way they all live happily together. The people of that place, the Griquas, make sure that they more or less keep the peace. And there's talking like you cannot believe, day and night. Sometimes they talk about war too, but most of the people are not looking for trouble. As long as they keep the Gariep between themselves and the Colony, everybody is satisfied. Many of them have started farming already. It's a dry world, but close to the Gariep there are green fields. And there's more than enough grazing for cattle and sheep and goats.

If it goes so well, says Labyn, then why did you come back? It sounds like a good place to stay for the rest of your life.

To stay, yes, Floris agrees. And that was what I also wanted to do. Even took myself a wife. She was a good woman, and good to look at too. He gives a soft groan and turns his head away. But then she got sick and she died, and the Gariep is a place without mercy for a man on his own. That's why I thought I must rather go back to where I come from. One of these days they going to let us go anyway, then I'll stay here for the four years the Meester will still take care of me, and afterwards I can think again. It's bad when a man got no woman with him. It's bad, I tell you. It's bad shit all the way.

After Floris has spoken, it's his turn to ask them about their own lives. And as the conversation wanders along, the sky goes on wheeling overhead with its stars, big and small, like a slow dust-devil that refuses to be hurried on its way.

From all the talking stories gradually emerge. This is how it has always gone on this farmyard and all the other farmyards in this land-without-end. It is Floris who begins, telling the story of how the chameleon was born: how he had no father, but two mothers, the moon and the rainbow, and how he was born before there were any people in the world. The moon gave him light on his way – because he was so slow he never needed much light to see by – and the rainbow knitted a little coat for him that helped him to change colour all the time, so that one couldn't see him easily. Only the sun got very grumpy and kept out of the way whenever the moon or the rainbow was around. And that, says Floris, is why he used to keep the little one under his shirt or somewhere out of reach of the sun, so that he wouldn't be scorched to death.

Philida keeps asking Floris questions about the small creature, and his stories grow more and more wonderful. This little man has come a hell of a long way with me, he tells her. I found him when I was still on my way to the Gariep, or perhaps it was he who found me, in a thin little stream with thorn bushes on both sides.

And weren't you scared to bring him with you? asks Philida.

No, why should I be?

My Ouma Nella always say I must watch out for them, for they bring death.

Ag, no, he's a good little man, his eyes see everything and if there's any trouble on the way, he always tells me about it long before it comes.

Somewhere during the long night, after Philida has brought out her breast once again to nurse Willempie, she drifts off from pure tiredness while the stories are still running into one another like strands of wool in a loose piece of knitting, and only at the first light of the new day does she wake up again from a giggling and scurrying all around and over her. It's the children, she discovers, who are watching Kleinkat playing with the chameleon that has come to hide in the crook of her arm. He is sitting there without making a sound, his mouth wide open, hissing, while the cat flips him upside down and rolls him to and fro to get to him with her small sharp teeth.

Stop it! cries Philida, grabbing the cat behind its neck. What are you doing?

Kleinkat tries to wriggle herself loose, but Philida holds on. Only when the cat begins to calm down in her grip does she relax and sit up.

Now you listen to me, she tells the cat very sternly. He is my new little friend and you're going to let him be. Do you understand what I'm saying?

Kleinkat hisses and forms a small, deep growl in her throat. Philida tightens her grasp again and lightly shakes her.

I say, do you hear me? Are you listening?

Another muttering of protest.

No, I want an answer from you. I won't have what you're doing. You not touching this chameleon, you hear? Not today, and never again. He's mine, Kleinkat. Do we understand one another?

For a moment it is very quiet. Then the cat stops fidgeting. With her grass-green eyes she looks up at Philida and makes a curious little chirping sound Philida has not heard before, like a small bird.

So, do you agree?

Once more Kleinkat utters the small sound.

All right, says Philida, then you may go. But from now on you let him be. Otherwise I'm sending you back to Frans.

The cat turns on her back and starts purring softly in her lap. Philida lets her go. Kleinkat gently crawls over Philida's thigh, stretches her neck forward, sniffs at the chameleon, then steps lightly over him, jumps down to the ground and goes her way.

It is the last time Philida will ever have any trouble with the small grey cat.

The encounter with the cat turns into a long game of teasing and giggling among the children, before it is time for a new story. And then another. And then Philida brings a new bowl of water for Floris, followed by still others, and Floris resumes his account of the Gariep and its people. He talks about crooks and *skelms*, about women who can knock you down with one blow of a fist, and men who can swallow live fire. He tells them about Griqua captains like Adam Kok and Willem Waterboer, he drops the names of a Jan Bloem and a Jager Afrikaner and one Stephanos, and his stories become so vivid that Philida can no longer make out whether the people are still around or long dead, as in his tales they are all so very much alive that they sound like his close friends. Not that it matters much, as he doesn't bother to make any distinction between the living and the dead, between night walkers and day walkers. He tells them about Griquas and Tswanas and Korannas, about missionaries and murderers. Every time when it seems he is getting too tired to go on, he begins with something new. And then some more. After which Philida goes to fetch a new bowl of water for Floris, and another. His speech gets slower, and the stories creep on like a row of chameleons, the stars of the Milky Way glide past them overhead and slowly the darkness turns more grey and a red smudge stains the underside of the sky, and here and there cocks start to crow and a new day begins.

The groans that come from Floris become deeper and darker as his body grows more weary and aching from lying stretched out like that, but at last that, too, is over. From time to time Philida offers her baby a breast, until she finally gets up to prepare him for the day. Delphina goes to the kitchen to make coffee and stoke the fire in the hearth. Afterwards the dough that has been left against the back wall of the hearth, and has risen over the tops of the long pans, is stacked in the oven, and the small door is pushed shut and smeared with cow dung, and everywhere around them cows begin to low and dogs are barking, and men stagger out in backyards with stiff legs to piss in foaming puddles, and before one knows where one is it is high day.

About that time Meester de la Bat emerges from his back door. He has a vicious-looking long sjambok in his hand with which he gives brief slaps against the black legs of his breeches, sending small puffs of dust up around him.

Morning, Floris, he grunts.

Morning, Meester, the man groans.

Slept well? asks the Baas.

Not really, Meester.

Are you ready for me?

Ready for Meester.

Meester de la Bat puts his long white hands with the knobbly knuckles on his hips, and asks: Where is Labyn?

Meester, I am here.

You can untie him now, says de la Bat with a small nervous grin towards Labyn. I think he's had enough of a scare.

Later, in the kitchen, while Philida is bustling about, the Meester comes in from outside and she overhears him saying contentedly to his wife Anna: It's important for a slave to be reminded regularly of who is the Baas.

Yes, Bernabé, she says meekly. As you wish.

Bring me my coffee, he says.

XXIV

The Narrative of what may be a Chapter from the Kind of Romance that was not uncommon at the Time of our Story, even though it may not be unequivocally happy

Only a day after Cornelis Brink has returned to Zandvliet from Worcester – his back aching, his rump raw from the long ride and in agony from the gland that gives him hell – he summons the whole family to report back. Janna is there, of course, draped over the full extent of the couch, and then the remaining children.

It is time for us to talk, announces Cornelis.

Complete silence, but all eyes are on him, both curious and in dread. With a father like this one can never be too complacent.

I have been to Worcester, says Cornelis.

Did Pa go to the de la Bats? asks Daniel.

Yes, I saw them.

Alida asks very quickly, Did Pa see Philida? When is she coming home?

She is not coming back, Cornelis says. She has no wish to leave from where she is.

But I miss her, wails Alida. It isn't nice to be on the farm when she isn't here. And I could do with a new cardigan.

We are getting on very well without her, sneers Janna from the couch; its legs creak in protest.

I don't know anyone who can knit like her, ventures Maria Elisabet.

Then why did she leave? Janna asks moodily. She must have known that we need her. But she always thought only about herself.

It wasn't her fault, Ma, says Maria Elisabet. What say did she have? Pa and Frans decided she had to go, so she had to go. I don't think they gave her any choice.

You watch out, warns Cornelis. I can see that backside of yours is itching to be tanned.

Well, I wish she can come back, says Alida. Did Pa tell her we'd like her to come home?

I said nothing to nobody. I won't allow that *meid* to set foot here again. She no longer belongs with decent Christian people.

How can Pa say a thing like that? asks Francois unexpectedly.

Philida went over to the Slamse, snaps Cornelis. She is with the heathens and unbelievers now.

I don't believe that, Pa!

I have said what I wanted to say, says Cornelis. What that means is that the road to Maria Berrangé is now open. For all of us, and that includes you. You better start moving your arse.

He was expecting Frans to object, but to his surprise his son seems unexpectedly amenable, as if for the first time he is beginning to understand reason.

I've begun to think, he says, that Maria Berrangé may not be such a bad idea. I've noticed that she has fine ankles.

What has that got to do with it? Janna asks indignantly, moving her massive legs on the sofa. Her feet protrude like two well-risen loaves. She adds: Her looks have nothing to do with it. What matters is what she *does*.

And if she can breed, says Cornelis. That, at least, the Berrangés can do. Seven sons and seven daughters.

One needs something for the eye too, says Francois. And

for the hand. He shakes his head. But don't get in too much of a hurry. I'll have to sound her out first. And I've heard she's not an easy one. She's choosy.

As long as you make a move soon, says Cornelis. That auction was a bad blow to us. Without you we'll never get out of the shit properly.

I promise Pa I'll do my best.

And just over a week later Francois makes his appearance under the high front stoep of the big house below the slope of Oranjezicht in the Caab. He has brought an anchor of his father's red wine for Berrangé, and a jar of green-fig preserve for the lady of the house. For Maria he has a small sewing box he has made himself, with a delicate inlaid pattern on the lid.

I never thought I'd see you again, she says when she is called from her room to greet the visitor. She is wearing a yellowish, oldish dress and the bands of her embroidered bodice are only loosely tied. Also, she is barefoot. The expression on her mother's face makes it clear that this is not how Vrouw Berrangé likes to see her daughter — at any rate not in front of guests. But Maria has turned her head away, clearly deliberately. It's only when she discovers who the guest is that one can see she has no wish to be here at all. She half turns away towards her room, but Francois says quickly:

Afternoon, Maria.

She remains standing.

Perhaps you should first go and make yourself decent for visitors, her mother says.

It's not visitors, Ma, says Maria. Ma can see it's only Francois Brink.

He is not yet family, Maria. It's not fit for you to appear naked in company.

It's just my feet, Ma. She cheekily pulls up the yellow-brown dress almost to her knees. (Lovely calves, Francois notices. And yes, those delicate ankles. He thinks: Not such a bad idea indeed.)

Maria! Vrouw Berrangé says tartly. You will really make me grey.

Not just her ankles, indeed, decides Francois. He gazes unabashedly at her and takes in the deep blue of her eyes, the slight hint of moisture on her lips and the way her long dark hair is swept back from her forehead, and notices, too, the swelling of her breasts thrust against the striped dress from the inside and the graceful curve of her hips.

It feels as if he has never properly noticed her before.

To your room, says her indignant mother. She turns towards Francois, her face flushed. Please wait a moment. And Francois, please forgive what you have just seen. We're not always like that.

A few difficult minutes creep past before Maria reappears in proper boots.

You can make us some coffee, orders Vrouw Magdalena Berrangé. Maria throws back her long hair. But she goes to the kitchen without another word of protest. In uneasy silence Francois and the mother of the house remain waiting until her daughter returns, followed by a slave woman with coffee cups, a bowl of aniseed rusks and a deep plate with wild-melon preserve on a large yellowwood tray. Afterwards the slave remains standing behind Tant Magdalena's chair until such time as her services may again be required. A few of the other Berrangé children arrive to join them.

Francois has of course been here before. Before the Brinks moved away to Drakenstein, to Zandvliet, the children regularly came over to play and cavort in the loquat trees or in the barn or in the wide Oranje Street below the house. But since Francois's father and mother have first come to discuss their son's future with Maria's parents the children have become more distant and more self-conscious and today is the first time in a long while that Francois has set foot in the house.

In wooden silence everybody eats and drinks. Beside the long low coffee table a naked slave boy stands with a fan of ostrich feathers on a long bamboo which he waves to keep away the flies. One can see that he is tired – he must have been chasing flies since early morning – but on his buttocks is a pattern of dark lines from a previous hiding which must be the reason why he goes on waving the feathered bamboo so energetically with his thin arms to keep the flies at bay, to and fro, to and fro, to and fro.

Only after the coffee ceremony does Vrouw Berrangé get up. I suppose you two still have something to discuss, she says to Maria, but without looking at Francois. Why don't you go into the garden if it's too stuffy inside? He knows that this is just because he is a familiar visitor; otherwise a few of the younger children would no doubt have been sent to accompany them.

The slave girl carries the tray back to the kitchen; the children silently disperse into the house; only the naked boy remains to wave and wave his large fan of plumes. Maria keeps watching him for a while, as if she hasn't noticed him before. He seems to become conscious of her stare and moves his feet to turn his back. A slow smile tugs at Maria's full mouth.

You may also go, Jantjie, she says to the boy.

He scurries out.

Maria moves her head to look at Francois. He self-consciously looks away.

Did you see? she asks deliberately.

Did I see what?

That slave boy is growing up fast. Soon he'll be a handful.

I didn't notice, says Francois gruffly.

Would you like to go into the garden?

If you want to. He gets up and lets her walk ahead of him, so that he can look at the graceful sweep of her long skirt.

It's a long time since you've been here, she says when they come outside.

We're kept busy at Zandvliet.

With what?

You should know. I got to help Pa on the farm.

And is that the only reason?

What else could it be?

I started thinking that you had somebody else in the eye.

He nearly misses a step. Like who?

She doesn't answer. Instead, she asks in her disconcertingly direct way: What is it you want of me?

Francois thinks fast, then says: I want to ask you something. It's an invitation.

And what is that?

You must come to visit us at Zandvliet again, he says. I'd like to show you the vineyards now that the summer grapes are beginning to swell. And I want you to see the bamboo copse. It is a beautiful and shady place in this hot weather.

Who says I want to see it? she says.

If you've seen it once you will know what I'm talking about. And then you'll want to see it again.

I wonder to how many people you've already shown your bamboo copse, she says.

He feels flustered, but tries to pull himself together. To nobody, he says, trying urgently to believe his own assurance. You are the only one I've always waited to show it to.

I have something to tell you too, she says.

And what is that?

I heard about the slave Philida, Maria says very calmly.

There's nothing to know about her.

They say you have children.

Maria! He indignantly pulls up his head, but the young woman does not look back at him.

If you have any plans with her, she says, flowing gracefully down the steps into the garden, you'd do well to stay away from me.

He feels his face glowing, but does his best to control it. This is the Caab, Maria! You know what things are like here.

You're making as if that is something very common!

Well, it is. It happens on all the farms.

I don't believe you, Frans.

Surely you cannot pretend to be shocked about it, Maria!

Of course I am. And if you think we can be married while you – We can't have something like this standing between us.

Whatever you may think happened between me and that slave Philida has been over for a long time now.

You may just as well be honest with me, Frans. Or do you think it's good for a husband and a wife to have silences between them?

You're not supposed to know about such things, he protests.

I have a father, she says calmly. I have brothers. I don't want my husband to be like them one day.

I won't! he promises precipitously. I swear!

Swearing is against the Bible, she says. And she turns round to face him squarely. All I'm telling you, Francois Brink, if you want to marry me, then you will have to stay

with me for the rest of your life. I won't share my husband.
Once we're married I don't want slave women in my bed.

If we get married, I shall stay with you. And with no one
else.

And this Philida? And her children?

They are already gone. Into the interior.

You went to visit them in Worcester the other day.

How do you know that? he asks.

A woman knows these things. Her voice grows more
vehement: My mother has fourteen children. That doesn't
mean that she doesn't know.

Francois hangs his head. Maria, I promise you –

Don't start promising me things. You'll first have to *prove*
to me that I can trust you.

I swear –

She presses a forefinger to his lips, so hard that it bruises
them. Don't swear to me, Frans! And after a silence she
adds: All you need to do is to *prove* what you said. Once
you've done that we can talk again. Otherwise you'll stay
at Zandvliet and I'll stay right here.

How can I make you believe?

There's no need ever to *make* me believe. Just make sure
you don't betray me. Because I shall know.

All I'm asking is for you to give me a chance.

I'll give you enough of a chance. But I tell you before
God: I shall know. And if I find out that you have lied
to me, it will be better for you never to come here again.

You can believe me, Maria.

Have you seen what they do to a young bullock?

Involuntarily he presses his knees together.

You will miss your balls, Frans. But then it'll be too late.

He doesn't know why he should think of a thing like
that now, but he says: You mustn't think I didn't notice!

Notice what?

It flusters him, but it also makes him angry: The way you looked at that slave boy in the *voorhuis*.

What are you talking about, Frans?

You're not the only one who can look where your eyes don't belong, he says.

Unflinching, she looks him straight in the face: That's the only way I can find out about things. And that's why I'm telling you to watch out. Because I shall know exactly what you're doing or what you're trying to do.

I tell you I won't try anything.

That is something only you can decide. I already told you what will happen to you if you lie.

If you marry me –

If I marry you, your eyes and your thing will stay at home. I don't want any Philidas in my home. And I don't want to bring up another woman's children like my mother did.

You can trust me, Maria.

Then it will be all right. You can go back to your Zandvliet now. Use the chance and think about it. And when you come back you can tell me.

I can come back tomorrow, Maria.

She gives a laugh. No, not tomorrow. That is too soon. I'll give you a chance. I'll give you a year. Then you can come and tell me. And then you will do as you said.

But a year?! Do you know how long a year is?

I know exactly. And I'm not a child any more. I am twenty-seven. I've been waiting long enough. But I refuse to be hurried.

After a long silence he pulls his breath in deeply and slowly. Then he says: All right, if that is how you want it.

I do. Because I have to make dead sure.

I give you my word.

I'm not all that eager to take a man's word. But if you can wait for a year and I can see that you mean what you said, then I shall give you my answer.

But Maria!

I don't want any But Maria, Frans. If you prefer, you can turn round right now and go home. I won't blame you, because you're a man. But if you come back in a year and give me your word once again, then I may believe you. She calmly looks him in the eyes. And Maria Berrangé says: Then you can do with me what you want, Francois Gerhard Jacob Brink. And then I may want to do it with you.

She turns away quickly, back to the house. But halfway up the garden path she looks back over her shoulder, drops both hands and picks up her dress by the seam of her skirt and briefly lifts it up to her knees. Just a moment, then she drops it back. Over her right shoulder her teasing eyes look back at him. Without knowing why, something in her gesture makes him feel unbearably sad.

When he gets onto his horse soon afterwards, what amazes him is that it is not Maria who keeps coming back into his head, not even her ankles. What does return to his mind, over and over, is a name. Philida. Just that: Philida.

But it is different from other times. The name carries a feeling, a sound, a weight. It is a name that belongs to the past. But not a past that is irrevocably behind him. It is a past which will never again, even if he tries to make it happen, let go of him.

Philida.

XXV

In which there is Talk of three Messages:
one from the Past, one from the Dead and one from the Moon

The news of Frans's visit to the Berrangés in the Caab travelled, like many other items of scandal, beyond the mountains to Worcester where it also reached Philida. This did
not always happen quickly, because the route to the interior
wasn't easy, no matter which road one took. Some horsemen
followed new and different short cuts, but that was mostly
asking for trouble, if not death. And yet, when all was said
and done, there was nothing that could stop news from
travelling. Not that it upset Philida much to hear about
Francois and Maria. Especially after Kleinkat had returned
to her, life began to continue on its way at a tolerable pace.
But there were some interruptions.

One of the first of these comes early on a winter's day,
when the frost turns the grass brittle and white, when
Meester de la Bat and his wife and children leave on the
Cape cart to visit friends, the Jouberts, on a farm just outside
the village. Setting aside his work on a few new coffins,
Labyn comes to tell Philida: I want you to come with me.

She looks up from where she sits knitting on the back
steps of the house: nowadays she works more and more in
an array of colours, which demands a lot of concentration.
This day's woman's cardigan is in a rusty red, dark yellow
and olive green. She asks: Where do you want to take me?

We're going to the Drostdy, you and me.

To do what?

There are people we got to see. You can say we got an appointment.

Who you talking about now?

You remember the day the Meester took us into the Bokkeveld and told us about the slaves that killed their Baas a few years ago?

Yes, I remember. But –

He told us about five that were locked up here at the Drostdy for hard labour. Two for fifteen years and another three for life.

The chameleon which now sits almost permanently perched on Philida's shoulder watching the world with its protruding eyes, she first leaves with Floris where he is making shoes as always; afterwards she goes to put away her knitting in the dark brown painted cupboard in the kitchen. Now I'm ready, she says eagerly. Let's go. The baby stays behind to play with Lena at Delphina's feet.

Labyn takes a short cut to the prison that forms the back part of the tall white Drostdy. He carries three bulging flour bags in his hands. In the backyard several prisoners are toiling with picks and heavy hammers and chisels to break large rocks into smaller and smaller ones until they are reduced to gravel. Against the farthest wall is a massive treadmill with steps hollowed by years of wear and rungs covered with dark stains, on which another eight or ten prisoners are chained, treading on and on like mules on a threshing floor, under the supervision of a Khoe guard with a long whip. Their clothes are soiled and hanging from their emaciated bodies in filthy tatters. Presumably they are forced to make do with whatever they were wearing when they arrived here, whether they are serving a sentence of five or ten years or lifelong imprisonment, summer and winter. A few of them are completely naked. Some look quite young, others are older, three or four ancient and doddering. Labyn must have arranged the visit with the guard beforehand, because he takes Philida straight to two men working in the farthest corner of the yard. Another Khoe guard, this one armed with an assegai, quickly scrambles to his feet and stares suspiciously at them, but then he recognises Labyn and withdraws again. He doesn't look much stronger than his prisoners, but at least his biltong body is more or less covered by a dilapidated red-and-white uniform.

Labyn motions Philida in the direction of the nearest prisoner: This one, he says, is Achilles. And then the oldest, who is Ontong. The old man, as rickety as a stick insect, has a wretched look about him, with spidery legs, hollow cheeks, and dull eyes set deeply in their sockets, like two old, extinguished coals. He doesn't look up when the visitors arrive beside him.

Achilles comes from Macassar, says Labyn. He is a Slams like me. So is Ontong, but he is from Batavia.

They say you come from the Bokkeveld? asks Philida.

Achilles shrugs his bony shoulders.

I heard about your uprising, says Philida.

He gives her a quick glance, then continues with his monotonous chopping-chopping-chopping.

My new Baas went to show me Galant's head on a pole in the Bokkeveld.

For a moment it seems as if he is going to say something, but then decides against it.

That must have been a really big thing, says Philida.

Another quick glance from Achilles, but he remains silent.

I am a Slams like you, says Philida.

This time there is a hint of fire in the embers of his dull eyes.

Philida stares intently at him, which forces him to look up. She says: I really came to say thank you.

Why? he asks suspiciously.

One of these days, she says, next year, all of us, all the slaves, will be free. As I understand it, it's really owing to people like you.

It doesn't help us, he says with unexpected vehemence. We sitting here until we die. But that will not be very long now, *Inshallah*.

Labyn told me, says Philida. The people have not forgotten about you.

Another shrug of the small, thin shoulders. He is so skinny and bent that it looks as if there is a hump between them.

It's not as if I did such a big thing, he says unexpectedly. The others did most of it. I was just there.

Sometimes it is enough just to be there, says Philida.

Even little Rooij did more than me, he protests. He was only a child, barely fourteen. If you ask me, he just went because he was too small to say no. But when the time came to shoot, he did. And I? I just stood there, out of the way.

Suddenly his tongue seems to loosen.

All my life I know just one thing: I am far away from my land. Nothing that is here is mine. So how could I let them drag me into murder and killing? All I did was to try and make sure it didn't get too bad. And when the Nooi got hurt, I tried to help. She said she would ask the big Baas people to look after me. But did she? Here I am still. Breaking stones. For fifteen years. So what now? Even if they let me go, even if they free us all, I shall never find the way back to my land and see the *mtili* trees moving in the wind. He remains silent for a long time. Then he looks up with a small, sad smile: I always thought it was those *mtili* trees that made the wind blow, but now I know better. The wind doesn't take orders from anyone. It just blows. And one day when I am dead it will still be blowing. Only I shall not be there to see.

After a while – chop-chop-chop-chop – he resumes: In the early days at Houd-den-Bek I often run away, but every time they bring me back and beat me. He draws his breath in deeply before he concludes: In the end one no longer try to run away. But what does that help? Here they still beat us every day. Look at me.

Without warning he turns round. Around his skinny shoulders and across his bare back they can see the bloody traces of beatings, some old, blackish, bluish stripes stained into the skin, others less old and covered with scabs, still others looking fresh, with red blood and yellow pus oozing from them.

Every day, he says with quiet resignation. But I am not complaining. Who am I to resist the will of Al-lah?

He glances quickly at the guard, who responds with a brief gesture of his head. It must be time to go. Labyn hands one of his small bags to Achilles, who very quickly thrusts it under one of his arms while the guard keeps his head turned away. Now they must move on to old Ontong.

Like Achilles, he is breaking stones, only much more slowly. He is evidently more exhausted than his friend. The hammer is clearly too heavy for his thin arms, his face looks wrinkled and bruised like an old fruit long past ripening, which has rotted and dried out. But when he starts talking, it comes more easily than with Achilles. He, too, has been here for almost ten years. Another five or six to go. It doesn't sound like so much, but he reacts vehemently when Philida asks about it.

Not so much? he asks, narrowly missing her with a gob

of spit. Come and sit here or try to walk on that long mill and see how you like it. Then try to think how it will be if you do it for fifteen years or for the rest of your life. Every day is like a year. Just five years, six years, and you are an old man. Death soaks into you like snow into these mountains in the wintertime.

Philida goes down on her haunches to listen as he speaks in a toneless, tireless voice. How he came out on the ship from Batavia to the Caab when he was barely ten years old. About the time on Houd-den-Bek and how he helped to bring up the boy Galant. How he and Nicolaas and the little girl Hester grew up like three small plants in the same vegetable bed. How they began to grow apart. Until the day Nicolaas nearly beat Galant to death after he'd flogged a horse, and how Hester later went to cut the thongs from which he was hanging in the stable, and how she told Ontong to cut down the slave that had been like a brother to him. How Ontong was always the first to stop them when trouble threatened to break out. How he once prevented Galant from setting fire to the house with all the people inside. But what good did it do him? All right, in the end they didn't hang him like they did Galant and the others. But sometimes he wonders if it wouldn't have been easier just to be hanged and have done with it, than to sit here for year after year crushing stones or treading the mill.

And yet, he says at last, a kind of weary pride in his voice, I learned to bear it. I lasted. A reed can bend without breaking like a stick, you see. It's just that I'm getting old so quickly now. Will there be any life left in me by the time I get out? The white people know very well how to wear a man out before he's dead.

Philida listens with a kind of awe to what he says, because in his voice there is something she has never heard in anybody else. It makes her think of what Ouman Cornelis Brink used to read from his Bible about the man Lazarus that rose from the dead and came back to his people and how at the time she always thought of how weird it must be for someone like that to come back among the living. Because Lazarus had been on the Other Side. He'd been dead. And even if he comes back to life, it must always feel to him as if he is looking on from very far away at what is happening on this side. It's like that with old Ontong. What he has seen, what has happened to him, must make him unlike other people. He must know more. Everything must look different to him. It must feel as if he has been to hell and come back through the flames to be here again. A *here* which can never be quite the same as other people's *here*. In a way he must look at his world like that Galant's head stuck on the pole in the Bokkeveld, staring through the empty hollows of his eyes, at everything that happens around him but which is no longer part of him. Fire he has seen, and murder, and killing, the things that people do to people, things that should not be seen or known about but which go on happening all the time. Every bloody day of his life. Every bloody day for which he, Ontong, is still sitting here breaking stones until they turn into gravel and disappear into dust under his blunt chisel, every day they chain him up here on the treadmill where he's got to tread and tread and tread and tread and tread, day after day until time no longer exists, past the ends of the earth, every day they go on beating and beating and beating him, without ever stopping. Every day – may Al-lah hear him, Al-lah the Compassionate, Al-lah the Merciful – every day he must remember those people, their eyes and their hands, their mouths that go on shouting and shouting in his ears, in every muscle and bone and sinew and drop of blood in his tired old body. *Jirre*, Ontong! You must be older than all the other people in the world. Older than Al-lah or the LordGod himself. You know too much. You know more than any living person ought to know. You could have been my grandfather. You could have been my father. I who don't even have a father to know about.

To Ontong Labyn hands another of his small flour bags with food and rolled tobacco and a cardigan which Philida really meant for Meester de la Bat. For the guard, too, Labyn has brought a *pasella*: a jug of wine, tobacco, *meebos*, dried fruit.

There isn't much time left, but they must visit another part of the Drostdy yard inside the ring wall, to look from a distance at the other rebels who were with Galant: those sentenced, not to fifteen years of breaking stones, but to life. The three Khoe men. The young Rooij who at the time of the revolt was still a child and only went with the others from curiosity, and then was persuaded to stay with the grown men and to shoot and kill the farmers. Hendrik who arrived from the Karoo with his Baas at the farm only in the late afternoon of the murder, in search of a runaway mare. Klaas, the *mantoor* on the farm, who intervened to save the lives of the women, but who didn't hesitate at the critical moment to unlock the front door of the homestead for Galant and his co-accused Abel.

It is as if another world is opened to Philida like a strange and terrible book. At the same time it is a world she knows only too well. It may be true that the night of murder and violence stands between them like a wall: but at the same time it does look like her own world. The rhythms of work during the summer or winter days, as precise and orderly as a knitting pattern, the bell that rings in the early morning, the farmyard coming to life, the seasons following one another, cold and hot and everything in between, rain and drought, food and beatings, slaves and masters. Then, one day, suddenly, everything is disrupted, a murder happens among them, and nothing is the same – and they discover that this frightening violence has been hovering among them all the time, pretending to be asleep, like a dog on the back stoep, but never really sleeping after all.

And now? Is that dog still lying there, pretending? How tame these men seem today when you look at them, how ordinary, how everyday, how subdued, how torn and tattered. All violence and will drained out of them. And yet – !

Are we all like that? she wonders. Is it lying in wait for all of us? And what will it take to make it break loose again? What do we really know about ourselves?

Labyn is getting agitated. The guard has warned him that they mustn't stay too long, or he will get into trouble. And soon, too soon for her liking, they must go on their way to the de la Bats' house in the Church Street. They do not talk much. The day lies heavily on them. Philida already knows that this morning will not readily let her go. Yet something happens upon their arrival which changes the feeling of the day for ever in her mind.

A horseman arrives from the Drostdy in Stellenbosch with a message for Meester de la Bat. Something about the preparations for the first of December, the day the slaves are to become free. Well, not completely free. Everybody knows by now that each will remain indentured with her or his Baas for four more years. But it does mean that something has started happening and that the Caab will never be the same again.

But that is not all the visitor has to say. He has a special message for Philida. It comes from Zandvliet.

Ouma Nella has died.

Quietly in her sleep, just over a week ago. Philida has always expected it to happen in a different way. It has never been in Ouma Nella's nature to allow anything just to happen quietly, almost unnoticed. She would always put her foot down, and resist. Yet now this has come to pass and suddenly there is only an emptiness that remains. An emptiness surrounded by wind, a wind that seems to be coming from all sides and has no beginning or end. But in a strange way the wind is also comforting in its wild dance.

And so, on the day the message comes, Philida's thoughts also slowly come to rest. In the heart of the emptiness she does not move until long after the messenger has left. She has no tears left to weep, all she can do is to remain sitting. But it is an emptiness that slowly begins to be filled with stories, all the stories Ouma Nella has told her over so many years. The children soon realise that their mother is not to be disturbed. And they quietly accompany Delphina when she takes them to where she is busy ironing. Even Kleinkat remains very quietly on Philida's lap, her small striped head resting against a knee, quietly purring as if she is trying to comfort Philida.

Unthinking, Philida lifts a hand to remove Floris's chameleon from her shoulder. The little creature sits quietly in her cupped hand. Only its eyes keep turning slowly this way and that as if it is watching something.

Ouma Nella's stories, she thinks, are all that remain now. Perhaps, when the end comes, they are all that can go on living.

Look at that little creature. You know *mos*, people say it is through him that death came into the world, but that is not fair, Ouma Nella always said. That story is just not true, it was all a misunderstanding.

Then what is the true story, Ouma?

Philida allows free rein to her thoughts, letting them run like water in a furrow in the vineyard.

It was the Moon, the same Moon sitting up there now, showing off its bulging tummy, pretending not to know anything, but actually knowing it all very well: one day, the Moon, that was one of the chameleon's two mothers, remember, sent the chameleon to give the people down there on Earth a message. Because the people were still new on the Earth, they didn't know anything about dying and that kind of thing. So she told the chameleon, Go and tell them they got nothing to be scared of. Because look at me, I am the Moon: sometimes I am round and full – like now, as you can see for yourselves – and then the darkness starts gnawing at me and I grow smaller and thinner, until at last I just disappear. You are still looking at me, then suddenly I am no longer there, I'm just goner than gone. But after some time, before you know what is going on, I start swelling again, like a cow with a calf inside her, and one day I am full and shiny and full of life again. Well, this is how it goes with you people too. You also grow old and get thin and then you die. But not for long, because soon you get up again to start a new life. This is the message I'm sending to the people. What lives must die, and then life begins again, and nothing is ever past. A message of hope that never dies.

All right. So there the chameleon goes. Little step by step, very carefully, treading very softly.

Up in the sky the Sun is looking at what is happening down there. He is surprised by the chameleon that walks so slowly and endlessly without getting tired or hurried. And he gets so curious that he cannot take it any longer. First he makes sure that the Moon will not see him, and then he slides all the way down to the Earth to find out what is this story that is happening. He calls the hare to find out what is going on. The hare is in such a hurry that he catches up with the chameleon from behind, and he asks: Where you going in such a hurry?

He is joking, of course, but the chameleon is concentrating so much on his slow walking and walking and walking that he doesn't even realise that the hare is pulling his leg. And when at long last the cha-me-le-on has slow-ly fin-ish-ed tel-ling his long sto-ry, the hare runs off in such a hurry that there is gravel and sand and dust scattered in every direction, until he gets back to the Sun and tells his story.

The Sun smiles in the light rays of his beard.

Look, he tells the hare. You are the one who is too fast. Calm down and listen carefully. Look at me. I am big and round and shiny and I burn like fire from morning to night. But tonight I lie down behind the mountains and then I'm dead and everything grows black with death. This is how it will be for people too: They are born and then they live, and then they die and the whole world gets dark.

And off goes the hare, even faster than the first time, and he runs right past the chameleon until he comes to the people, and he tells them:

Listen to the message from the Sun. He says: Look at me! In the morning I am born and then I keep shining right through the day until evening comes, and then I die behind the mountains. This is how it will be with all of you.

The people believed the message, and from that day death lives among them.

A long, long time after that the poor little chameleon arrived with the message sent by the Moon. But by then it was too late. The people had already heard and believed the message, so it could not be changed any more, and now we are stuck with it.

Philida still remembers the first time she heard the story from Ouma Nella and how furiously she protested, and how Ouma Nella laughed and said, That's how people are, my child. They always believe the worst, and if you're born stupid you will die stupid. But let that be a lesson to you. If you get a message, make sure you understand it right. Otherwise you will just see your own backside.

For a long time Philida remains sitting in the backyard with the chameleon very peaceful in her hand. There is so much she wants to remember. How they used to work and talk together. How Ouma Nella taught her everything about knitting. All the stories, all the laughter. How they slept together at night in Ouma Nella's *bulsak*, and how soft and warm and downy and happy and safe it was. How they picked the first crystal grapes of summer together, and the sweetest hanepoot at the end of the season. And the deep yellow loquats, and the purple Adam's figs, and how rotten figs and chickenshit slithered through her toes in the backyard, and how day after day Ouma Nella got angry with the stupid hen Zelda that always cackled about the eggs of other chickens without ever producing anything of her own, and how nobody ever dared to disturb them when they were together in Ouma Nella's room, and how on that last visit to the Caab they walked through the whole of the town in search of work after Frans had betrayed her and refused to acknowledge his own fair children, and how she'd gone to say goodbye to Ounooi Janna before she left for Worcester, and how her whole life through spring summer autumn winter has always been made true by Ouma Nella, and good and evil and everything else has been given their names by Ouma, and how the Ouman wanted to force her to kneel for him in the bamboo copse, and how he looked on while the two boys in the backyard were taking turns with her, and how all the pain in the world grew less painful when Ouma Nella was with her. And if she now has to be buried in a coffin like those made by Labyn, but never as beautiful and perfect as Labyn's, it will be a whole life that is put away. For evermore. My poor old Ouma. Poor, poor me.

XXVI

A Chapter about a Day that is as blue as all Others
while it is also completely different

For years it has been hovering like a smell in the sky, a
heavy smell that could make you drunk and light-headed.
A smell like young wine or must in a farmyard. But even
when hope turned to knowledge, it was not yet ready to
be believed and accepted. For too long it has soaked into
one's flesh and blood and sinews and deep into the marrow
of one's bones. Now, suddenly, it is there and, God knows,
true. Monday, the first of December, in the Year of Our
Lord, 1834.

The slaves are free.

Well, not yet free in the way one can talk about swallows
or even bobtails or sparrows or *janfrederiks*, because for four
more years – that is, forty-eight months, one thousand four
hundred and sixty-one days (including the leap year) for
those prepared or able to count so far – each and everyone
has to remain indentured with a baas. But still: free.

For Philida the day begins in an ordinary enough way
with getting up early, feeding her children, and then going
to sit in the back garden and watch how the street slowly
comes to life. There are a number of revellers trying to
dance or run about, people making bonfires in the street
and cavorting wildly around them. The magistrate's helpers
try very quickly to put an end to it, but it soon becomes
evident that no one will be able to douse the exuberance.

It is like a New Year's Day. From all sides slaves come running towards the Drostdy square, even from farms around the town, and soon the whole place is like a broken antheap. Many people have brought their own music, fiddles and ramkies, a few accordions known here as Christmas worms, the odd trumpet, and they all let go in an explosion of celebration.

In the de la Bats' backyard Philida moves away for a while from the shade of the oak tree where she has been knitting since early morning, to stare, with her head thrown back, into the bluest blue of the sky as if she's trying to prise loose something up there. There's *got* to be something different, something new, something completely extraordinary, about a day like this. Something that would make one realise that this day is unlike any other. Not so? But the blue up there seems the same as the blue of any other day, neither paler nor darker. As if blue is nothing but blue. A colour like other colours. Like red, or green, or yellow, only blue. What she wants to see is a blue that will be bluer than blue. A blue that means: sadness. Or: happiness. Or: longing. Or: I. No longer just a colour.

But at first sight this day, the first of December, 1834, is no different from any other day.

In the end Philida becomes tired of staring up at the sky. At her feet Kleinkat keeps on playing. This little cat can always find something to keep her busy. A ball of wool. A bobbin. A mouse. A cricket. A gecko. And when she cannot find something tangible, she may simply invent or imagine it. Something only she can see. Make-believe cats or story cats or ghost cats. On this Monday morning it may be a ladybird, the orange-and-black kind. Kleinkat stalks the little thing as if it were some huge animal, much larger than herself. A dassie or a mongoose, a leguan, a pangolin, a lynx, or even worse: a leopard, a lion. She creeps up on it, charges it, brings it down, throws it up, jumps on it with arched back, makes a somersault, growls deep in her throat and makes a sound that would scare off any intruding beast. While Philida is around, Kleinkat is prepared to take on anything. A hippopotamus, a rhinoceros, an elephant, a bugbear, a satan, a monster as big as the house, as a drostdy, as a Caab staggering under a southeaster. To Kleinkat this Monday is indeed no ordinary day. And in the end, just as suddenly as she began, she abandons it, curls up in a tiny bundle and starts purring. And falls into a deep sleep.

Then Floris approaches round the back corner of the house with an exuberant call like a fish bugle: I say, I say! Aren't we also going to churn up a bit of dust?

Don't be silly, man, Labyn scolds him.

But Floris won't be stopped. Look what I got here! he shouts as he reveals what he has been hiding in an old folded jacket under his arm. It's shoes, honest to God. Shoes he has made for everybody in this backyard: for Philida and Delphina, for Labyn and himself, even for Philida's children, Lena and Willempie. Each pair cut and sewn exactly to size: one can see that he has taken every single measurement very precisely by screwing up his eyes. They all sit down on the ground and start trying on the shoes. Labyn and Floris immediately jump to their feet and start dancing a reel. Floris scoops up Delphina and Labyn and Philida, and the dust gets churned up as if a few dust-devils have come to life like ghosts in bright daylight.

Until Meester Bernabé de la Bat, in top hat and black suit, comes out on the back stoep and sternly demands: What is going on here today?

For a moment they all stop in their tracks, from sheer

habit. Then Philida calls over her shoulder: Doesn't Meester know then? We're *mos* free today.

Free and happy, Meester! laughs Floris, showing all his teeth.

Meester de la Bat cautiously takes both his gloves in one hand, as if to prevent them from getting soiled. We shall talk again later, he says. His nose in the air as if there is chickenshit on his upper lip.

Usually, this would be enough to silence everybody. But today there is something let loose among the people.

And this is how it goes for the rest of the day, in the village of Worcester and everywhere else in the Colony, from the Caab to way beyond the farthest line of bluer-than-blue mountains. Another week or two, and they will get news of all that has happened on this day. On some farms, and in Stellenbosch and Franschhoek, and in the more distant Swellendam and Graaff-Reinet, it even got out of hand. Two or three farmers have been attacked, one stabbed to death at Tulbagh. And on the burgher side some of the men have taken rifles from the shelves in the *voorhuis* and started shooting. Two slaves killed in the region of the Twenty-Four Rivers, another seriously wounded at Trawal. In the Caab it even led to a brief general outbreak of violence, and the garrison had to be called out to restore the peace with force. Vrouw Magdalena Berrangé made it known that on the day in question, 1 December 1834, a drunken slave she didn't know from Adam, arrived at their home in the Oranje Straat, and had the temerity to demand to speak to her personally; and when she appeared in a rage to tell him to go to hell, he made an elaborate bow in front of her and boldly announced: I been told that Vrouw Berrangé got a whole brood of daughters, so I just come to tell you: four years from today, when our time of indenture is over, I'll be back to marry one of them. A nice chubby one that will just fit into the crook of my arm. And before she even had time to fetch her husband's gun from the shelf, he was gone again. He could be heard laughing several streets away.

But here in Worcester it grew quiet earlier than elsewhere. In the evening new fires were lit at first dusk, and more reels were danced. But the magistrate and his helpers made sure that action was taken very rapidly.

For much of the day Philida goes on knitting on her seat in the backyard, neither faster nor more slowly than usual. The only difference compared to other days is that she keeps on her two shoes. And from time to time she still glances up quickly, almost guiltily. As if she isn't sure of what she will see there. The day remains blue, deep blue and very quiet, and empty after the wind has blown everything away. And bloody hot, causing the blue to start melting and turn limp and exhausted.

And then, in the midst of all this blue, something breaks loose inside Philida. Suddenly it feels as if all the aimlessness in the day changes course and starts moving in a new direction. Now she knows what it is: until this moment it has been like one of those occasions, so very long ago, when she and Frans found themselves together in the bamboo copse and, inexplicably, nothing would come of it. They would just be there, she and he, she lying in his arm, and she could feel desire beginning to grow in him and slowly insinuate itself into her own body. But it would remain shapeless, aimless. If he put his hand between her legs, she would start thinking of the knitting she still had to do in Ouma Nella's room. Or she would become conscious of the male *kiewiet* calling outside and her body would tighten as she waited for the female to respond, but it wouldn't happen.

Something would remain unfinished, incomplete, unfulfilled. She would feel the urge gathering inside her, and be aware of the same happening to him, yet nothing would come of it. And this blue day was exactly like that.

Until it happened by itself, without her knowing how or why. All of a sudden, as a turtle dove started calling in the bluegums outside, Philida sat up, knowing: *This* is what I have been waiting for! *This* is what must happen now! And she thrust her knitting back on the bench and ran into the kitchen. As she ran she could feel all the thoughts in her head tumbling into place, everything exactly where it had to be. From the large water barrel next to the hearth she filled two wooden pails. And then she hobbled across the yard to a spot of shade just behind the big loquat tree, where one could be completely protected and invisible from either the slave quarters or the kitchen, because today she couldn't bear to be interrupted or seen.

Back in the room she shares with Delphina and the children, she takes two toys from under the bed: a mealie-cob doll for Lena on which Labyn has drawn two round eyes and a big red mouth, and in a small wooden box a little tortoise he has picked up in the veld. The boy is still too small to play with it, but he keeps grinning at it and sometimes even laughing out loud as he watches it scurrying about on its short crooked legs. These toys she puts inside their box in the shade of the loquat tree before she hurries off again to where Delphina has been keeping the kids occupied.

Lena is playing with the quick, deft movements of a bobtail, while Willempie grins through gobs of spittle as he keeps on trying to grab the little tortoise as it scuttles about. Philida waits until both are so occupied that they become oblivious of everything else before she grabs the two wooden pails and upends them, one by one, over the children. Both gasp for breath and howl blue murder, making such a row that Juffrouw comes running from the kitchen to see what is going on. Even old Labyn comes running, clutching an unfinished chair leg in his hands. Only Meester de la Bat seems to have remained unaware of the commotion as he continues to work, unperturbed, on his documents at the dining-room table.

It takes quite a while before peace and order has been restored in and around the home. Only then does Labyn, still flustered, ask Philida: Can you please tell me what on earth has happened here?

Nothing, she replies quite unruffled. I just baptised the children.

You what? he gasps. But, Philida, you can't do that!

I can, she says calmly, and I just did.

But why in Al-lah's name?

On a day like this I had to do *something*, she says quietly. It was high time. And if it doesn't happen by itself, I got to do something, not so? I been waiting for heaven knows how long, and where can we find a better day for it? You and I are free, and the children are now baptised in the name of Al-lah, so now we can go on from here. With shoes on our feet and all.

I told you one cannot be baptised in the faith of Islam. The imam will never agree to it.

It wasn't a baptism for *Islam*, Philida points out. It was only for us. No one ever needs to know.

But it's sinful, Philida!

Now you talking like Ouman Cornelis. You and I know better than that, Labyn. We did it to praise Al-lah. In a way the two of us started a new church here today.

You know my people don't believe in a church.

Then make it a new mosque, she says, unperturbed. We can call it the Free Mosque Church of the Cross and the Crescent, if you wish.

And Al-lah is in charge of it?

Both Al-lah and the LordGod, if you want, she says, a laugh in her voice. Her head is racing ahead of them now. I'll tell you what: we can add Muhammad and Jesus to it, they both prophets, aren't they? And what about A'isha and Mary as well? We can't leave them out, can we? I tell you what: our place for prayers will be the best there ever was. It will have room for everybody.

Well, when do we start? asks Labyn. But before she can reply, he changes his mind and shakes his head with a sigh. No, wait. Let's keep it to ourselves for the moment. Some things are better in dreams.

That is enough too, Philida agrees. Just look at how blue the day has already become. Blue and blue and blue, wherever you look. Al-lah's sky and the LordGod's sky.

And after Labyn has returned to his workplace, she thinks: So this is Monday, the first of December, 1834, the day everybody been dreaming about. I think it's been worthwhile after all. Now I know what it really feel like to be free.

She knows: it started with the children, with the first little one, that day she'd held him in her hands, as small as a cat. That was when she understood: What happened has happened and I cannot change it. It *had* to happen. But never-ever again. If there must be another child, children, they stay with me, they will live. If Frans try anything or want me to do something again, I shall wait until he sleep and then I shall do what I must do and that will be that. But the child, the children shall live with me. When little Mamie is born everybody can see right then that she will not live long, so there is no need to do anything. Later, with Lena, the stories about freedom are already everywhere and I know I must just wait. From the first day with her I know I must hope, and wait. From that day I live with the hope and it keep us alive. I shall never again think I am Al-lah or I am the LordGod and decide for myself about living and dying. And today with this baptism I can say it openly. These children are mine and they will live. That is freedom for me. And for them. For now and for ever.

And it is only three days later that she hears the news from the Drostdy: all the slaves have been called in by the Commissioner and ordered to chop the treadmill into small pieces for firewood. Only that, nothing more. No word about breaking the stones into little chips. For Ontong and the others, that punishment continues, but there is no more stepping on the treadmill.

The following Monday, when Philida comes in again to tidy up the Commissioner's office, she casually remarks: I just want to say thank you to the Meester.

He looks at her, suppressing the frown on his forehead, pretending not to know what she is talking about. And mumbling, as if to himself: There's nothing I did. Nothing at all.

And all Philida can do is quietly to finish her dusting as she says: So I want to say thank you for nothing, Meester. Adding as an afterthought: But it's a good nothing to say thank you for, Meester.

PART THREE
~
GARIEP

XXVII

In which Everything unravels and comes together again

It is on that same Monday that I think: Today is the day I been waiting for all my life. Even when I was a child, I always thought: Surely, this cannot be all. This *cannot* be all. One day something will happen that will change everything. Because it's impossible that this can be all there is. It was worst on the days Ounooi Janna beat me, which was most days. But even any other ordinary day, as I carry out the shit bucket or the piss pots to empty them in the big hole at the back, or to feed the dirty old sow in the pigsty, or even on the good days when I can just sit and knit for hours, I used to think: Jirre, no, this cannot be all. And then it will come into my mind, no matter if the sun was burning me or the moon is caught in the branches of an oak tree: One day there must be something else and something new. One day – one day – one day.

Now this must be the One Day. Because if it isn't, I rather not be here.

But of course one also get used to it. You learn to think: This is what it is to be a slave. Just this, and nothing more. This: that everything is decided for you from out there. You just got to listen and do as they tell you. No matter if it is a piece of knitting you got to unravel and knit again, or to kneel when some baas want to beat you. You don't say no. You don't ask questions. You just do what they tell you. But far at the back of your head you think: Soon there must come a day when I can say for myself: This and that I shall do, this and that I shall not. But such a day never come. Until that Monday. When the people come running up and down the street, and singing and dancing and kicking up dust, and the sky stay just as blue as it always was. A Blue Monday, as they say. And from now on blue will be my colour. That is when I say to Labyn: From now on everything will be different.

Say who? he ask, with a laugh.

Say I, Philida.

And how will you make that happen? You know we will be slaves for another four years.

That may be so, Labyn. But to be a slave will now be something else.

Just try, and see what happen, he say.

I will try, and *you* will see what happen.

This is when I decide in my own head: All these years it was they who decided they got the right to say: Philida, you a slave. But they don't have the right to say: Philida, now you free. That is something only I can say. And this I say today: Today I am a free woman.

But saying, I know, is always easier than doing.

It begin on the long-ago day with KleinFrans, but I do not even know it myself. Because that is the most terrible day of my life. The day we never speak about. Not ever. I remember the look in his baby eyes. He was so small. Like a little kitten. He half lift his head to look into my face. The small frown between his eyes. He know what is coming. There is just a feeble struggle. A smothered sound. Then nothing. He go limp in my hands. He put out one of his tiny hands and touch my cheek, so softly one can barely feel it, like a leaf stirring. He touch me the way Kleinkat sometimes do when I'm sleeping and she touch me with one of her little paws to wake me up. Just like him. Like KleinFrans that day. Only, he don't want to wake me but to say goodbye. But I know: he know what is happening. I swear he know. In that one moment he know who I am. He know I am his mother. And I am doing what nobody on the LordGod's earth got the right to do.

There is only one reason why I got to do it. And that is to stop Frans from doing it. I do it to stop *him* from killing our child. You can say I do it to save him. From the man I love. Because I know I cannot live with that. I who am his mother. Now and for ever. That is where the world begin. With a man and a woman. Just the two of them. And then with a child they make between them. And then I kill him. To stop Frans.

To stop Frans from killing him, to go and drown him the way he do with kittens and puppies that are not wanted on the farm. I decide I must rather do it myself, and take him out of his hands. So that he won't become a slave like his mother was a slave. That's all.

Six years old, that is what he'd have been today. Six years, four months and thirteen days. That is how I learn to count, and when all my learning begin.

There's one specially good thing about being free, you know, I say to Labyn.

And what would that be?

That no baas can ever be a baas again.

How do you get that?

Because a baas without a slave cannot be a baas, I tell him, which is what Ouma Nella say to me long ago. But today I *know* it for the first time.

I don't think *they* know it, say Labyn.

It don't matter if they do, I say. You and I know it, all of us that were slaves until yesterday.

I'm not so sure, he say with a frown of deep thought on his forehead. A man needn't know that he is a baas. He just *is*.

No, Labyn, I argue. It can only come with knowing. A thing isn't something before you know it. And that is why I'm happy about today, and why the next four years is not important.

You better watch out, say Labyn. For these four years and all the other years that still lie ahead. Remember, a man can only step as far as his legs are long. And they keeping our legs short.

You forget one thing, I say. We can *jump*. And I'm not going to step carefully if I know I can jump. Remember, I wearing shoes now.

Labyn sit in silence for a long time, looking down at his feet. This Floris knows about making good shoes, he say. That's for sure.

I look at the work he been doing in the light of his oil lamp. And you, I say, you know about making a good coffin.

He grin. This is for a baas, he say. Don't forget, when *we* die they just roll us in an old blanket.

When I die one day, I say, I want *you* to make my coffin. *Inshallah*, say Labyn.

Outside it is still afternoon, the kind of afternoon that happen only in Worcester: a heat that push you down against the ground to burn all the wetness out of you, here among the mountains, where nothing can get out and no air can come in.

If we stay here we all going to burn to death, say Labyn.

I stay quiet for a while, then I say: Well, then it must be time for us to go away from here. There is nothing in this place for us.

Where can we go to? he ask.

Between here and the Caab they're pushing us against the sea, I answer. But you hear what Floris say: if you go far enough in this direction, you come to the river they call Gariep. From there, the land is open and everything is free.

And how do we get there?

With our feet, I say.

You got two small children with you, Philida.

Nothing is pushing us. We got time. We got all the time in the world.

Meester de la Bat will never let us go, Labyn assure me.

Nothing stop us asking.

He paid a lot of money for us. Not so long ago either, for you. To white people money is important.

Then we buy ourselves free.

How?

You with your coffins. And I can knit.

You will knit yourself to hell and gone. And I got to go on making coffins until long after I'm dead myself.

We can start now. My Ouma Nella always said that from a few drops of rain at a time the dam get full.

He shake his head. I notice how grey he is now. But I don't want to give up. I know that from giving up too soon one's wool start unravelling and then the stitches no longer stay in neat rows and the knitting get loose and tatty.

He say, You know, Floris says we must just make life so difficult for them that they'll be happy to let us go, for then they will be rid of us.

But I shake my head. No, Labyn. If you ask me, it will be harder for the white people than for us. We can still manage, one way or another. But what will become of them? We are like the foundation of their house. Their lives and everything is built on us. This whole land is built on our sweat and our blood.

They just got to learn to get on without us. We all of us still got a lot to learn.

If we don't try we won't get anywhere, I tell him.

But how do you want to start?

By talking to them straight.

How?

I'll go to the Meester and ask him to let us go, and then we go.

So easy?!

I'm not saying it will be easy. But we got to see what that Gariep look like. We got to find out for ourselves. The way Floris tell it, I don't know if it's going to be all good and wonderful. But unless we make sure in time, we'll still be here when we die.

And you think you can go and speak to the Meester?

Yes, I do.

And the very next afternoon, when Meester de la Bat comes home from his office, I go to him.

Yes, Philida, what do you want?

I tell him about what Labyn and I discuss. That we must go to the Gariep to see what it look like. Then we can come back here and talk again.

It turn out like Labyn say: the man will not listen to anything. When I tell him we need a pass to go to the Gariep, he look at me as if I am now mad in my head. But I keep on: Before we know what is for us at that far place, we can't do nothing and we can't go nowhere.

He sound ready to get difficult: And what if I say no?

Then we shall just have to go without a pass, I say.

Philida!

I shrug my shoulders. This is not how we want to go, Meester. We want to stay with the law. But we got to go and that is how it is.

How do I know that you'll ever come back?

I shall give the Meester my word.

And you want me to just believe you?

Yes, I say. Why not? Did I ever lie to the Meester?

Then he say what Labyn told me was coming: Do you know what I paid for you and your two children?

Yes, Meester, I say. One hundred and twenty-three pounds two shillings and sixpence. That is my price.

He stare at me, blinking his eyes. Yes, that is so. I see you kept your ears open at the auction.

I do not answer.

And suppose you go away and stay away, how will I ever get my money again, Philida?

I told you *mos* I will come back, Meester de la Bat.

We will talk again, he say quickly and he turn round and go into the house.

In the early evening we can hear him and his wife arguing in the kitchen. Their voices get loud. But Labyn and I and Floris and Delphina remain sitting very quietly on a bench in the backyard, listening but not talking. The children are lying like little mice, Lena with a small stuffed doll I make for her, Willempie with two short offcuts of wood. Kleinkat is with us too, playing with a cricket she catch.

So ordinary, so everyday, I think, it is when one's whole life is decided by other people. And that is precisely what I got enough of.

I still don't know what would have happen then. For five, six days there is nothing from the big house. It is *mos* not for us to decide, is it? The way it always been, as if that Blue Monday never happen. But then there is something no one could have expected. Like when you sit fidgeting with a tuft of wool that Kleinkat unravelled: you struggle for hours, sometimes for a whole day, and nothing happen, but then suddenly you get hold of a loose end, and you pull at it, and everything unwind and your thread is untangled, all the way. What happen this time is that an unexpected visitor turn up from the Caab. A young man in a black broadcloth suit with a top hat on his bony head, as thin and yellowish white as a gut that got scrubbed for making sausage, and he look pretty sick to me. Don't know him from Adam. But it turn out he is called Jan Fredrik Berrangé, and he is on his way to a village far inland, Driefontein, where he want to talk to the people before he travel away over the sea to study as a dominee.

A lot of talking to and fro until sometime in their discussion he ask about the slave girl Philida, which of course is me. At first I want to find out which way the wind blow, but I'm curious at the same time, so I go closer. That is when he take a whole bag of stuff from his saddle and give it to me. Not really a present, but things left to me by Ouma Nella. You can blow me over with a feather. A cardigan knit by Ouma Nella, more beautiful than anything my own two hands can make, all pale blue and yellow. And a pair of ivory knitting needles that I know since I was small, she always say she bring them from Java, and a snuffbox with a fine inlaid wooden lid. A heavy soup spoon she once find on the beach. A bolt of heavy red-and-white cloth. And a bamboo box half filled with coins: several handfuls of rix-dollars and seven gold pounds. Also a heavy golden ring that I remember from very long ago.

Surely all of this can't be for me? I ask.

There was no one else she could leave it to, say the thin pale gutman. Francois Brink brought it to us when he heard I was on my way inland. I think you know he is engaged to my sister Maria Magdalena.

Are they still to be married? I ask without meaning to.

Yes, still, he say. But the Good Lord alone knows when.

She keeps on putting it off, and nobody has any idea for how long.

I feel a smile tugging at my mouth, but try not to let them see it.

And how are things at Zandvliet? I ask.

He shrug uneasily. Well, I suppose, he say. I prefer not to ask them too many questions. I hear that Oom Cornelis has got a bad pain in his fundament, he says it is his old man's gland, and now your grandmother is no longer around to help, of course, and Tant Janna grows heavier by the day, she can barely walk, but they are all still alive by the grace of God.

Then it's good, I say. Now I'm in a hurry to look at the things he brought with him, but I don't want the others to see how eager I am.

It is only afterwards, in my room after I put the little ones to sleep, that I count my money in the pretty little box over and over, and change the pounds into rix-dollars. No, I soon discover, it is no way enough to buy my freedom, and certainly not Labyn's. Not even if we add the golden ring to it. But there must be more than enough to leave with Meester de la Bat until I come back, to show him I am serious. I don't think he can object now.

Or can he? With white people one can never be sure.

Well, possibly, yes, say the Meester when I offer him the money the following day. Then he look hard at me with narrowed eyes, and he ask, But what about the children?

What about the children?

If you leave the children with us we may think about letting you go.

I can feel my mouth dropping open. All I can think of saying is: And will Meester give them a teat to drink? Or clean their bums when they shit themselves?

· 289 ·

He stare at me as if I winded him. Philida! How on God's earth can you – ?

I just asking, Meester, I say. Now I begin to speak more freely, as I can see he is no longer quite so sure of himself.

Meester de la Bat pull himself together like a rooster getting ready to crow.

I think about it, he say very quickly and he get ready to go inside.

At last I can breathe more freely again. Because I can see that it is all over. There is no crowing left in him.

So the very next morning Labyn and I are told that we may prepare to leave for the Gariep. We can have the pass. The only condition is that we mustn't lengthen the road by wasting time along the way, is that clear?

Very clear, thank you, Meester.

But what about Floris? I ask. We need him to go with us, he been there, he can show us the way. But when Labyn go to ask him, he say that he don't want to go. Why should he? he ask. He been there, he know what he know. It's up to the others who don't know the way yet, to decide if they want to go or not. And Delphina don't want to go anyway, she too scared, she will rather stay in a place she know well. She know she may be sorry afterwards, but for now she prefer not to risk it, this land is too big and too wild for her.

And so we go to pack our bundles, just the most necessary stuff, because the road is blarry long and it's only Labyn and me, and we still have to carry the children. Meester de la Bat hand over the pass, and there we go. The greatest sadness is about Kleinkat who must now stay behind. But it won't be for long, I tell Nooi de la Bat, because I'll soon be back. In the meantime Delphina will look after her, they already know and trust each other.

What make me feel better is that at the last moment, as we shoulder our bundles to set out on our way, Kleinkat come from nowhere to lay down a small yellow flower at my feet. She do that every morning, a flower or a small branch or a beetle or a half-dead mouse she catch. On this morning it make me feel a kind of peace inside me, because now I know she understand what is happening and everything will go well for us.

Just before we go, Floris come from the small room where he been working on some new *velskoene*, and offer me the little chameleon to take with me on my shoulder.

Look after him, he say. He'll take good care of you too. And make sure you bring him with you when you come back.

Now we are ready to go.

At the last moment we decide to look in at the Drostdy prison to take our leave, but at the gate to the backyard the guard who let us in the last time come out to tell us that old Ontong is no longer with us, he die quietly a few days ago, and so we decide not to ask about Achilles too, it is too sad to find out that they disappearing like this, one by one. So off we go. Out of the village, where we are lucky to be picked up by the driver of a mule cart who is off to the Bokkeveld to fetch some wheat on a nearly empty wagon. Once again, in passing, we greet Galant that we met the last time. This time we do not stop, but drive on along the Skurweberge as far as the turn-off to the farm Houd-den-Bek. From there the mule cart go on while we must turn right to the farm.

At first I am not so sure, but Labyn insist that we must go. Too many ghosts around this place, I think. I know about ghosts, but the ones that haunt this place, I feel, still carry fresh memories of death inside them, and I'm not sure that it will be safe. But then I remember Kleinkat and her flower, and that make me decide to risk it after all. We follow the thin path to the farmhouse that squarely block it as if it don't want anything to do with the outside world. As we draw closer, a lot of dogs in the farmyard start barking furiously. The back door open and a woman come out. She is thickset and carries a long muzzle-loader in her hands. Her hair is tied back in a long, loose plait. She is still quite young, yet her hair is completely grey.

When we are still some distance away the woman put the gun to her shoulder and call out very sharply: Whoareyouwheredoyoucomefromwhatdoyouwant?

This get on my nerves, but Labyn quietly take me by the arm and that make me feel calm again.

Morning, Juffrouw, I say. I first wanted to say Nooi, but that is something I will no longer do.

The woman give no answer. The rifle keep pointing at us.

We are free people, Juffrouw, I call out. I am Philida of the Caab and this is Labyn from Batavia. We have a pass and we're on our way to the Gariep.

The Gariep do not run this way.

We know where it run, Juffrouw, and we know it is far from here, but we are on our way. We just come to hear if Juffrouw got something to eat for the children.

The woman look angry and scared, but more tired than anything else. I don't think I ever seen any other person look so tired. She wiggle the gun tighter under her arm and say: I got nothing for layabouts. Get off my farm!

We came to bring you news, Juffrouw, Labyn say.

What kind of news? the woman ask with bad weather in her voice.

It's about Ontong, Labyn say calmly. He died.

Well done, say the woman. Glad to hear that. I wish they'd all die.

Ai, Juffrouw, say Labyn.

You can stuff your *ai* up your backside! All of a sudden her eyes are full of tears. It's not that she is crying, the tears simply streaming quietly over her hollow cheeks.

There is a wild expression in her eyes as she start talking and cannot stop. My son Nicolaas and Galant grew up together, she say. They were inseparable, like two lambs of one ewe, a brown one and a white one. How could he do a thing like that?

I have no idea why she talk like this to a stranger like me, but Labyn put his hand on my arm to hold me back. I am very sorry, Juffrouw, say Labyn, as if he is to blame.

Voertsek off my farm! she suddenly shout. Or I'll shoot.

Behind her, leaning over the kitchen's stable door, a big man say: What's the matter, Cecilia? What is this scum doing here?

Without warning, she pull the trigger. Not over our heads but straight at us. About ten paces to our left a small cloud of dust fly off the bare earth.

We do not wait any longer. Labyn grab me by the shoulder and pull me out of the way. Little Lena start screaming like a little pig. The dogs barking like things gone mad. By the time we reach the road again, a second shot go off, but this time it is far off target.

I want to shout something bad at the woman over my shoulder, but Labyn keep dragging me away until we are well out of reach.

He mumbling beside me. I don't even try to listen, but by this time I know his words well enough to make out what he saying: *Al-lah leads the hearts of those who believe in him. Al-lah has knowledge of all things.*

And so we move on from Houd-den-Bek. Only Lena keep on sobbing. But Labyn give her Floris's chameleon to hold and that make her feel better. A few more deep sobs, and it is all over.

The children slow us down a lot. But why must we hurry? We know where we are going and we know we'll get there, even if take a lifetime. At least it isn't a treadmill like the one old Ontong knew. Step by step, day after day, we move on. Now and then another cart or wagon come along. Sometimes there are long days in between. On a specially busy day there may be two. Some of them stop to offer us a ride, which may be for a very short way, just to the next turn-off, or sometimes for much longer, for days and days.

Once it is a very rickety little wagon, coming from behind. It don't look as if it will get far before it collapse. On the front chest sit a small man, all shrunk from age and weakness and possibly hunger, as small and thin as a praying mantis, grey with dust and years. Next to him is a skinny woman in a worn chintz dress.

Hokaai! the little man shout at his four thin oxen as he pull them up next to us. My brother, my sister, my children! he call in a voice like a thin little cicada. Where you going to?

To the Gariep, I tell him. Is it still very far?

For us it is far, he say. For the Lord nothing is far.

And not for All-lah either, say Labyn sharply. He is everywhere.

I don't know anything about this Al-lah, say the small man on the wagon chest. But I know a bit about the Lord. If you like to know more, you can all get on the wagon, then we can talk, because the Lord called me to speak about him.

For the children's sake we can get on, say Labyn. But

don't talk too much, because they're small and they get tired quickly.

What about you? the driver turn to me. You women usually make better listeners.

To tell you the truth, I answer, I hear more than enough about the Lord from the bloody Ouman I worked for on the farm called Zandvliet. I want to hear more about *you*. Please tell us who you are and what you doing in this Nothing-from-Nowhere?

I am Cupido Cockroach, say the stick man. I am a missionary of the LordGod, on the other side of the Gariep, on the other side of Kuruman, on the other side of almost everything.

And I am Philida of the Caab, I tell him. This is Labyn from Batavia, and these are my children, Willempie and Lena. We are on our way to the Gariep.

I can take you in that direction, say Cupido. Not all the way, mind you, because I must turn off to go and look for a few of the members of my congregation that ran away. But perhaps a day or so.

It turn out different. Because before we rode another hour there is a grinding, gnashing sound under the sad little wagon and we find it is a wheel that broke and fell out. There is no more time for talking about the LordGod and Al-lah. Just as well, I think afterwards, otherwise this little Cupido Cockroach would have talked us all the way to hell. All we got time for is to get down from the wagon so that the children can play with a dead *toktokkie* in the thin shade of a thorn tree while the woman Anna and I give a hand to the men to repair the wheel. This take us right through the hot afternoon to nightfall, when we prepare to sleep.

Until the break of day, and then we get up again to go on working, searching for wood to make spokes and patch the wheel together. In a way it is a good feeling to see the two men work together. Labyn, with a sore back, because he is not young any more, and the spidery little man with the stick legs. The stranger passes on the spokes for Labyn to fit. And by the evening of the second day the wheel can start wobbling again, following the oxen.

First we got to test it to make sure that it work. Then the two men go off into the veld and return, a miracle, with a steenbok that the driver has shot with an arrow, and Anna and I skin the little thing and roast it on a fire and one way or another we all share the bit of meat. Afterwards we sleep in a circle around the dying fire, our filled stomachs turned to what is left of the flames and the embers, until it get light again. At the first light of the dawn we get up.

We women embrace. The men shake hands. One of them say, May God go with you. The other one say, May Al-lah go with you.

Then we go our separate ways without needing to talk any more – Cupido and Anna on the shaky little wagon, following the oxen that are so thin it seem the daylight must shine right through them; and the two of us with the children, towards the Gariep.

After a while I start laughing quietly to myself.

Why you laughing, Philida? ask Labyn.

And I say, No reason, Labyn. Just about you two men.

What so funny about us?

Nothing, Labyn. It's just that when the two of you meet, it was just God and Al-lah all the way. I thought there was a hell of a lot of talk coming to us. But in the end it was only the fixing of the broken wheel.

That is Al-lah's way of working, say Labyn.

And I suppose if you ask Cupido he'll say it's the LordGod's way of working.

As long as the wheel turn, he say with a little laugh. Then we all get to where we want to be.

Who know? I say.

And then we move on again.

On our long walk Labyn talk about many things. Sometimes I wonder about his stories. But in the end it always get back to the Gariep that we are going to.

You can say it's our Promised Land, Labyn like to say. You remember that Al-lah showed Moses how to trek through the desert? We just got to go on and not give up.

I never know what a blarry long way it will be, Labyn!

Don't forget about Moses and his people going on for forty years! he say. I tell you, once we get to that Gariep and we see the land of Canaan, it will all be worthwhile. Just grit your teeth and go on.

So on and on we go. Sometimes we make a halt. For a day or a few days or a long week. The first time it happen we are on a farm where somebody just died, a child that drowned in a dam, and then the people find out about Labyn's work and they ask him to make a coffin. This happen a few more times. And once the farmer is so pleased with his coffin that Labyn is asked to make coffins for everybody that live there. It's good to have your coffin ready before they dig you in, and in the meantime you can use it for raisins or dried apricots, or peaches, or for buchu and even dagga, it is such a good smell for a coffin and it must feel good for a dead person to lie in it, and if the people pay for the coffins we have another handful of rix-dollars to take along with us.

Getting to the Gariep, say Labyn, must already be like a halfway station to heaven because listen what Al-lah say about it in the Koran: *He who obeys Al-lah and his Prophet will live for ever in gardens watered by running streams.* This can only be the Gariep he talk about.

Still we go on and on. Often it feel like another desert we are moving through, like the one Moses go through, or even worse. They call it Bushmanland, they call it the Richtersveld, this desert got many names. But somewhere, somewhere you must come to its end. Somewhere anything and everything come to an end.

It is not an easy way, God know, Al-lah know, it is an uphill road. Even when it seem to go downhill it is still uphill.

And I have a hard time. The children are small and they are skinny with their chicken legs, and they are like stones that get heavier and heavier as you carry them. And it is not just Willempie and Lena I must carry. There is also Mamie, but the heaviest one is KleinFrans. He is not just in my arms but deep inside my body.

There isn't a day, not an hour, that he is not with me. He is inside me like the taste of bitter aloe in my mouth, in every breath I breathe in or out, in every step, even in my standing up or in my lying down. KleinFrans. KleinFrans. KleinFrans. Who come out of my body and who Frans want to drown. And who I got to smother in my arms to save him from a life of slavery. There is nothing else I can do. LordGod and Al-lah, help me to carry him. Help me to believe there was nothing else I can do. How can I leave it to Frans to kill him? He is mine and he is Frans's too. But first of all he is mine. Just believe me, Philida, he say to me. Allow me to take you and let us make a child, then I shall make you happy and I shall buy your freedom. And we shall both walk with shoes on our feet, for ever.

And so he make sure. And so what else could I do?

And now we shall be free anyway, whatever he did or did not do, whatever he promised or lied to make me lie with him.

I know now that I am free, not because somebody said that on such-and-such a day I must be free. I am free because I am free. Because I myself take my freedom. I take it and I choose it. It is, I think, a freedom like the sun and the moon and the other stars. The sun do not rise because somebody tell him to, but because coming up is its nature and because nobody can tell him not to. This is my freedom and this is who I am and what I am. I kill my Little Frans and I set him free. We are both free now.

We shall all go through that Gateway to Paradise together, he and I and our children and everybody.

Frans. Frans. KleinFrans.

This will be the last night we spend on the road. I know, because one can already see the dark green of the bushes and the trees that mark its course. If the children were not with me, I don't think I will have stopped. But now that we are here, I am glad to have this last night. It is not quiet. In the distance there are many voices, all the time. Lots of people talking, some shouting, some fighting, women's voices crying. This is what it mean to be with other people again. If I think of it, I must admit that perhaps it was better when it was just old Labyn and me and the children in the desert. That silence we hear there. The stillness of the night and of distance that go on and on, for ever. I am glad, of course, to know that we are here now, that this long, long walk is over. But perhaps I am a bit scared too, because I am not sure what is going to happen in this place, if one can call it a place. When old Labyn talk about it to me in Worcester, before we set out, it is only a cross on a map and it seem like a real spot one can reach, where perhaps one can rest or stay over, and from where one can set out again. But this is not a map where we are walking. It is sand

and hard earth, and scorching hot underfoot. It is as if this whole land is stuck to the soles of our feet. It will go with us wherever we go. We can never get away from it again. Nor do we want to.

I suppose I must now be happy. Is this not the end we been waiting for all along? Except that it don't feel like an end. It don't feel like anything. It is like that blue day when all the slaves got free and then the sky stay just as blue as it always was.

And yet it was good too, and I feel happy because I could baptise my children. And now? What difference can it really make?

We are here. We come a long way, an almost endless way, and now we are here. Where is *here*?

I remember on that trip to the Caab when I ask Ouma Nella: *Ouma Nella, where am I not?*

Am I here or am I not?

Am I a slave or am I not?

Am I Philida or am I not?

Are these two little children here or are they not?

Is KleinFrans here?

If I lie very still and try as hard as I can, I think I can hear the river in the distance. This Gariep we been looking for all along.

Now we are here and I still do not know where is *here*.

It is while I am lying here, so still in the endlessness of the night, that I suddenly hear something. I cannot even be sure that I hear it, that it is really there. But it sound like a cat mewing in the dark. A small cat or a baby. I know it cannot be Kleinkat, and yet while I am here alone in the dark I can believe it is she.

And that is when I know: This is why I cannot feel as if this place is here or there: because it is nowhere. Yes, it is the Gariep, it must be. They say it is. But this is not where I must be: this is not *my* place.

Where is *my* place? Ouma Nella, where am I not? And where am I?

I put out my elbow and I poke old Labyn in the ribs. He is next to me, as always. I don't know if he asleep or not. But I can touch him in the dark, and I ask him very softly, because if the children are asleep I do not want to wake them.

Labyn? I ask.

And he say, as I know he must: Yes, Philida?

Labyn, I think I hear a cat calling.

Yes, he say, I hear it too.

You think it was Kleinkat?

I don't think she could have come so far, he say. But if that is what Al-lah wish, then Kleinkat will be here.

Do you know what that mean, Labyn?

What do you think it mean, Philida?

If you ask me, I think she want us to go back.

Back where? he ask.

Back to Worcester. Perhaps that is now our place. We only know that now because we come all this way, to the Gariep, to hell and gone. It is only because we come all this way that we know where we must go to, where you and I and the children belong.

You know how far that is, Philida?

I know every blarry step of the way, Labyn.

And you say we must go back?

We must go back, because now we shall know the place for the first time. Our place. I once ask my Ouma Nella: Ouma Nella, where am I not? And tonight, in this night under the stars, I know at last: In this place I am not. The only place where I am is back where I come from. And the only way to know it is to come all the way here to find out. The Gariep is the name of the place where one find out what one do not know before.

We stay silent for a long time.

Then I ask him: And you know what, Labyn?

No, I don't know, Philida. But you tell me and then we shall both know.

We *had* to come here, Labyn. It was the only way to know.

If you say so, say Labyn.

I say so because that is what I know. I can tell you something about knitting: In the past I hate correcting a dropped stitch, or two knitted together, or a purl too soon, but now I know that one of the best things that can happen to you is to find a mistake in the knitting. When you find it you feel so happy because you can make it right. You unravel and you unravel until you get to the right place, and then you pick up the wrong stitches and you knit them right. Now you got a beautiful piece of knitting that is perfect. There is nothing, nothing wrong with it. Every stitch is just where it must be. Now you cast off, it is finished, everything is right. And now you can sleep in the night.

I know this Gariep show us where we go wrong. So we can undo the wrong rows and go back and knit it right. Now we can be really happy, Labyn. To find what is wrong and then to make it right. There is nothing better than that, Labyn.

And as I say it to him, this is what I know inside myself: In the brown waters of the Gariep I shall wash myself clean. I do not want to be whiter than snow as the Ouman use to say. Brown is what I am and brown is what I want to be. Like stone. Like soil. Like the earth. Brown like everything that is worthwhile. Brown I will wash myself. A new person I will be. Brown.

This river, this Gariep: where do it come from? They say that if you want to know where it begin, you must first find out where the sky end and where the world begin. They say it come from everywhere: not here or there or somewhere else, but everywhere. They say you cannot count all the rivers and streams and brooks and watercourses and creeks and fountains that run together into it, it really is from everywhere, it bring this whole land with it, all its sand and stones and rocks and boulders and mountains, all its trees and bushes and forests and copses and coppices. It bring with it all the feet and all the bodies and all the people that ever walked and came and were and lived here, it bring together everything that never been before, it come from all places and all times, they say that on its way it run through Paradise itself, where Adam and Eve live and lie together and where they swim *kaalgat*, where God or Al-lah or both of them walk together in the evening breeze and eat of the fruit and give it to the people so they can also eat, where Adam taste Eve and Eve taste Adam, where everybody and everything is just fruit that can be eaten. They say it come from everywhere, it is the whole land and the whole blarry earth, they give it a name, they name it all the names that ever lived in a tongue, they call it Gariep, they call it Orange River, they call it Vaal River. To many people it is the Great River, the Always River, the Ever River, the People River, the river where wind and dreams are born, where the sun and the moon and the other stars all swim together, like the love of the LordGod and of Al-lah himself. For ever and ever, amen.

This Great Gariep. My Gariep. To drink it into me so that it can for ever be part of me and I of it.

We coming closer, Labyn. I don't really know to what, but I know we coming closer. Old Labyn is here. And Lena is here. And Willempie is here. And Mamie. Deep inside me KleinFrans is here too. I am here. I, Philida of the Caab. This I that is free. The I who was a slave and who now is free, who is a woman, and who is everything.

I

ACKNOWLEDGEMENTS

In which a Professor and Vintner, a Historian,
some Authors, two Film-makers, various Characters,
a Lady, many Friends and a small Cat called Glinka,
without whom this Book would not have been
possible, are most profoundly thanked, and in which
certain unspecified Critics are not mentioned

I owe more to Mark Solms than I can ever say. Without him there could have been no book. It was Mark, Chair of Neuropsychology at the University of Cape Town, lecturer at the St Bartholomew's and Royal London School of Medicine, director of the Arnold Pfeffer Center for Neuro-Psychoanalysis at the New York Psychoanalytic Institute, and exceptional wine farmer of the farm Solms Delta, originally Zandvliet, who first introduced me to the slave woman Philida. She worked as a knitting girl on the farm from 1824 to 1832. The discovery that her master Cornelis Brink was a brother of one of my own direct ancestors, and that he sold her at auction after his son Francois Gerhard Jacob Brink had made four children with her, triggered this novel. In the remarkable little museum on the farm Philida's history was first briefly narrated, and I am deeply indebted to the historian attached to this museum, Tracey Randle, for the incalculable help and information she provided, over many months and later years, with endless patience, unquenchable energy and great dedication, throughout her pregnancy with little Maya, and in spite of numerous other duties and obligations. She was always prepared to field questions, on topics as wide-ranging as details of Philida's life story or the lives of other slaves and of the Brinks, the Berrangés, the de la Bats and other families, the fabrication of ink, wine prices (here Mark Solms also stepped in), slave prices, slave registration rolls, Day Books and Reports of Slave Protectors, travelling routes in the Western Cape in the nineteenth century and different modes of travel, mortgage bonds, the clothing of prisoners and methods of punishment – including the treadmill – in Cape prisons, exchange rates between sterling and the rix-dollar, water resources at Zandvliet and elsewhere, compensation to slave owners after emancipation, and much, much more. It is thanks to her that a demanding undertaking eventually developed into a project providing so much excitement, fulfilment and enjoyment.

Through Tracey I could also become absorbed in the painstaking research of her colleague Jackie Loos, writer of the fine study *Echoes of Slavery* (Cape Town: David Philip, 2004). Among the many other illuminating studies of slavery at the Cape, particularly during the years surrounding emancipation, I became drawn into Nigel Worden and Clifton Crais's *Breaking the Chains* (Johannesburg: WUP, 1994), Wayne Dooling's *Slavery, Emancipation and Colonial Rule* (Scottsville: UK-N Press, 2007), Robert C-H Shell's *Children of Bondage* (Johannesburg: WUP, 1994), and many others. On the Gariep I am indebted to William Dicey's exciting *Borderline* (Cape Town: Kwela, 2004) and, as in the past, Nigel Penn's *Forgotten Frontier* (London: Swallow Press, 2006).

In using historical sources it is of course necessary always to remain conscious not only of what is narrated, but also of what has been left unsaid. For example, in Francois Brink's reaction to Philida's complaint to the Slave Protector in Stellenbosch in 1832 about his relationship with Philida, what he says is that his own words are 'just as true as they are false'. What, exactly, does that mean? Another example: in her deposition Philida alleges that she and Frans have 'made' four children. But in the Slave Rolls and other official sources only three children are ever listed. Surely a mother would not make such a mistake – especially if it concerns her firstborn?!

Often in such tricky situations it is only through discussions with informed and caring friends that light can be shed on such puzzles. That is why I am so indebted to Ariel Dorfman for many unforgettable conversations, most especially one during a visit to the farm Solms Delta which helped to make many things fall into place. It sent me back to Cape history where slave infanticide regrettably was not uncommon. One of the best-known incidents concerned the Khoe woman Sara who had cut the throats of her two children to prevent their being returned to their 'Nooi', Christina van der Merwe. In another instance a slave mother drowned her two small children in the sea to save them from slavery. A most striking narrative based on such a historical event in South Africa is undoubtedly Yvette Christiansë's novel *Unconfessed* (New York: Other Press, 2006).

It is unknown exactly what role the aged slave woman Petronella Johanna Cornelia really played in the life of the Zandvliet Brinks. That she was manumitted and given her own room inside the *langhuis* of the Brinks' (unlike any of the numerous other slaves in the household), and that her possessions were left untouched when those of the Brink family were sold, is historically true. Once again it seems to me justified to draw one's own conclusions in the light of the relations between masters and slaves as recorded in Cape history, as in the history of my own ancestors.

A warm thank-you is due to Jean-Marc Giri and Jean-Marc Bouzou for an unforgettable revisit, in search of origins, to the Cedarberg rock paintings. Also to Imraan Coovadia (and through him to Saarah Jappie and Shahid Mathee) who helped with references to Islam and the Koran. In this respect Reza Aslan's *No God But God* (London: Arrow Books, 2005) also proved invaluable. And special thanks to Karen Jayes for the enthusiastic and moving way in which she shared her own conversion to Islam with Karina and myself.

Where possible, I tried to keep strictly to the available sources. The bankruptcy auction of Cornelis Brink, for instance, was recorded in extensive detail and has been incorporated here as an invaluable key to people and mores of that period at the Cape. But from time to time I took some liberties with the historical sources: in this way an alleged affair mentioned here, between Dominee Jan Fredrik Berrangé and a slave woman, was really inspired by an incident in the biography of another pious dominee. From the moment Philida is sold and almost totally disappears from recorded history, I had no choice but to rely on my imagination – but supported throughout, and meticulously, by what has actually been recorded in sources on that period at the Cape. Even an episode like the slave auction in Worcester and the case that preceded it, concerning the court's attempts to investigate the death of the Khoe man Kees to establish how many blows he had been given before he expired, are based, in all the unbearable and macabre details, on historical fact.

Names like *Caab*, *Helshoogde* and others are written to conform with spelling conventions of the time.

The brief reappearance of some characters from the Bokkeveld uprising of 1825, on which my novel *A Chain of Voices* (1983) was based, is effected, not only because it was historically probable, but because the structure of *Philida* is a conscious corollary of the earlier novel, in order to highlight both the similarities and the differences between the two. And the fact that Daniel Fredrik Berrangé, whose daughter married Francois Brink in due course (after a delay which had to be accounted for in narrative terms), was indeed the secretary of the court that tried the Bokkeveld rebels provides further motivation for such a link.

It was impossible to keep Cupido Cockroach of *Praying Mantis* (2005) from making a reappearance in this novel. In many respects his story paved the way for this book.

The scene in the *voorhuis* of the Berrangés', with the slave boy chasing the flies, is based on an illustration from Sir John Barrow's *An Account of Travels into the Interior of Southern Africa* (1801–04). The extravagant size of Lady Anne's chameleon was enough motivation for reincorporating the familiar Khoe myth about death and the chameleon so prominently.

For the cosmology of the Khoekhoen and other early inhabitants of Africa I am once again indebted to L. Schapera's *The Khoisan Peoples of Southern Africa* (London: Routledge & Kegan Paul, 1930) and, obviously, to the Bleek-Lloyd collection at the University of Cape Town, as well as to Lady Ademola's three-part *African Proverbs* (Ibadan: Bookcraft, 2008), while much of our human existence between the natural and the supernatural has been inspired by the Occitan writer Max Rouquette, whose beautiful *Vert Paradis* (Paris: Le Chemin vert, 1980) has accompanied me on many a voyage, geographically and in the mind.

The writing of this book is, in itself, an acknowledgement and an expression of deep gratitude, to Jan Rabie and Marjorie Wallace, for a friendship of nearly fifty years.

In a very special way, and like so often before, my editor and dear friend Geoff Mulligan was indispensable in shaping the final version of this book.

Cape Town, February 2012

www.vintage-books.co.uk